THE
ORCHID
EATER

Also by Marc Laidlaw

Dad's Nuke
Neon Lotus
Kalifornia

THE ORCHID EATER

MARC LAIDLAW

ST. MARTIN'S PRESS

NEW YORK

This is a work of fiction. Names, characters, places and incidents either are the product of the author's imagination or are used fictitiously. Any resemblance to events or persons, living or dead, is entirely coincidental.

Design by Junie Lee

Library of Congress Cataloging-in-Publication Data

Laidlaw, Marc.
    The orchid eater / Marc Laidlaw.
        p. cm.
    ISBN 0-312-10515-0
        1. Serial murders—California, Southern—Fiction. 2. Teenagers—California, Southern—Fiction. I. Title.
    PS3562.A333O73 1994
    813'.54—dc20   93-43648
                                                                          CIP

First Edition: March 1994

10 9 8 7 6 5 4 3 2 1

For Robert S. Gillespie

And for my brother Brian

(This book owes its life to Tim Ferret)

Sandstone walls appear in leaping bursts of bluish light that come with a roar and fade, like the flame of revelation in a nightmare that shows a monster's grin for an instant, then shuts off and strands you in darkness.

This is a darkness full of laughter, full of fingers digging into your flesh, pinning you to the ground.

When the light flares again, you see a blue tongue of flame licking from the nozzle of a blowtorch. Hissing and spitting, it kisses your cheeks, singes your eyebrows, then goes away somewhere out of sight.

Somebody says, "Get his pants."

You can't believe where the flame goes next. . . .

PART ONE

THE ONE-WAY GANG

The reek of the Greyhound's chemical toilet woke him shortly after dawn. The aluminum door banged open and an old man emerged in a cloud of cigarette smoke, hacking into a handkerchief. He dropped down in the seat next to Lupe.

Looking down and sideways through half-open lids, pretending to sleep on, Lupe saw a pint bottle clamped between knees so bony that a three-inch gap showed between the skeletal thighs. Filthy checkered trousers hung slack from the bones.

A fly buzzed, circled, and settled on the old wretch's undone zipper. Scabby sunburned hands with swollen knuckles worked at the bottle cap, and suddenly Lupe smelled rubbing alcohol. He gagged, twisting away from that and all the other odors, urine and sweat and infection mingling like a human compost from which anything might grow.

A hand fell lightly on his leg. He sat up, blinking at the old man, seeing thin hair dyed red, a scalp spotted with freckles that looked like burst bloodscabs, his nose a mass of blue webs and pores. He wore a tattered suit, gray shirtfront stained with coffee, vomit, booze. The hand stayed.

"Hey, kid."

Lupe stared at him, digging deep into the pocket of his coat, finding his security there.

"Want to make some easy money?"

With his bottle open, wafting its medicinal odor across the seats, the old man went working his fingers into the flaps of his gaping fly. Before he could do any more than that, Lupe laid his switchblade on the checkered lap.

"Now, now," the old man said. "Now, now."

The blade looked as if it might float up between them, under its own power.

Lupe turned back to the window. The old man, wheezing and groaning, struggled out of the seat and down the aisle. A few rows toward the front, the geezer stopped and looked down into another seat. "Hi there, sweetie-pie." He lowered himself out of sight.

Rubbing gummed eyelids, dreams in full retreat, Lupe looked out through a tinted window blurred by a million tiny scratches and the accumulated breath of ten thousand riders. The bus was on a narrow two-lane highway, headed down a dry canyon where night's shadows had already begun to evaporate. The low sun laid its fingers on the crowns of hills, making dead weeds shine like gold. Tire tracks scored the grass, running parallel to power lines. Green clumps of cactus, penned in by barriers of sagging barbed wire, huddled together like frightened sheep in the shadows of weathered ridges.

An outcropping of wind-gnarled sandstone drifted past, looking like beige dough that had been folded on itself a billion times before hardening. His pulse quickened when he saw that the doughy rock was pocked with holes like mute gray mouths. No true caves among them—even the deepest looked no better than a shallow shelf or pocket—but the sight made him straighten in his seat to search the hills more carefully, fully awake now. The stink of the old man's booze and trousers was finally starting to leave him. Face pressed against the glass, he sucked in the tepid recirculated air that seeped up from vents below the window. He could almost smell the stale cool desolation of real caves somewhere near, the deep winds blowing up from underneath the world. He would find them, sniff them out. Dr. Brownhouse would be proud to learn how Lupe had conquered his fears. He had mastered them completely.

The hills piled up higher the closer they came to the coast. Headlamps of Mercedes, Porsches and BMWs cut through the persistent gloom at the bottom of the valley, purring past and then gone. The hollows in the hills were dense with vegetation, dusty pines and eucalyptus with peeling silver bark and leaves like long green daggers. The first houses appeared among the trees, rusted cars and catamarans on wheeled trailers parked in dirt lots around them, surfboards propped against fences. The bus passed a boatyard, then a corral where several grimy horses stared sleepily at traffic. No Porsches parked down here in the canyon. Wind chimes of abalone shell and colored glass dangled from the eaves of dark-shingled shacks with clumsy driftwood fences. He could almost hear the chimes, a sound like chattering teeth. On came junkyards full of metal scrap in advanced decay. Then what might have been a churchyard, its bare parking lot prickly with crosses, presided over by a battered trailer with black hand-lettering all over the side.

Lupe pulled a Baggie of dried figs from his pocket and began to chew, wishing for something to help wash them down. An old scavenger with the look of a faded athlete—bare chested in a baseball cap, his sunburned teats hanging nearly to the waist of his shorts—sauntered down the highway as though it were midday, stabbing beer cans with a spike and dropping them in a burlap sack. Lupe shuddered. Old men!

Above the eucalyptus and the auto shops, he could still see the hills; but no more sandstone, no sign of caves. On the ridges, seeming to revolve into sight, were buildings of stained wood and glass and polished steel gazing west toward the sea. Others, just as elegant, bore roofs of curved Spanish tile, whitewashed stucco walls, arched gateways. Porsches up there, he'd bet.

The hills stepped back from the road. Four lanes now. Ahead he saw the square, drab, ordinary buildings of the town.

The driver's voice crackled from a speaker: "Bohemia Bay. We'll be stopping here five minutes before heading on to San Diego."

Lupe had seen plenty of bus stations. They had a way of turning their surroundings into slums. It was as though a gas emanated from the lounges, souring the faces of old houses that might otherwise look merely quaint, exhaust fumes turning green lawns gray. It was no different here. The shacks in the canyon had looked comfortably weather-worn, but for the space of one block around the bus station Bohemia Bay had the look and feel of a ghetto.

Standing at the edge of the parking lot, knapsack over his shoulder, Lupe leaned against a cyclone fence and stared down into a dry aqueduct as he finished the last of the figs. The cement channel was deep enough to accommodate raging winter torrents, but it held nothing now except a trickle of stagnant water; banks of sandy mud held fast to a litter of blown-out tires, beer bottles and bloated wood. A rancid briny stench hung over the canal, a stronger but staler version of the smell that blew up the streets from the beach. Across the viaduct, a black child peered down at him from a tenement window that backed up directly on the foul-smelling trickle.

Inside the station Lupe bought a cup of scalding cocoa from a machine. The phone book, stolen from the booth, was survived by a frayed tether of steel cable. He drank the chocolate in two gulps—pouring it past his tongue, head tipped back—and studied a large yellowing map of the town mounted on a bulletin board. Later he would buy a pocket map, but for now this gave him a sense of the place, a thinly inhabited crescent with empty land on one side and emptier sea on the other. When he could see it with his eyes closed, he went back out.

The morning air was humid and warming, though a sea chill lingered. The canyon road led straight toward the beach; beyond a traffic signal, he could see the silvery swell of waves. Their sound carried faintly. Shops were opening. He passed a florist, a dress shop, a five-and-ten, two ice cream parlors. Across the street from the beach, a Jaguar came rolling out of a corner gas station. Lupe spotted a phone booth at the nearest edge of the lot; the directory was still intact.

A kid in a greasy blue uniform, with long sun-bleached hair under his blue cap and skin tanned brown as Lupe's, watched him approach the booth and pick up the book. Lupe could feel the attendant staring as he paged through the D's.

Diaz.

There was only one of them, first initial "S."

Too easy. In L.A. he'd had to look for days before learning that Sal had left the city around the same time he had. It was the first time a little whitebread town like this had ever made his life easier. Sal must be feeling pretty safe here, so far from the old neighborhood, to go listing his name. Guess he figured he'd put everything behind him.

Lupe tore off the lower half of the page, taking what he needed. He wasn't too good at remembering numbers.

"Hey, asshole," said a voice.

He turned and saw the pump jockey standing behind him.

"The fuck you just do?"

The boy was taller than Lupe. He had strong arms, grease-smeared hands. Lupe didn't say anything, only stared up into eyes like pale blue broken crystals. The sun topped the hills right then; he felt its first rays burning on the back of his head. He could almost smell burning hair.

"What are you anyway?" the boy said. "You a guy or a girl? Takes some kind of nerve for a faggot like you to go ripping off public property like that."

Lupe started to step around him. The kid grabbed him by a sleeve.

"Where you going, greaser faggot?" Fingers clenched in the baggy sleeve of Lupe's green army-surplus jacket, twisting him closer. "You look like a girl, you know that? Do you even shave? Come on, you fucking queer, hand it over."

Lupe's hand was in his pocket where he'd tucked the phone book page. His fingers stroked the warm bone handle as he thought of the cold polished metal folded up inside it. His thumb played across the silver button in the handle, stroking it as he would a nipple. He hadn't wanted to waste it on the old man, but now . . . given this and the burning . . .

The sun felt like a blowtorch turned up to full, searing the back of his skull, boring into the center of his brain, destroying the wall between the halves. He caught the stink of charred flesh and blood.

Caught unsuspecting in Lupe's shadow, the kid thrust out his hand again. "Stupid fucking homo, give it here."

Lupe took his fingers from his pocket and started to lay the crumpled paper in the pump jockey's hand, imagining that it was the blade of the knife. Seeing the silver cut down into the fleshy whiteness of the grimy palm, seeing the blood well up.

He looked into the pale blue eyes, seeing them full of respect now. And fear. A rich mix of emotion in those humiliated eyes. He had tasted this blend before; not that any two were ever exactly alike. The flavors of fear could keep him busy forever, tasting them, stirring up new varieties.

Then the pump jockey grabbed Lupe's wrist and fingers and started bending them back. The paper dropped to the ground. Pain chased the fog of dreams from Lupe's eyes, and as his vision cleared, he saw that there was no respect in the pump jockey's face, not really. No fear of him, either. Only an angry, smirking disgust.

He wished for his knife, but it was too late.

"Stop," he gasped. "Stop or . . ."

"Or what, faggot?" The kid's face swam closer; Lupe's fingers were going to break. "Or what?"

A car glided up to the pumps and beeped its horn.

The pump jockey dropped Lupe's hand and backed away, grinning. "You're welcome to try me, cocksucker. I see you around here again, I'll show you *or what.*"

He turned away, exulting in Lupe's humiliation, striding proudly toward the pumps. For a moment Lupe couldn't feel the sun, which was a relief even in his misery.

But the feeling wouldn't last. He couldn't stand here all day. It would be hot and bright soon, hotter than he liked it, his shadow withering as noon approached.

More cars pulled in off the street. The kid hustled to handle them, and a stocky older man, also in uniform, rushed out of the station office to help.

With no one looking his way, Lupe bent and snatched up the crumpled phonebook page, stuffed it back in his pocket. Aching fingers stroked the blade.

"I saw that!" the pump jockey called. The other man grabbed him, steering him toward a customer, sparing Lupe another assault. "Next time, faggot! Next time you're mine!"

Lupe ran across the street to the beach, looking back once to see the pump jockey watching him as he violently sponged a windshield.

Lupe was shaking now. His guts were all twisted. Hard to keep calm. At least the sun didn't seem to burn, and he couldn't smell the charring.

He walked over a patch of grass, then a splintered boardwalk, and stepped down onto sand. His steps turned slow and awkward; it was like moving into a dream, except for the sand grains already chafing in his boots. A string of pelicans bobbed up and down on the waves; otherwise the shore was deserted. The sun cast his shadow ahead of him onto the sand, beside the longer shadow of a tall white lifeguard lookout that reminded him of a prison gun-tower. One of the windows was broken, a corner piece of glass missing. Something gray hopped around inside, then stuck out its head and flew toward him. It was a seagull, carrying what looked like something bloody in its beak. As it swooped overhead he saw that it was part of a hot dog, dripping ketchup. He felt a small disappointment.

He looked around casually, expecting nothing more than sand and birds. The lonely calm fed him as little else could. But far south down the beach, a yellow jeep appeared around a sandstone point, bouncing past cliffside apartments, high houses and hotels. An official-looking vehicle. Fluorescent orange floats strapped to the roll-bar startled him with their brightness. Lupe turned away, looking for a refuge, and was amazed to see a perfect circle of darkness awaiting him.

The pipe emerged from the sand beneath the boardwalk, taller than a man and infinitely deeper. From its lower lip a shallow pool of water drooled, flecked with bilious brown foam, fringed with rotting seaweed like a tramp's beard, and swirling with flies. He could see the sheen of liquid stretching back like a tongue in the black throat. He almost gasped with anticipation, feeling himself on the verge of some critical event or revelation. But his life was always like that: fraught with tension, always *about* to happen. Change was in the air, but for Lupe it never came.

Before the mouth could call his name, he hurried into it.

The storm drain swallowed him. Broken glass snapped under his boot soles as he sloshed through muddy water. He knew that if he kept going he would end up in the aqueduct behind the bus station. Sudden thunder filled the tunnel. At first he thought it was cars on the Coast Highway above; then he recognized the sound of surf, echoing and amplified.

A short distance into the pipe, speckled light filtered down from holes in a manhole cover. The passage divided here, changing from a circular tube into two broad, squared-off, low-ceilinged corridors, each with its flotsam of Styrofoam and low banks of mud. Choices. Forward, to right or left? Or back, to wait for the jeep to pass? He brought his knife out and held it in the faint light. He tried to make his mind a bright, hard, sharp thing, like the knife, to cut through this problem.

Behind him, a presence announced itself with silence. The crashing of waves snuffed out, and he knew they had caught up with him.

Lupe turned slowly, keeping his knife in plain sight.

The entrance to the drain looked no bigger or brighter than a dime held out at the end of his arm. What little light it gave was eclipsed by his boys.

Seven of them. Same as last time. They stood in their usual

poses, some looking tough and defiant, others pretending not to notice him. The Hopi and the Virginian leaned against the curved walls of the tunnel, sharing a cigarette that smelled like burning meat. The Musician, a lean and sullen black boy, carried a silent battered guitar slung over his shoulder on a homemade strap. The one he called the Marine had been shaved nearly to the scalp, and his blank face was rigid beneath stubble that never grew. The Cherokee had hair to his shoulders, hair that fell across his dark eyes like a veil of mourning. The Junkie picked at his chancred lips and ragged fingernails, refusing to meet Lupe's eyes. The littlest one, Miguel, always looked as though he'd been caught crying.

Seeing them, he sheathed the switchblade and slipped it back into his pocket.

"I missed you," he said. "I been lonely."

They didn't say a thing. A few didn't even look up, though he knew they heard him. He didn't expect affection, didn't ask for their respect, though he had won it long ago. It was good to know they were still with him. He had spent too many nights in bright bus terminals, in fluorescent stations, in the homes of people he barely knew. His boys were shy. He feared they might have gone away. Sometimes he thought he saw them, but he was almost never sure. Once he had been able to summon or send them away at will, but that ability had weakened with time, as the gang grew in number. At first they had shown themselves only when he willed it, calling them up as an act of concentrated need; but things had gone beyond that point. He couldn't help but see them when they chose to appear; and if they decided to leave, it was their decision and not his own.

Not that they had anywhere to go. They needed him for guidance, that was why they hung around and clung to him, waiting with bored infinite patience. They were his forever, never to change—no more than he would change.

"I'm glad you're back," he told them, as if they needed reassurance. "There's something we have to do together. Someone to find."

That caught their interest. The Virginian's cigarette fell to the tunnel floor, drowning without a sizzle. He still couldn't hear the surf. The boys closed in around him, cutting off all light from the beach. Even the rays from the manhole cover dimmed, though that might have been a car idling overhead. For a moment he felt suffocating panic. He was in the dark again, in the First Cave, surrounded.

He shook it off.

No. They're mine this time. I've got my gang. I never have to be alone again.

When he felt calm, he dried his palms on his jacket and reached into his pocket for the torn phone book page.

"Did I ever tell you about my brother?"

"This morning I'm going to talk about the life of the Fightin' Jesus," Hawk told his congregation.

"Any relation to the Rootin'-Tootin' Jesus?" someone said. There was scattered coarse laughter.

Hawk shut the Bible and looked down at his boys. They sat in a semicircle on log stumps he'd arranged on a flattened part of the hill behind his trailer. He stood above them on the slope, behind a crude-hewn pulpit, so they had to look up at him. Most of the boys he knew fairly well, but they were encouraged to bring friends along to the Saturday Sermons, and today there were a few he didn't recognize. The one who'd spoken was a tall, muscular kid with downy jaws and the fixed expression of a born smartass. Hawk held him with his eyes until the kid looked down.

"As a matter of fact," Hawk said, "they are one and the same. Our Savior goes by many names. Some of you might even laugh at some of them."

That silenced the other boys.

"Now, the thing is, this Fightin' Jesus, he had a reputation as the Fastest Gun in the Middle East. Carried a pair of silver six-shooters, he did, though these guns of his didn't shoot real bullets. They fired something much more powerful."

"Hollow-point parables!" the fuzz-face said.

Hawk stamped down the hillside, raising swirls of dust. He walked right up to the smartass, grabbed him by the collar of his T-shirt, and hauled him to his feet.

"What is your name, son?" he said through clenched teeth.

"Scott."

"Scott? Who brought you here today, Scott?"

The kid seemed unwilling to say, as if it would have been a betrayal. Hawk looked around at the other boys until finally Edgar Goncourt raised his hand. "I did, Hawk."

"Why?"

Edgar, long-faced and bony-nosed, with shoulder-length thin brown hair, shrugged. "He's cool."

"Did you force him to come here, Edgar?" Hawk looked at Scott. "Did Edgar force you?"

Scott shook his head.

"You came of your own free will? So you're really a guest here, aren't you? We didn't abduct you, nobody forced you to listen to me, nobody even asked your opinion. So why are you making such a pain of yourself?"

"Sorry," Scott said.

"Do you want to leave or listen?"

"I'll listen."

"Maybe you have something you want to say before you listen? Any important information I might not have heard about the Fightin' Jesus? Anything me and my friends can't live without?"

Scott shook his head.

"Okay, then." Hawk let go of him, and the boy sank back down.

Hawk hiked back to his stump, wondering what the hell he'd been meaning to say. A good preacher should be able to hold on to his thoughts even in the face of interruptions. He should be able to reach out to these boys on their own terms, which included plenty of insecure backtalk disguising legitimate questions. But somehow he couldn't stand the feeling of things getting out of control. There had to be something in his fucking life he could keep a grip on. These boys were his project. He couldn't fail them.

They were watching Hawk with fading interest, picking their teeth, scuffing at the dirt, whispering. He had wanted to improvise something they could relate to around the Fightin' Jesus image he was so proud of, but the thoughts were no longer flowing.

He cracked open the Bible at random. *"Thou shalt by no means come out hence until thou hast paid the uttermost farthing."* Now, what the hell did that mean? A farthing was some kind of old-fashioned English coin, wasn't it? How could they have farthings in the Bible lands? The kids wouldn't understand that kind of time travel.

He looked at the sky, blazing blue between the shifting eucalyptus leaves, and allowed his mind to wander. They wouldn't know the difference.

"The Fightin' Jesus . . . he used to say . . . *'You can't get out of jail, until you've paid your bail.'* "

That's more like it, Hawk thought. See, you hang in there, take a chance, it comes to you. Lord's work, Lord's words.

"Now, a few of us have been there, haven't we? We know what Jesus was talking about. You have just that one phone call to make—and who's it gonna be? Your parents? You expect them to come pick you up? Hell, it's 'cause of your parents you're in jail in the first place. If they'd loved you, let you be yourself, everything mighta turned out better. No, you can't call your parents. What about a lawyer, then? A gold-toothed, shiny-suited, briefcase-carrying lawyer. Hell, you'd have to rob a bank just to pay his fees. Forget about lawyers. You got one call, now. You gonna waste it? You think you can scrape up bail all by yourself? Think your friends can get it for you, when they're just as lost and unlucky as you? Man, they'd just end up in the cell next to yours, tossed in for robbing a gas station trying to get your bail. Nope. The best call you can make right then, your best bondsman, the guy who's gonna pay up and get you back on the street, back on your feet—is Jesus. Jesus said, 'Dial my number and I *shall* pick up the phone. Call and I will answer.' When you call Jesus, you won't get a secretary saying, 'I'm sorry, Mr. Christ is out to lunch right now, you'll have to leave a message.' "

They were laughing now, even Scott.

"And I'll tell you this. Jesus will not only pay up your bail, right to the last penny, but he'll also represent you in court. He will file the necessary papers, bargain with the cops who busted you, and stand at your side on the Judgment Day. He'll do everything he can to save your ass. He will not forsake you. He may reduce your sentence, or get it commuted completely, or maybe even get your whole case thrown out of court. You might have to do some community service, but that's okay. For Jesus is the Great Public Defender."

"Is he the Great Parole Officer, too?" Scott said daringly, though without such a smartass tone this time, making it easy for Hawk to smile.

"That he is. I see you do understand."

"Sure. I watch 'Perry Mason' like everybody else."

Afterward, most of the boys scattered, but a core remained in Hawk's gravel yard alongside Old Creek Road, working on their bikes among the heavy black crosses he had mounted at the edges of the lot. They'd had to learn not to dangle greasy rags or chains from the arms of the crucifixes, but otherwise Hawk let them do what they wanted. Sometimes they asked his advice and he gave a few pointers, though he refrained from actually working on the bikes. He didn't ride them anymore, so repairing them was out of the question. Once he started, did a bit of work, he'd just have to sit astride the hog and kick the starter, listen to the roar and feel the throb; and then he'd just have to take off for a spin, only a little test drive to make sure everything was running smooth . . . and the next thing you knew, he'd be back in some sweaty lodge, snorting rails, picking fights, grabbing the first heavy tool that came to hand and wailing down on somebody's skull or kneecaps, caught up in a drugged and drunken battle over meaningless bullshit like whose bike was a piece of shit, whose colors were allowed in that particular bar.

No . . . no, he'd never get caught in those gears again. And the best way he knew to avoid the trap was to swear off bikes forever. Two-horned steeds of the Devil, that's what they were. Of course, not everyone saw them that way, and they made a nice contrast, parked in his lot. What was right for him, was right for him; he couldn't speak for others. And the constant temptation of bikes around the place was good for his soul; it made him strong in his struggle, forever vigilant.

The Saturday traffic was up to its afternoon peak, a steady *whoosh* of cars heading toward the beach. Occasionally the revving of motorcycle engines drowned out everything.

Hawk sat on the trailer hook in a narrow band of shade and leafed through the Saturday paper, holding its edges down with the toes of his boots while sipping a Mountain Dew. He had just reached a troubling headline when a shadow fell over the paper.

"Hey, Hawk," Edgar said. "I didn't get a chance to introduce him before. This is Scott Gillette."

Hawk glanced up, holding out a hand dyed dark with grease and oil, which Scott clasped firmly after a moment's hesitation. "You're all right, Scott."

"Thanks. You make those Old Testaments sparkle like new."

Hawk wasn't sure if Scott was ridiculing him specifically, or simply in the grip of an unfocused, uncontrollable sarcasm. He decided on the latter. There didn't seem to be much malice in him; his face betrayed the usual stew of adolescent gripes.

Edgar, on the other hand, looked decidedly nervous about something. His eyes kept flickering toward the ground and away again. Hawk picked up the paper and held it out to him.

"You in the news again, Edgar?" he said. "Is this you?"

" 'Rash of break-ins . . .' " Edgar started to recite. Then he backed off, shaking his head without looking any further at the page.

"Shangri-La," Hawk said. "That's your neighborhood."

"Lots of shady people live up there, Hawk," Edgar said edgily. "Hell, Sal and his buttboys are right down the street from me."

Hawk stared at Edgar, hoping to unnerve the truth out of him, but Edgar, sadly, had learned some new defenses. Scrutiny merely toughened him, made his excuses more casual.

"I don't know anybody doing that shit," he said. "Not anymore."

It's him, Hawk thought.

"I hope you're not that stupid, Edgar."

"I'm smart, Hawk. I'm smart!"

"Well, I wouldn't go that far," Scott said.

"Keep an eye on him for me, would you, Scott? See he stays out of trouble?"

A look flickered between the boys. Scott's smirk returned.

"You ever been to jail, Scott?" Hawk said.

Slowly the smirk vanished. Hawk spied an involuntary surge of surprise and fear, but it was quickly shrugged off.

"You think that was all just poetry, what I said about posting bail, that one phone call? I speak from experience, friend. I've been in jail more than once, and so has Edgar here. Now, sometimes when your friends go places, it can be pretty hard not to follow. You understand me?"

Scott nodded, his Adam's apple bobbing, no comeback at the ready. But he didn't look fearful anymore; he looked exquisitely bored.

"And you, Edgar. Keep your nose clean."

Edgar sniffed and toed the dirt, fingering the flexible gold band of a wristwatch Hawk had never seen him wear before. One that was several sizes too big.

3

"Mike, where are you?"

The woman's voice startled him, coming from right outside the supply closet. Mike James nearly dropped his clipboard. He'd been drawing a dragon with a dripping torso hanging from its fangs. He made sure that the vacuum bag inventory list completely covered his sketch, then he stuck his head out of the closet.

"Right here," he said. She was standing several feet away, with her back to the closet. When he spoke, she jumped visibly.

"Goodness," she said, turning a startled face toward him.

It was the middle sister, plump, pale and sort of pretty. She looked around the store, flustered and embarrassed, then moved closer.

Is this it? he wondered. Finally? Is she going to push me back in the closet and do it to me here and now, with her sisters and all the customers right outside, and her father in the back room? I guess she's okay looking enough—I mean, she's a *woman!*

She came very close and lowered her voice. It was sweet and almost husky:

"Mike . . . could you go count the floods in overstock and see if there's anything we need to put on order?"

"Okay, Miss Glantz." He tried to keep his disappointment

from showing as he saluted her with his ballpoint pen and headed toward the back of Glantz Appliances, past rows of blenders, clocks and toasters, under racks of swinging mock-Tiffany lamps, past the counter where the other two Glantz sisters stood arguing over the week's receipts. They were all "Miss Glantz" to him; he knew their first names but didn't use them, couldn't even keep them straight.

The door at the rear of the store opened into a dark region of handmade shelves crammed with junction boxes, lead pipes, Bakelite sockets, spools of coaxial cable. Old Mr. Glantz, father of the women out front, stood at his workbench in a pool of light, dissecting a toaster, mumbling to himself, oblivious to Mike's presence. A wooden ramp led up between the shelves to the delivery entrance at the rear. He paused at the door, looking out at the parking lot and alley behind the building, where the asphalt seemed to seethe and simmer, soft as wax. He was almost glad to be indoors on such a day. Almost.

Mike went into a storage area near the top of the ramp and started rummaging through boxes so light they felt empty, counting indoor floods and outdoor floods in various wattages, in shades of amber and green. He noted the totals on a clipboard. Someday, if he worked here long enough, he could look forward to keeping all the different kinds of lightbulb straight in his head, like Mr. Glantz, who could instantly name the order number of any replacement part, like some Houdini of household appliances.

He calculated he could spend a good ten minutes back here before anyone disturbed him; so, resting his clipboard on a dusty wooden shelf, he peeled back the inventory lists and returned to filling in bloodstains on the dragon's teeth with a red pen, drawing big splashing pools of it on the ground below the victim. He used a little red to touch up the victim's nipples as well.

Scarcely any light came through the delivery door into the storage area, and while he was drawing even this went dim. Two guys blocked the door, in silhouette. The tallest one was his best friend, Scott Gillette. The other was lanky Edgar Goncourt, whom Mike scarcely knew except by reputation. Mike could smell a faint whiff of incenselike musk coming off him—a weird cologne he associated with the Alt-School crowd.

They peered down the ramp toward the front of the store, not seeing Mike in the shadows. Scott said, "This is where he works."

"Old Glantz's place? Man, that sucks. Imagine that hardass for your boss."

"Hey," Mike said. "Over here."

Scott blundered into a case of three-way bulbs and knocked it over. Little packages pattered down the ramp.

"Watch what you're doing!" Mike hurried to prevent further disaster, gathering the boxes.

"You get off soon?" Scott said.

"Pretty soon. Why, what're you guys doing?"

"Edgar lives up in Shangri-La, right where you're moving. We were going to head up there. You want us to wait for you?"

"It won't be till like a quarter after five," Mike said. "I have to sweep up and stuff."

"That's cool," Edgar said.

"Mike?" called a perpetually hoarse voice. "Who's up there?"

He looked up from repacking the carton Scott had spilled. Mr. Glantz was coming toward the ramp.

"Just some friends of mine," he said.

"That's Edgar Goncourt! Get him the hell out of my store!"

"Just leaving," Edgar said. "Don't sweat it."

"Meet you at the library," Scott said.

The two of them hurried into the alley, laughing. Mr. Glantz trudged up the ramp in his heavy boots. "I didn't know you hung around with boys like that. I thought you had more sense. You should choose your friends more carefully."

Mike started to say that he hardly knew Edgar, but although it was true, it sounded like betrayal. He and Edgar did not exactly occupy the same orbits, since Edgar was in the Alternative School, which had a building to itself adjacent to the main grounds of Bohemia High. The Alt-School students took lots of field trips in a broken-down, painted-up hippie bus, and had legendary parties where faculty and students alike supposedly took drugs, listened to Led Zeppelin and engaged in orgies. In that notorious pantheon of spectacular rebels and tragic, hollow-eyed losers, Edgar Goncourt was only a minor figure, neither demigod nor semidemon. Quiet, secretive, all but anonymous, he had never spoken even one word to Mike until just now, on the shadowy ramp. The thought of all the things Edgar might know—the wild world to which he was privy—turned a key in a lock at the top of Mike's skull, opening a magic door in the back of his dull little world. He was not about to throw away that key, or stop that door from swinging wider. He'd always been curious about Edgar and his friends—envious of the kids who, because they didn't do as well on tests, were allowed to create their own lessons. The girls in the Alt-School all looked worldly, experienced, even somewhat jaded in their bell-tasseled tie-dyed skirts, with their hairy legs and unshaven armpits he couldn't help but imagine sucking on. Girls straight out of *Zap Comix,* R. Crumb women, sexy and seductive, who never noticed Mike (though they weren't stuck up in the same way as the ordinary Bohemia soshes and cheerleaders and surfer chicks) because he looked so . . . so normal, in his striped T-shirts and flared trousers.

Mr. Glantz stood over him while he finished repacking the box.

"You just ask some of the other merchants if things don't disappear when that Edgar comes around. He's been arrested more than once—and not only on this street. There's better things to do with your time than go around with hoods."

Mike shoved the box back onto the shelf as hard as he could, hoping something would break. His mind was a cloud of Alt-School orgies, vivid pictures of all the things he'd missed out on because he was so damn square.

"Better things than working here," he muttered.

"What's that?"

"You don't even know me, Mr. Glantz. How do you know I'm not just like Edgar—or worse?"

Mr. Glantz stared at him. Stared and swayed, holding on to the wooden rail that ran along the ramp. In the dim light, his face lost all expression and his anger sloughed away. He wasn't looking at Mike now, or at anything. Something might have come out of the toaster on his workbench, crawled up his arm and eaten a piece of his brain. His eyes had melted.

Mike's mouth went dry; he felt sick all of a sudden. Poor old geezer wouldn't hear anything else he said right now. Probably wouldn't remember the encounter with Edgar and Scott either. Mike brushed past him, on his way into the store.

Up front, the oldest and youngest Glantz sisters stood near the register arguing about hearing-aid batteries. He didn't see the middle one.

"Your dad's having another one of his, uh, diabetic things," he said. Several customers looked his way. He jerked his thumb back at the ramp.

The two women looked peeved and worried at the same time. The older one grabbed a container of orange juice sitting on the back counter and hurried toward the storeroom. "You should have been watching the clock."

"*I* should have been watching?" said the younger. "Mike, could you hold the fort for a minute?"

"I don't think so," he said, and watched her face change. "He just gave me the rest of the day off."

"Well, we could use your help right now. Couldn't you stay just another few minutes?"

"I'm sorry, Miss Glantz, I've got to be somewhere right away."

He grabbed his unseasonably heavy jacket from behind the counter and walked out the front door, avoiding her frustrated look. She had no reason to doubt his lie, and what could she do to him anyway? He wasn't her slave.

Mike hurried through the shade of a dozen awnings, past

stores that sold unicorn jewelry, driftwood sculpture, sand candles, health food and vitamins. How could he waste his whole summer counting light bulbs? This job was worse than his paper route, worse even than the week he'd spent with blistered palms hoeing trenches at the experimental farm down in Dana Point. When he was counting vacuum bags and unpacking tortoise lampshades and sorting batteries, he felt a gray suffocation sinking down on him; something thick and heavy and inescapable, like a soft ceiling crushing him, turning his mind to paste. The clocks on the shelves slowed to a halt and the seconds dripped like Chinese water torture. *That's* what had happened to Mr. Glantz. It wasn't diabetes. The job itself was a coma—a coma that paid three bucks an hour.

He turned the block and went up to the alley that ran between Glantz Appliances and the library. The sisters' voices echoed over the parked cars like the cries of parrots. He hurried away from the doomed sensation it gave him, and came upon Scott and Edgar hanging around on benches near the main doors of the library.

Scott Gillette was tall and husky—some might say massive— yet he moved lightly, at times furtively, wearing a heavy olive-drab army coat in all but the hottest weather, including today's. At the moment, without any effort, he had wrapped both hands around the lower branch of an avocado tree that spread above the benches and was shaking the bough, causing little withered bombs of inedible fruit to pelt Mike as he approached.

"Watch out for tree gonads!" Scott shouted.

Edgar sat in Scott's shadow: smaller, thinner, wiry, his eyes constantly darting above a broad, sly smile.

"Hey, it's not five yet," Scott said. "What'd you do, quit?"

"I wish," Mike said.

"That's one wish could definitely come true," Edgar said. He closed his eyes and tipped back his head, as if entering a trance. "You just have to visualize it clearly and it'll manifest in your life. Close your eyes and picture yourself walking up to old man Glantz and saying 'Kiss my ass, dick-breath!' "

"I suppose that would work," Mike admitted. "Is that what they teach you in the Alt-School?"

Edgar's eyes opened slowly, his grin broadening. "Naw. My mom taught me that one."

"Let's get going," Scott said. "We've got a sortie to plan."

"A sortie?" said Mike.

"I think he means a raid," Edgar said. "Right, Scott?"

"I was just lamenting the fact that all the avocados get picked or shaken from this tree before they're ripe enough to eat. Edgar let on that he knows a few trees that are peaking even as we speak."

"Gah," Mike said. "I wouldn't care if you had a whole orchard. I hate avocados. All that greeny brown smoosh."

"You must never've had a really fresh one," Edgar said. "Right off the tree, they're sweet as butter." Edgar licked his wide lips. "When they're even slightly past their prime, they get all gray and gross. You've got to catch them right at that perfect moment. Which happens to be today."

Scott said, "Mike's still a ripe avocado virgin."

Mike shoved Scott, who hardly budged.

"So where are these trees?"

"There's a grove in this old farmer's back pasture, halfway up the hill to Shangri-La. He doesn't have any friends to give them to, doesn't sell them or anything, so I just help myself. They just fall and rot otherwise."

"It occurred to us," Scott added, "that we should invest in a few giant grocery bags. Between the three of us, we could bring home quite a booty."

Mike shrugged. "What are we waiting for?"

They walked abreast down Glen Ellen Boulevard, the thoroughfare of choice for local traffic, now that the Coast Highway was perpetually clogged with its summer load of tourist cars. Striding along with a raid in the offing—an adventure of almost mythical promise—Mike found himself laughing for no reason. Well, there were good reasons really. He was out of school, so why waste his summer in an appliance store? It's not as though he had a family to support. Hell, his mother's boyfriend Jack was buying a house, freeing them from the tiny two-bedroom sea-cliff apartment they'd been living in for a year. Mike and his brother Ryan would have their own rooms for the first time. No more moving from place to place. He was set!

They went into the Glen Ellen Supermarket. Edgar idled before the snack rack with great deliberation, picking through the assortment of candy and gum. He finally settled on a small packet of Chiclets, but not before a man with a push broom came out of an aisle and stood behind them. He followed them to the register.

"Will that be all?" asked the checker, a fat woman who kept staring suspiciously at Scott, enfolded in his thick army coat.

"Yes, please," said Edgar, handing her a few coins. "I'll bag it myself."

He reached around the end of the counter, pulled out a large paper bag, and shook it open. The woman glared at him as if she wanted to hurry him up. Mike at first assumed he wasn't attracted to her, since she was fat and all, but even so he couldn't help imagining her with her clothes off, as a sort of thought-experiment. He realized, with faint humility at the stirring in his underwear, that he would have accepted it even from her. If she'd have him.

Edgar, meanwhile, had taken out a second bag, shaken it open, and shoved it down inside the first.

"What are you doing?" she said.

He unfolded a third bag and fit it into the others, straightened the edges, thumped it several times lightly as if to check the sturdiness of his construction. Then he picked up the tiny packet of Chiclets and tossed it in.

"I don't want the bottom falling out," he said, lifting the triple-lined bag in his arms. He grunted as if it weighed a ton, staggering toward the door. Mike looked at the woman, shrugged apologetically, but couldn't meet her eyes. He was still seeing her as a pale opulent mass of sticky, sweet-smelling, seductive flesh.

He ran after Scott and Edgar, all of them straight-faced until they reached Glen Ellen. They had gone nearly a block before they could speak without choking. Edgar scooped out the Chiclets and folded up the bags, then started pulling handfuls of candy from his pockets.

"Who wants what?" he asked.

"I pay my own way," said Scott, shaking a Snickers bar out of his sleeve.

Edgar offered candy bars to Mike. "Three Musketeers, Baby Ruth, or Rocky Road?"

Mike looked back down Glen Ellen to see if anyone from the store was watching, then shrugged and took the Rocky Road. "How'd you do that?" he asked as he tore the wrapper with his teeth. "I was right there watching you."

"So was the manager," Edgar said. "That's the challenge."

"I can't believe it."

"Listen to you," Scott said. "As if you never stole a thing."

"Yeah, Mike?" Edgar said. "I'll bet you could get away with anything, innocent-looking guy like you."

"Well, I haven't—I mean, nothing big. But I always think it would be great to be like, you know, an international jewel thief. Planning big heists. Wouldn't it be great to commit the perfect robbery? Like that movie *Gambit*. Do it once and make a million bucks, then retire."

Edgar shook his head, laughing. "Man, you think big, don't you?"

"It would sure beat fixing broken toasters the rest of your life."

"I always took you for a . . . well, I won't say it."

Mike choked on the last bite of marshmallow. "Just 'cause I don't hang around with the Bathroom Gang? I could plan crimes those guys would never even think of."

"Yeah? But could you pull 'em off?"

"Sure. Anyway, who'd suspect a kid?"

"Maybe they wouldn't—a straight-looking kid like you."

"We should start our own gang."

Edgar laughed. "That's too much work. You just have to find the right one and join it. Right, Scott? Should we tell him about Hawk?"

Scott smirked. "You mean the Sunday School gang?"

"No, man, Hawk's cool. Don't get the wrong idea. He was on his Jesus trip today, but he's not always like that."

Suddenly Mike felt like a bit of an outcast.

"Hawk?" Mike said tentatively, aware he'd been left out of something. Usually he knew exactly what Scott was talking about—knew better than anyone.

"Forget it," Scott said. "He's no international jewel thief."

"Hawk's the real thing, man," Edgar said defensively. Mike couldn't figure out what they were talking about, so he said nothing.

His sense of camaraderie slightly tarnished, Mike turned his eyes to their goal, the curving range of coastal hills that hemmed in Bohemia Bay. The slopes, which grew green for a few months in winter, were yellowish brown by now. The highest, hindmost peaks of Shangri-La were hidden by the lower hills mounting up to them. From here at sea level, the heights were cloaked in the slithery silvery green of eucalyptus. They stopped walking at the base of Shoreview Road, which ascended and vanished among these leaves.

Edgar said, "From here we hitch."

They took a stand by a stop sign where a constant stream of cars came up from the Coast Highway, heading into the hills. Edgar stuck out his thumb. Scott and Mike stood behind him and watched the cars. A few drivers glanced at them without slowing. A woman in a run-down VW gave an apologetic shrug, as if to say her car would never make it to the top with the added load. One man held up his thumb and forefinger as if pinching a dime. In response, Edgar spread his arms as wide as they would go. The man grinned and kept driving.

"Comparing dick size?" Scott asked.

"No, man, he was only going a few blocks, and we're going all the way."

All the way, Mike thought.

He could see a big black van at the bottom of the hill, turning off the Coast Highway. What if it stopped for them and there was, say, a beautiful blond beach-bunny driving, and this amazing brunette in a bikini next to her, and they offered us a ride and we got in and the whole van was *packed* with these girls, sexy and horny and just dying to get ahold of a virgin, really show him how it was done. Of course, they could do stuff with Scott and Edgar, too, that'd be okay, but mainly—

The van drew closer, stopping at the sign across Glen Ellen. It was only then Edgar noticed it.

"Holy shit!" he shouted. "The enemy! Get back, fast!"

Edgar shoved them into a hedge. They huddled down and watched the road through the bushes.

"See this van?" Edgar whispered. "Burn it into your memory."

A huge black van rumbled past, gathering speed for the climb. It was shiny as a new hearse, freshly waxed and polished.

"That's Sal Diaz," Edgar said. "When you see him coming, boys, you'd better get out of the way. If he pulls over, say you're not hitching. Whatever you do, don't get inside that van."

Mike watched the van heading uphill, toward the ceiling of trees. "Why?"

"Sal is lethal. He's a self-defense instructor, but he only teaches *boys,* if you know what I mean. Get in that van with him, he'll ask if you know how to protect yourself, offer you some free lessons. Next thing you know, he's grabbing your cock."

Edgar bent closer, pitching his voice low as if telling a ghost story: "And if you say you don't want a lesson, he'll just pin you down and do it to you then and there. Right up the ol' poop-chute."

"While he's driving?"

"His boys chauffeur him around. He's the most dangerous man in Bohemia Bay, believe me. Hangs out at the Rock Lobster watching the surfers. If he sees someone he likes, he hunts 'em down and fuckin' rapes 'em. Course, those surfer jerks don't go down without a fight, but Sal likes that. He just sort of toys with them."

Mike crept cautiously out of the hedge, a bit awestruck to think of such a psycho loose in Bohemia Bay. He looked after the van, but saw instead an all too familiar yellow Volvo cruising downhill toward them. It was Jack's car. He almost jumped back in the hedge, but the presence of the other two froze him.

The Volvo eased to a halt across the street. Jack Harding was driving, Mike's mother next to him. "Hey, guys!" Jack called. Mike crossed the street reluctantly. The other two followed.

"We were just up at the house," Jack said.

"Roddy and Nathaniel are all moved out," said his mom. "Everything's ready for us. What are you boys up to?"

"Oh, uh, this is Edgar Goncourt. He lives in Shangri-La. He's going to show me around the neighborhood."

"Edgar?" she said. "Are you Nan Goncourt's son, the child psychologist?"

Edgar blushed. "Well . . ."

"How nice to meet you! Your mother consults for some of the district's counseling programs."

"That's my mom," Edgar said softly, with mixed pride and embarrassment.

"Have you seen the house yet?" Jack asked, with explosive heartiness.

"Only from the outside," Mike said.

"Let me give you a key." Even before Mike could answer, Jack was digging into his pocket and hauling out a ring. "The three of you can take a tour."

"Wow, cool," Mike said. "You mean we can all go in?"

"Why not?"

His mother said, "The house is so beautiful, you've never seen anything like it. I already know which room Mike will want."

"Great," Edgar said.

"You boys just . . . be careful," she said in a slightly sterner voice. "The phones aren't hooked up yet. I don't want you in there after dark."

"Would it be all right if Mike stayed at my house tonight?" Edgar asked.

She looked over at Jack, who could hardly suppress his grin as he worked the key off the ring. "Well, there is still a lot of packing to be done, but Ryan somehow slipped away for the weekend with Dirk's family, so . . ." She shrugged. "Just be sure you ask Edgar's mother first. If she has any reservations, we'll come pick you up."

"She won't care," Edgar said.

"Oh, don't say that. Say she won't *mind.*"

Jack tossed Mike the key.

"Thanks! This is gonna be great!"

"We've got Sunday brunch planned, so don't come home too late. You've still got packing to do."

Mike dropped the key in his pocket and patted it for security as the car pulled away.

"Your mom's pretty cool," Edgar said.

"She's all right," Mike admitted sheepishly, as if a cool mother were a source of humiliation. He felt he should do something to counteract the image Edgar had of him, innocent and with an easy life. He didn't feel innocent. He wanted to be seasoned, tough, mature, experienced, worldly—even a little bit dangerous. But he couldn't even get the nerve to ask a girl out on a date. He was terrified of school dances. He could easily *die* a virgin.

Yeah, at least death was reliable—the one experience he could count on having. For that reason, he looked forward to it with a morbid curiosity.

"We don't have to stay at your place," he said suddenly, shoving away all the assumptions and expectations he felt piling up on him. Why was everyone so sure he was a "good kid," so sensible and innocent? His soul wasn't so simple that a stranger could read it at a glance. Mike himself didn't know its depth.

"She'll never know if we sleep in our house," he said.

"It's no big deal," said Edgar. "We've got blankets at our place."

"I mean, it's my house, too."

"But you don't have any furniture," Scott said.

"I'm just saying, we can if we want to." He let it go at that, slightly deflated by the realization that they really didn't care if they stayed in the house or not.

"What I want right now is an avocado," Edgar said. "Come on, these drivers are jaded. Let's get their attention."

Edgar dropped to his hands and knees. "No one can refuse the human pyramid."

Scott laughed and got down beside him. "Come on, Mike. Climb up."

It was an embarrassing stunt, but that had never stopped him before. He clambered on, gouging them with his knees, arms wide and waving to the oncoming traffic.

It's summer, he thought. Anything can happen! Those beach-bunnies could still come along.

The very next car, with a nice old lady driving, gave them a ride.

4

From the bottom of Shoreview Road, as he turned off the Pacific Coast Highway, Sal saw three boys hitching. By the time he got to the corner of Shoreview and Glen Ellen, they had vanished. Bushes quaked near the roadside. He laughed, shaking his head as he drove past.

"You see that?" he asked Randy, who was sunk down in the passenger seat sucking at a yellowing roach clamped in an alligator clip.

"No. What?" Randy's voice sounded tight and scratchy.

"Hawk's boys. Scared shitless of me. You can imagine what he tells them."

"Fuck Hawk."

Sal laughed, stamping the pedal to the floor for the steep climb. "You wish."

"Don't Bogart that thing," said a voice from the back of the van.

"It's already dead," Randy said.

"So roll another. Humphrey Bogart, that's your name from now on."

"You roll it."

"Humphrey," other voices repeated. "Hump-Free!"

The van filled with high laughter. It was dark in the windowless back, where some of Sal's students and workers huddled on the floor. A youth with long bleached platinum hair climbed up between Sal and Randy, reaching for the glove box. He dug out a pack of rolling papers and a Ziploc Baggie containing several tight buds of gold-speckled sensemilla.

"Don't make a mess, Marilyn," Sal said. "I don't want seeds and stems in the carpet. It's a bitch dragging the vacuum cleaner out to the van."

"A bitch for who?" Randy said. "I'm the only one who does any cleaning. If it were up to you, this van would look like it belonged in the canyon. You know what Turtle Wax has done to my hands?"

"Bogart and Monroe, together for the first time," said a voice in the back, to more laughter. "Don't miss that cinema classic, *The Maltese Bus Stop*."

"*Maltese Butt-Fuck*, you mean."

"What is that, a new position?"

"Mm," said Marilyn. "Sounds like fun."

Sal slowed for the hairpin turn where cars were always going off the road and smashing into the shacky wood houses; he had to floor it again when the real climb began. The road snaked up through bare sandstone hills, past houses under construction and recently leveled plots where foundations had yet to be poured. The boys in back shrieked each time the van banked around a curve and sent them rolling. The van came out above a grove of avocado trees, the leaves all dark and glossy, with Bohemia Bay and the Pacific Ocean stretching out below. The boys' laughter made Sal smile.

The van began to lug on the next and steepest stage of the ascent; the boys shifted around as if redistributing the weight would help. The road leveled out in a terraced ridge community, apparently the top of the hill; but there was another climb ahead of them, and yet another after that. So they climbed through the long afternoon, up a long stretch of fairly level road with a huge sage-choked gulch on one side and a single row of houses on the other. New houses stood along the far end of the gulch, bearded by gravelly flows of excess cement that had dripped down the slopes during construction. He followed Shoreview Road to the easternmost edge of the Shangri-La development, a dirt ridge topped by barbed wire. Sal's house faced the Bohemia Greenbelt, hundreds of acres of dry-brush hills, canyons and gulleys and meadows preserved as wilderness, though ranchers had worked the land continuously since the early Spanish settlement of California.

As was usual for this hour, the neighborhood was quiet, the baking streets deserted. There was no sea breeze to cool the houses, no trees except a few silver-dollar eucalyptus saplings planted hopefully in the yards. Many of the houses were still unsold, unoccupied. It was not the most desirable region in Bohemia Bay, but Sal had paid nothing for his house, and the near-isolation suited him. Many of the places sold so far had gone to single gay men or couples; it was turning into a bit of a colony within the larger colony of Bohemia Bay. One of the Shangri-La developers, Buddy Loomis, was an old customer who had managed the deal in exchange for Sal's arrangement of a permanent Colombian connection. Buddy had probably earned back many times the value of the house by now, tax-free. Sal didn't mind the lost income; he never would have seen that money anyway, not without totally changing his image, repressing some essential part of himself. He didn't run with business-men. He preferred a lifestyle that allowed him free and open expression of his character. Buddy was almost certainly a closet-queen, judging from various neurotic quirks and the way he eyed Sal's students. Sal could usually tell when people were hiding their feelings, or hiding from them.

If Buddy had been twenty years younger, Sal might have tried to bring him out, goading him down the tricky paths of insight and confession where he had taken many of his students. But Buddy was timid and lacked a young man's daring; his hopes and ambitions lay in business, where risk was all financial and all the paths were freshly paved. Sal had taken another, less-traveled course, struggling for balance until the struggle became second nature, and finally a discipline. That rugged road had led him out of a self-tormenting existence in Los Angeles, where gangs, drugs and violence had added to the more intimate torments of his spirit; led him to this house in quiet hills above the ocean whose very name meant peace. He had come a long way for a Cholo from the barrio, few of whose natives ever left; but he had been an outcast there. That world would almost certainly have destroyed him by now if he'd remained.

Randy jumped out of the van. The boys in back were slower, since they were hungrily watching Marilyn light the joint he'd rolled.

"Save that for later," Sal said. "I don't want you stoned when we work out, I told you that."

"But Randy smoked that whole joint by himself," Marilyn complained.

"He also did tai chi for two hours this morning while the rest of you were goofing off or sleeping late."

"That's 'cause he horned about a pound of coke while you were meditating. He couldn't sit still, in case you didn't notice."

Sal climbed out of the van, unsure whether he was angrier with Randy for taking his coke, or with Marilyn for ratting on him.

"Randy," he called, "we have to talk."

Randy stood at the side of the house, staring at the door. He put a finger to his lips and beckoned urgently.

Sal hissed at the boys to be quiet. He joined Randy at the door, the others following.

Randy pointed at the doorframe; the wood next to the knob was splintered. Someone had worked a pry bar into it. No one inhabited the house next door, and with the street so deserted it would have been easy to pop the lock in broad daylight. Hell, he'd done it himself in crowded neighborhoods. Sal couldn't tell if the intruder had succeeded or not.

"Go around the back," he whispered to the others. "Watch the windows and the back door, any way they can get out."

The boys scattered around the house. Sal slipped his key into the deadbolt. He was just about to twist it when Randy whistled softly from the back yard.

"They got in here," he whispered. "Window's broken."

Sal tried to figure how much he might have lost. He'd been sitting on over forty thousand in cash, most it owed to his suppliers. He also had large new stashes of grass and coke yet to be sold, and fresh sheets of acid in the freezer. Everything in quantity.

All that was bad enough. Worse was the question of who'd hit him. If it was only a common burglar, that wasn't so bad; the guy had struck it lucky once, and next time around Sal would be waiting for him. But if it was an associate, someone he did business with, well . . . that added a whole new element of mistrust to what was already a routine founded on suspicion. The thing was, he'd never know who hit him. He couldn't call the cops, couldn't do much of anything. He was helpless in a case like this.

He let himself in, peering sidelong down the hall into the living room. Most of the drugs were kept upstairs. At least, he saw, the thief hadn't wasted time slashing furniture. The painting on the main wall, in particular, was safe: a cityscape of Los Angeles, its downtown skyline rendered at night against a backdrop of bizarre splotches like hallucinated galaxies. The picture was garish and awful, but it meant everything to Sal, who had sold its like from door to door, in bars, motels and waiting rooms, when he was trying to start a legitimate life away from the easy money and brutal stress of hustling. That shitty sales job had seemed pointless for a while, selling crap art instead of his body. He had almost given up on it when the door into money opened. A salesman—whose face meant less to him now than the lurid streaks of color in the ugly nightscape—had seen in Sal some of the qualities necessary to deal drugs. He had never stopped selling the paintings, although now they were a front for his other sales. This painting was the first he had done himself, when he was learning the assembly line trade. It had been done by the numbers, built up in layers, simultaneous with a dozen others almost exactly like it. But this one had sentimental value.

He was so intent on the painting that at first he didn't notice the figure lying in the dark on the couch below. A drab army-issue jacket had been thrown over one arm of the sofa, and a knapsack sat on the floor next to a metal crowbar that could have come from Sal's own garage. The fruit bowl on the coffee table was almost empty. Peels, cores and broken walnut shells were scattered on the glass.

"Hello, Sal."

Sal didn't move for a moment. He knew the voice, high as a girl's, but the body that went with it was all wrong.

"Guadalupe?" he whispered.

"Caught up with you."

Sal flipped on a light. He hadn't seen his brother in more than five years, and life had changed him in ways he never could have predicted. Lupe had always run to fat, slouching around like a sleepwalker, a born victim, natural prey for urban predators. But now he looked trim and strong, in need of no protector. His blue jeans and thin T-shirt were stretched tight over lean, dense muscles. His face, though . . . his face hadn't changed. Fat-cheeked, round and soft, like a baby's head on a soldier's frame, as though none of the body's hardships had been able to affect that grinning moon. His hands were scarred, his brow smooth.

"How'd you find me?"

"Wasn't hard. Why? Were you hiding?"

"It's just . . . you've been out of touch so long, I didn't know how to tell you where I went."

"You didn't tell many of your old friends either. I was in L.A. for a week, asking after you. Aunt Theresa . . . you didn't even tell her."

"I especially didn't tell her," Sal said, suddenly uncomfortable, as if Lupe had reached into an old source of shame and drawn out Sal's personal demons. He felt attacked. Lupe's appearance brought a flood of unwelcome memories, things he had been glad to leave untouched for as long as possible.

Sal heard steps in the back of the house. Realizing that his boys were coming in, he relaxed.

"I didn't want any of those fools following me," he said, wishing he didn't sound so defensive. "I wanted to leave all that shit behind. Like you did."

Lupe shook his head and laughed, a high-pitched childish sound. "I didn't leave anything behind. I went to meet it."

"So what'd you do? Join the army?"

The girlish face looked astonished. "You think they'd take me? No, I been traveling. All over the country."

"No kidding? New York?"

Lupe nodded. "I was there a while. I like the country better."

Sal found himself laughing. "Who'd have thought it? We're a long way from our roots—not many like us. You're a world traveler, and me . . ."

"Yeah. What are you, anyway?"

Randy stepped into the room.

In the instant of silence that followed, Lupe grabbed for his coat, fingers closing on the pocket.

He's got a knife, Sal thought. I wonder if it's the same one . . . the switchblade I gave him?

"What's going on?" Randy said. "Who is this?"

"This is my little brother Lupe. He's come for a visit."

Lupe stared at Randy.

"He couldn't wait till we got home?" Randy said. "He had to break the fucking window and jimmy the door?"

"Cool it," Sal said. "This was unexpected. For all he knew, I might have been out of town for a week."

Randy shook his head and went toward the back of the house. "Wait'll you see this," he called. "Sal has a brother."

"Who's he talking to?" Lupe said.

"My friends," said Sal. He could see that Lupe was disappointed they wouldn't be alone; Randy's appearance had jarred him. To be fair, he'd have to set aside some time to spend alone with his brother—send the boys out for a while so they could talk in private.

Meanwhile, he was curious to see how Lupe would react to the gang.

Marilyn was the first into the room, fingers toying with his long platinum locks. When he saw Lupe, he let his hands fall.

"This is Lupe," Sal said.

"Loopie?" said Marilyn, gaping. "Is that a nickname? You're not loopie, are you? Nuts, I mean? If you are it doesn't matter, not to me. I'm a little loopie myself. Just ask my parents. They're always trying to have me put away."

Marilyn extended his hand while he chattered but Lupe only stared at the long red nails. Marilyn pursed his lips, offended, and drew back his hand.

"I *don't* bite," he said. "Do you?"

Lupe pushed up from the couch, his smooth face contorted with disgust. The other boys were trickling into the room.

"Who are they?" he said.

Sal put a hand on Lupe's chest, calming him gently but forcibly. "Lupe, man, I haven't seen you in five years. Wherever you went, that was your business, your life. But I have my life, too, okay? These are my friends and students, and they work for me. I expect you to treat them with respect."

Marilyn shrugged. "It doesn't bother me, Sal. I get it all the time."

The other boys, picking up on Lupe's hostility, were treating him to their own brand of it. Randy and Douglas put their arms around each other and engaged in a flaunting kiss.

Well, Sal thought, so let them. He had meant what he said.

Lupe scowled and looked away from the boys.

"This is who I am, Lupe. If it bothers you . . ."

"I know what you are, Sal," he said.

Sal had to remind himself that Lupe had been through hell. His childhood had ended with a violent initiation into adulthood, of a sort. The boy had almost died. Sal, as he had so often before, regretted that he hadn't been there to protect Lupe.

Yet Lupe now looked steady and strong, sure of himself, nurtured by an inner source of strength.

"Okay, Lupe," Sal said, trying not to let a bittersweet compassion turn saccharine in his mouth. "These are my friends. Boys, this is my brother. I hope you can all get along. If you want to stay here, Lupe, you're welcome to."

"I don't want to put you out," Lupe said mockingly.

"It's no bother." He turned to the boys. "Is it?"

"Hell no," said Randy, with a smug grin. "He can take my bed, Sal. I'll sleep with you."

If the comment was supposed to get a rise out of Lupe, Randy must have been disappointed. Lupe only nodded then sank back down in the couch.

"I won't be staying long," he said.

"Stay as long as you like," said Marilyn. "There's always room for one more in Sal's house. Your brother is one of the nicest guys in Bohemia Bay."

Lupe smiled. "You mean he has a reputation?"

"In certain circles."

Sal sat down next to Lupe and put a hand on his shoulder. "I try to keep a low profile. Business being what it is."

"You're dealing," Lupe said, without surprise. "How else could you afford to live in a place like this?"

Sal shrugged. "It got me here, true enough. But that's only money. What matters to me is my other work. You don't see me wasting the money, you know, on a bunch of luxuries. I support my causes—gay rights, shelters for runaways. You'd be surprised at the number of kids who end up here. I teach tai chi, to bring mind and body into harmony, get things in balance. I've got a good life, Lupe. I've got friends. What about you?"

Lupe shrugged. "You know me, Sal. Nothing ever changes."

Sal hoped it didn't sound like he was trying to impress Lupe with his success and make all Lupe's accomplishments seem trivial. In the past, you could never be sure how Lupe would take things. Even the plainest statement of fact seemed to go banging around in his head, ending up twisted beyond recognition.

Maybe all that had changed now. Maybe.

Sal's students crouched down on the floor or dropped into chairs, watching Lupe—some openly, some covertly.

"God," Marilyn said, "I would die for your complexion. I'm allergic to hormone creams. Do you shave?"

Sal tensed up, waiting for one of Lupe's surges of rage, of violent temper. But apparently Lupe had mellowed enough to answer the question with a weary smile.

"Naw," he said. "I don't have to."

"Really? How come?"

Lupe plucked the last two walnuts from the fruit bowl and cupped them in his palm.

" 'Cause these here, see, are like the only nuts I got."

=5=

A green bomb dropped through leafy shade, barely missing Mike's head. He stooped to pick it up and toss it in his bag. In the branches above, Edgar clambered about like a monkey, reaching for another ripe avocado.

Mike and Scott had two bags full of fruit, some of it warm from the highest branches, some of it cool as the shade. They had crawled through a hole under a barbed wire fence near the roadside, then crept downhill under a continuous canopy of avocado trees. Mike had never seen so many in one place. Edgar scurried up one tree after another, plucking the rough-skinned bulbs and tossing them down.

Mike kept glancing down the hill, but the trees were so thick he couldn't see much more than a white flicker of the farmhouse.

"Keep your voices down," Edgar whispered from above.

"Why?" Scott said loudly.

At that instant, just down the hill, dogs began to howl.

"Oh, Jesus," Mike said, snatching up his bag, stuffing a spare avocado in the pocket of his coat.

Edgar leaped from the tree, landing with an *"Oof!"* directly in front of Mike. He got up limping. Scott was already halfway up the hill to the fence with one full bag under his arm. Behind them, fallen leaves crackled and branches snapped, but the dogs were silent, devoting their energies to the chase.

Seconds later, Mike shoved his bag under the fence and crawled after it. Scott was waiting. They grabbed Edgar's hands and yanked him to freedom on the bare hillside, above the trees. They ran up Shoreview Road, gasping for breath. The dogs were barking again, but getting no closer.

Mike and Scott glared at Edgar.

"I swear to God, there weren't any dogs last time," Edgar said. "Anyway, we got enough to last us. Two full bags? That's plenty."

"I don't even like avocados," Mike reminded them.

They started up the road, slowly catching their breath. It was a steep climb. Mike slung his jacket over his shoulder though Scott, perversely, kept his on.

"The avocado was the original fruit of knowledge," Scott said eventually.

"Oh yeah?" said Edgar. "Says who?"

"You think they had apple trees in the Middle East?"

"You mean Eve gave Adam an avocado?" said Edgar with a sour expression, still limping.

Scott nodded with a look of unimpeachable authority. "She would have, if Adam or Eve had ever existed, which they didn't."

"Don't ever tell that to Hawk."

"You can't argue with Scott," Mike said. "He knows everything."

"You can't argue with Hawk either. He'll just blow your head off."

"The Bible's nothing but symbols and metaphors, with a lot of old history mixed in," Scott said. "I'm sure Hawk knows that. Look at his Fightin' Jesus stories."

"Still . . . you can never tell with Hawk. I wouldn't tempt him."

"Not even with an avocado?" Scott said.

The road wound up and up. When it leveled off, Mike was

grateful, thinking they had reached the peak. Then Edgar led them up another three steep blocks. The last time he'd come up here, by car, he'd been reading in the backseat and hadn't paid attention to the road. By the time they surmounted the next rise, the sun was sinking behind them. He looked back at the ocean, far below. Ahead, the road went on for another quarter mile, rising more gradually. There were fewer houses to be seen, and only sparse chaparral vegetation. He saw a broad gorge with a row of houses lined up along the far end.

"One of those is our new place."

"Which one?"

"I'm not sure. It's kind of hard to tell them apart."

They did look alike, stacked tall and thin on the canyon's steep wall. Their westward-facing sliding glass doors glared bright orange with the setting sun. Below them, the canyon was a darkening lake of shadow. As the boys walked along the edge, Mike looked down into it, thinking of all the hiding places and forts he could build down there, if he were still young enough to care about that sort of thing. His brother might enjoy it, although Ryan was mainly interested in sports these days. Better than forts, though—it was a place he could go with a girl, when he met one. Down there under the bushes, naked on a blanket, he wouldn't care if he got dirty or if bugs climbed all over him. It would all be worth it when she wrapped her legs around him.

When they finally reached the houses, they turned and walked along the row. At the fifth one, Mike stopped. "This is it."

There wasn't much to see except an empty carport identical to every other on the block. That was about all he'd seen of the place. A black Cadillac was parked in the carport next door. Mike walked across the oil-stained cement and over a redwood porch linking the carport to the front door. He slid the key into the lock.

Inside, it smelled like a house that had been lived in till yesterday. Odors of butter and garlic, faint and fading even now, slipped past him as he stepped inside, like the last ghosts of the prior residents. Scott and Edgar followed him in. As they got a good look at the place, all three of them let out exclamations. Mike's mother had mentioned that the walls were painted, but he had never imagined anything like this. One of the two men who'd lived here before, Roddy, was an interior decorator, and he had partitioned the top floor into three areas. The walls were midnight blue. A square of gold carpet lay in a small dining area, divided from the kitchen by a wooden counter. Beyond the kitchen was a big living room, with sliding glass doors opening onto a balcony at the far end. Stairs ran down into the house, colored stripes running with them, zigzagging past one landing and ending at a second two floors below.

"Wow," said Edgar, shutting the door. Scott stepped onto the square of yellow carpeting and stared at the wall opposite the kitchen. It was one solid mirror.

"Get out of there, Scott! Jesus, your feet are dirty!"

Scott gave him a look he usually reserved for morons. Mike found himself wondering if he could actually live in a house like this. It was like a place in a magazine. He was afraid to put his own feet down.

They took the stairs to the second level, which held two bedrooms. The biggest opened onto another balcony. Three huge overlapping colored circles decorated the main wall. The color scheme continued into a private bathroom.

"This has got to be Mom and Jack's room," Mike said.

He backed into the hall and saw Edgar opening a door next to the stairs.

"Look at this!" he said.

Scott and Mike followed him into the room—stopped in awe when they saw where they were.

They had walked into a fairy tale. A full, silvery indoor moon hung in a luminous blue sky, above rolling hills layered in shades of green, seeming to go on for miles. The landscape covered every wall, except where a large walk-in closet opened under the stairs. The design continued right on into a second bath-room, which had a second entrance leading back into the hall.

"Unbelievable," Scott said.

"This is *my* room," Mike said, determined that it would be. He had never dreamed that such a room could exist. It was like something out of the Narnia books: a plain wooden door opening onto a secret world.

"You are one lucky dude," Edgar said. "Lucky, lucky, lucky."

Mike couldn't possibly disagree.

The rest of the house was an anticlimax. They followed the colored stripes down the stairs to the third level, a large white room with mirrored tiles on opposite walls, so you could stand between them and see your image reflected to infinity. It was too bright for Mike, who preferred dark woods and cool shade, but for Ryan, who could spend all day on the beach without getting burned, it seemed fine. He began instantly thinking of it as Ryan's room. It had a balcony of its own, like the master bedroom. A private back door opened onto a mossy patio full of ferns and dichondra, like a cool cave tucked beneath the house.

A flight of spiral stairs penetrated the floor of Ryan's room, leading down to a tiny, wood-paneled room that smelled of new carpeting. Sliding glass doors opened directly onto the edge of the wild brush canyon. A slender young eucalyptus tree swayed beyond the glass.

"TV room," Edgar said.

"Library," said Scott.

"Who cares? As long as I get the moon room."

They hiked back up to the second level. They had dropped their bags of avocados on the landing. It was getting dark—especially in the house—and as they entered Mike's room, he could almost believe he was stepping outside. He couldn't imagine what it would be like to live in this room, to wake and sleep in such beauty every day. It would be like inhabiting a painting. He could only imagine that his own artwork would soar when he worked here. It would inspire him every day. And imagine . . . if a girl ever saw it? She would have to love this room. They would lie on the floor under that fat white moon, among the green hills, and do everything imaginable.

Edgar said, "Let's stash a bag of avocados here for later, in case we sleep over."

Suddenly Mike wasn't sure he wanted them here at all. He felt protective of the room, as if it were already his private territory. He wondered if he would have to battle Ryan for possession.

"But there's no furniture or anything," he said.

"I've got sleeping bags and blankets at my place," said Edgar.

"I don't know. You heard my mom . . ."

"How's she gonna know? I mean, you can stay at my place if you want, but just look at this. . . ."

"I'll think about it." Mike stashed his bag of avocados in the big closet, which went far back under the stairs. He felt he was marking the room as his own. With extreme reluctance, he went out into the hall and shut the door on the nightscape.

It was dusk now, the houses around them gray as the sky, most of the windows dark.

Edgar lived less than a block away, up Shoreview Road. Mrs. Goncourt wasn't home, so they fixed sandwiches and went down to Edgar's room. He had a sliding glass door of his own, facing on the dark, weedy expanse of cactus and brush behind his house. While they were eating, someone rapped on the glass. Mike looked up to see two faces grinning in from the night, two guys carrying skateboards. "Hey!" he said, sliding open the door. "You guys are just in time."

"For what?" said the first kid in, a skinny blond named Kurtis Tyre. Kurtis was another student from the Alt-School. Mike had never spoken to him, though occasionally he'd held his schoolbooks tight to his chest when Kurtis passed, in case the kid tried to knock them out of his arms.

"We're figuring out what to do tonight," Edgar said. "Hey, it's Mad-Dog!"

Mad-Dog Murphy, Kurtis Tyre's inseparable companion, nodded a greeting and slid the glass shut behind him. He was dark-haired and gap-toothed, with a crazed look exaggerated by the way his eyes wandered off in different directions. Kurtis propped his skateboard against the wall; Mad-Dog dropped his on the floor and sat down on it, rolling back and forth in great agitation.

"You talked to Hawk lately?" Kurtis asked, ignoring Mike and Scott.

"Saw him at Saturday Sermon," Edgar said. "Where were you?"

"Avoiding him, man. Craig warned me he's coming down on us for scratching 'S.S.' on dirty cars. Says the cops are bugging him about it."

"What's wrong with 'S.S.'?" Edgar said.

Scott chuckled deeply and everyone turned to look at him. "It's a Nazi emblem," he said. "For the *Schutzstaffel,* the Black Shirts."

"Really? I thought it stood for Silver Skaters," Edgar said.

"It does," Kurtis said, irritably. "What's he doing here anyway?"

"Scott's cool," Edgar said. "Hawk likes him."

"You another Jesus freak, Gillette?"

Scott didn't deign to answer. Instead he rolled his eyes at Mike, who suddenly didn't feel quite so isolated. But if Kurtis Tyre and Mad Dog could show up out of the blue, some of those Alt-School girls couldn't be far behind.

"I get so sick of that Jesus stuff," Kurtis went on. "Making out like he's such a fuckin' saint. So what if the cops think we're Nazis? Maybe they'd give us some respect."

Edgar picked up the phone.

"Who you calling?"

"Craig Frost. See if him and Howard want to come up, bring the other guys."

Kurtis turned his attention to Mike. "Never thought I'd see you here, James. You trying to join the club or something?"

Mike shrugged. "I don't know about any club. I'm just with Scott."

"And with me," Edgar said, covering the phone. "Mike's moving in down the street. He wants to be a master thief."

Mad-Dog barked his patented hyena laugh.

"A master thief?" said Kurtis in disbelief. "Oh, man, what is this? Are you serious?"

"I saw a murder once," Mike blurted.

For a minute, Mad-Dog stopped laughing. Edgar was muttering on the phone but even he looked up.

Kurtis gaped. "What does that mean? Do you want to see another?"

"I was just . . ." Forget it, he thought. He wasn't going to tell the story.

"You're full of shit, Kurtis," Edgar said.

"What kind of club is it, anyway?" Mike said.

"It's Hawk's One-Way Gang."

"One-Way?" Mike said.

Edgar pointed a finger at the ceiling. "You know, straight up. To Heaven? We're all in it."

Mike looked at Scott. "You too?"

Scott shrugged.

"Not if I have anything to say about it," Kurtis said.

"Hawk likes him. That's what matters."

"Yeah, Kuuur-tis," said Mad-Dog mockingly, laughing till Kurtis grabbed an ear and twisted it.

It was almost an hour before Craig Frost and Howard Lean showed up. In that time, Mike and Scott had to endure so many of Kurtis Tyre's jibes that it was a relief to see new faces at the glass—even these faces, which were not the most comforting in Bohemia Bay. Craig and Howard were several years older than the others. Craig was out of school completely, though he hadn't graduated. Everyone knew his story, the high school was so small. He was a grease monkey at the Central Beach station now. Howard was still in school, though he had been kept back at least twice. His orthodontist father and realtor mother wouldn't let him drop out like his idol, Craig. They had big plans for him, apparently.

"So, Frost, you got a car tonight?" asked Kurtis.

Craig shook his head, looking embarrassed. "No, man, we hitched."

Kurtis chortled. "Never heard of a mechanic without wheels."

"My engine's laid out all over my fuckin' garage. Never shoulda let Dusty touch it."

"So tell him to steal you a new one. Or do it yourself. You got to brush up on crime, man, unless you plan on *working* the rest of your life."

"Howard, put a fist in his mouth, would you?"

Howard smiled, showing gray chipped teeth crammed in rows like a shark's. He stooped toward Kurtis, fist soaring in slow motion. Kurtis lightly batted it away.

"Guess who we saw today," Edgar said. "Sal Diaz!"

Howard's face grew even sallower. "That queer? Did you suck his dick this time?"

"No, I bit it off and brought it for you." Everyone but Howard laughed. "He was trawling for chicken in his black van."

"That guy makes me sick," Craig said. "Why hasn't somebody firebombed his house?"

"Let's us do it," Howard said.

"Guy thinks he's a Mexican Bruce Lee," said Kurtis.

"Well, he's only a block from here," Edgar said. "We could do it."

"You're not going to firebomb somebody's house," Scott said suddenly.

"Who is this pussy?" Howard asked.

"Meet Albert Einstein," Kurtis said.

"Don't worry, Scott," Edgar reassured him. "We'll just go over and moon the guy. Bug him a little."

"Oh, he'll like that all right," Kurtis said. "Give him a nice whiff of his favorite food. I mean, don't do the fag any favors."

"This room is suffocatin'," Craig said. "Let's get out of here."

He slid open the sliding glass door and stepped outside. Everyone tumbled after him, though Edgar hung behind a moment and Mike watched him take a small glass vial from his pocket. He uncapped it, touched it to his fingertips, then dabbed himself behind the ears. Mike smelled the strong odor he'd caught from Edgar all day—the hippie, Alt-School smell.

"What is that?" he asked.

"Patchouli oil. You want some?"

Mike wrinkled his nose, shook his head.

"It's for protection, attracting money . . . and sex."

"Sex?"

"Yeah. Drives girls crazy."

Mike put out a finger. "Maybe a little."

It didn't smell *that* bad.

6

It was good to get outside again, into the air, especially since he regretted the patchouli oil immediately. It made his eyes water and his nose begin to itch and run. He didn't feel much like an adventure now, not with these guys. It was becoming pretty obvious that no girls were going to turn up. They wouldn't be acting like this if there were. Going to bother queers wasn't going to get him any closer to his first lay—not the kind he was hoping for, anyway.

He was half tempted to walk away from them, go back to the new house and stare at the moon on his wall. He thought Scott would probably come along, but then he saw Scott arguing with Edgar over what they should do and say when they got where they were going. He was laughing, having a great time. Mike kicked himself mentally. How much excitement did they have in their lives anyway? He spent most of his time wishing for something to happen; and now here it was, happening, and he was already trying to get out of it.

Screw it. Screw fear.

Besides, it was dark. It wasn't like Sal would see his face—or even his ass—in this light. Nobody was going to catch them. He'd been doing this sort of thing all his life. When it came to pranks, he was practically a pro.

Dried grass hissed in a warm wind along the embankment. All the houses were on one side of the street, facing undeveloped land on the other. Barbed wire marked the boundary. Most of the homes were dark, but he could hear the steady *thud, thud, thud* of disco up ahead; the only sign of life in the development. As they got closer to the sound, he saw Sal's black van sitting in a driveway.

The seven boys stopped in the middle of the street.

"Somebody go ring the bell," Craig said.

For a paralyzing moment, Mike was certain they would choose him.

"Mad-Dog," said Kurtis.

"Yeah-yeah-yeah!" Mad-Dog agreed with a sniggering laugh.

Mike relaxed. Apparently he wasn't cool enough to be considered even for the dirty work.

"The rest of you get ready," Craig said. "About fuckin' face!"

They turned their backs to the house, strung across the street in a straggling line like a half-hearted human roadblock. Mad-Dog, meanwhile, scampered past the black van, up to the door. Looking over his shoulder, Mike saw Mad-Dog capering under the porch light, then he touched the doorbell and came tearing back to the line-up.

The muffled music died.

"Hey, queer!" Howard called.

"We know you're in there, you faggot!" Kurtis joined in.

Thumbs hooked in the waist of his trousers, still twisted around, Mike saw the door open. A man appeared in silhouette, leaning against the doorframe looking out.

"Pervert!"

"Fucking homo!"

"Queer!"

"Cocksucker!"

"Buttfucker!"

"Goddamn faggot!"

"Queer!"

"Suck my dick, you quasar!"

"Kiss my ass!"

Sal—if Sal it was—stayed perfectly still.

Craig said, *"Now!"*

The sound of zippers and snaps broke out along the row, as the boys yanked down their pants. Mike felt the breeze on his cheeks, and craned around to look at the luminous doorway. The man had gone back inside. The door hung open like a mouth about to speak. Mike sent his own voice hooting out with the others, barking like a fool, his blood foaming with an adrenaline rush.

Giddy, feeling wilder than any of them now, he clutched at the pocket of his jacket and felt the bulbous avocado inside, where he had stuffed it when they were running from the grove. He dug into the pocket without another thought, screaming and yipping and laughing—yes! He was a wild man! Part of the pack—invincible!

He lobbed the green fruit as hard as he could, and watched in amazement as it sailed—as if expertly tossed—straight through the open doorway and exploded on the wall within. Guacamole splattered; chunks of green pulp gleamed on the white plaster. . . .

"Holy shit!" Edgar said. "Run!"

The command was unnecessary. None of them would have stood still another instant. And they had good reason to run.

Shrieks poured from the open door. Mike saw a blur of silhouettes merging with darkness. His own scream came involuntarily. He yanked up his jeans, trying to run without tripping. For a minute he thought he heard Mad-Dog's laughter echoing down the empty street, but Mad-Dog's mouth was clamped shut. The seven fled in silence. The sound he heard was Sal's gang, howling hungrily for their blood.

Mike could hardly see where he was going, even though his eyes were used to the dark. Edgar hissed and pointed them down a hill street; halfway down the block, they dodged into a walkway between two houses. Mike felt like a frightened rabbit running for a hole. The cries of their pursuers faded in another direction. They bounded into the clear, coming out in a vacant lot. Mike stumbled and fell into deep dead grass. Sticker-balls from burr-clover buried tiny snags in his palms; sticky foxtails pierced his clothes, making ripping sounds as he tried to rise.

"Down!" Edgar whispered from somewhere nearby, unseen. Someone giggled breathlessly. They were all in the weeds, huddled down.

Craig: "Where'd they go?"

"Whyn't you go look?"

"Fuck you, Tyre. Edgar, how do we get to your house from here?"

"They know where I live, man. They're probably over there right now."

Mike raised his eyes—no more than that—above the grass. Just down the street, less than half a block away, a black Cadillac gleamed in a carport. He stifled a laugh. The other guys were about to enter into his debt.

"Hey, my house is right there," he said.

"No shit?" said Craig. "Is anybody home?"

"We haven't even moved in yet."

"Whoa, that's right!" said Edgar. "We got a key!"

"Let's do it," Craig said. "Follow the twerp."

Mike crept to the edge of the vacant lot; dry grass rustled behind him, the only sign that he was being followed. He looked up and down the street, saw nothing but darkness. As soon as he stepped onto asphalt, he heard a shout. Gray shapes swarmed under a streetlight up the hill. They had seen him.

A dozen or so long, leaping strides brought him to the porch. The other boys plowed into him, grabbing at the doorknob. "Hurry, man!" He dug into his pocket for the key.

"What the fuck's wrong?"

"Let us in!"

"Come on, Mike!"

"Get it open, dipshit!"

"I'm trying, I'm—"

"They're coming!"

The key twisted in the lock. The street echoed with blood-thirsty cries. The door flew open from the pressure of seven straining bodies.

Suddenly the carport shook with new arrivals.

Mike nearly stumbled down the stairwell in the dark; he caught the rail and tried to grab the door, but it had already banged shut. He twisted the knob to make sure it was locked. The other six clustered around him, waiting, some pressing hard on the door as if they didn't trust the lock.

Just then, someone started pounding on the wood. It sounded as if they were using mallets. Mike could feel the jarring in his feet.

"Gonna kill you!" whispered a deep voice.

"Shit," Kurtis whispered, "did you see? Those guys had nun-chuks."

"You're dead in there," said another voice.

"Dead!" promised another.

"Must be like twenty of 'em," Howard whispered. "Oh, we picked a good night to hassle Sal. A real good night."

"They probably have swords, too," Kurtis said. "Like, those big Bruce Lee machetes?"

After a minute, Sal's gang left off pounding. The whispers of the seven fugitives sounded loud in the empty house. Mike went halfway down the stairs, listening to a thudding too far away to be his heart. He felt fairly sure that someone was running down the stairs between the houses.

"They're surrounding us," he announced.

"What are you talking about?"

Before he could explain, they heard hammering and pound-ing in the depths of the house. It sounded like the Diaz gang was about to shatter the sliding glass doors on the ground floor.

"Where's the light?" Howard asked.

"No, keep it off," said Scott. "They can't be sure we're in here. Maybe they'll try another house and get somebody really pissed off."

"Oh, fuck," Howard was saying. "We're going to die, man, we're really going to die!"

Craig: "Everybody! Just shut the fuck up! Especially you, Howard."

It was worse in silence, because they could clearly hear whispering outside, all around them, along with the sound of feet scurrying up and down the stairs and hillside. There were no more noisy threats, only the quiet persistence of determined assassins.

"Whose idea was this anyway?" Kurtis said.

"Yours," said Mad-Dog.

"But who the fuck threw that avocado?"

Mike swallowed apprehensively. He couldn't believe Kurtis was trying to blame this on him. He'd only been joining in the spirit of things . . . hadn't he?

"Forget it," Edgar said. "Let's check the balcony."

Edgar, Scott and Mike crossed the living room, opened the sliding glass door, and went out on the deck. The only illumination came from streetlights along Shoreview Road, far away at the edge of the canyon. Mike leaned over the railing and saw shadows moving around the base of the house. Big shadows. It took him a moment to realize that they were cast by the eucalyptus tree. He tried to look between the houses, but it was pitch black in there. He was sure he heard whispering and bootsteps crunching in earth. Suddenly three shapes rushed out from under the house, where they'd been busy in the little fern grotto. Mike jerked back abruptly.

"I can't see anything," Scott said, from the other side of the balcony, "but I can hear them."

"They're definitely down there," Edgar agreed.

As they went back in, rocks and gravel began to pelt the sides of the house, rattling on the windows and sliding glass doors. Mike prayed they wouldn't throw anything too big, but that prayer only opened the gates to deeper levels of hopelessness. He never should have fled to the house. He'd be better off out in the street, free to move without putting his house at risk. What if they busted windows? What if they spray-painted the walls? What if they broke down the door and massacred everyone? He had promised his mother he wouldn't go in after dark, and instead he had attracted the wrath of a gang of marauders.

"What do we do now?" Howard said.

"Gimme a minute to think," said Craig.

"I wish Hawk was here."

"He's not, so forget about it."

"Call him, Edgar," Kurtis said.

"There's no phone," Mike said. "I'm not even supposed to be here."

They ignored that.

"We gotta get Hawk, that's all there is to it," said Kurtis.

"Oh, and how the fuck do you plan to do that?"

"Somebody has to go get him, that's all."

Suddenly the pounding started up again at the front door. They all jumped. Mike stared at the door, expecting it to come flying open, torn from its hinges. He was waiting for the *real* destruction to begin. The guys outside weren't yelling anymore, but he could hear them whispering their threats, and that was even worse. Death, mutilation, torture—all this and more was in store for them. Jack and his mom would find the walls freshly painted in the morning—painted with his blood.

And you asked for it, Mike told himself. You had to invite everybody in.

If they'd caught him outside, it would have been quicker. At least the house would have been untouched. He'd have received a proper burial then, and the pity of his family.

As it is, he thought, if they leave any part of me alive, Mom'll finish the job they start.

He put his back to the door, as if he could hold it shut alone if they decided to batter it down. "Shit," he said finally.

"You can't think that way," Edgar said firmly. "We all have to start focusing on some positive images."

"Oh, get off that bullshit," Kurtis said.

"I'm serious. We can do it. Seven minds, working together.

We have so much untapped power. All we have to do is concentrate."

"You're worse than Hawk, man. At least the Bible really exists."

"The rest of you, then," Edgar said. "If we all focus on one thought, visualize the thing we want, it'll work. We can influence them, I swear to God. You just have to hold a clear picture of what you want, and that creates the space it needs to happen."

"What do you mean?" Mike asked. "Like, ESP?"

"It's mind power, brain power."

"But it only works if you have shit for brains, like Edgar."

"I'm just ignoring you, Kurtis. I'm seeing your negativity locked up inside a safe where it can't hurt us. The rest of you, close your eyes and try. See them going away, leaving us alone."

"When I close my eyes I see myself getting killed," said Howard.

"Come on, concentrate. Visualize them going away, leaving the house, going back to Sal's."

Edgar's voice was deep and slow, but could not quite manage to be hypnotic.

"Going away . . . going away . . . leaving us alone, like . . . leaving us alone . . . can you see it?"

Mike didn't need to close his eyes. Desperation made it easy to picture their pursuers slipping away like shadows under a strong light. It was his most fervent desire at the moment.

"Going away . . . going away . . ."

"Are you doing it, Scott?" Mike asked.

"Worth a try," Scott said.

"Imbecile," said Kurtis, but no one else was arguing. They seemed to be following Edgar's instructions.

After a few minutes, Mike didn't hear any more whispering or scraping around the house. The rocks had stopped clattering on the windows; no more threats crept in under the door.

"See?" Edgar said. "It's working."

As soon as he spoke, a scream erupted less than a foot from

Mike's head. They began hammering the door under his back. He flung himself away.

"That's it, Edgar," Kurtis said. "You're elected. Go get Hawk. Fucking call him by ESP if you don't want to run for a phone."

Edgar stared at Kurtis, his eyes gleaming in the dark as if he were crying. "All right," he said after a minute, defeat in his voice. "I'll go."

Mike felt sorry for him, but not sorry enough to argue with Kurtis. Whoever Hawk was, Mike would be glad for any help they could get.

"You can go out the bottom door," he suggested. "Someone should watch from up here on the balcony, to make sure the coast is clear."

Craig Frost said, "Me and Howard'll watch."

So Edgar, Scott and Mike groped their way to the dark spiral stairs. They discovered, upon entering the lowest room, that they were clearly visible to anyone outside, thanks to the street-lights glaring in through the sliding glass doors. There were no curtains or blinds on the doors. Fortunately, there didn't seem to be anyone around. But Mike half expected savage faces to appear at the glass at any moment, and then there would be no hiding.

"I thought for a minute there that it was working," Mike said as Edgar peered through the glass. "Your visualization thing, I mean."

"It would have, but Kurtis is way too negative," Edgar said. "I've been trying to get the whole gang to use it, so we can work in total silence."

"Edgar . . ." Scott said reproachfully.

"Yeah, so anyway, I'm going to stick to the underbrush as long as I can, but I've got to cross the street eventually. I hope they're not over there. When I come back, I'll have Hawk with me. Then we'll really take care of Sal."

"I just want to get out of here," Mike confessed.

"Well, that too."

Scott called up the spiral stairway, "All clear?"

They heard Howard relaying Craig's message: *"Go!"*

Mike flipped the latch and slid the door open. Edgar slipped out. He hauled the glass shut as fast as he could and snapped the latch back down. Edgar was already invisible, lost in the bushes. Mike felt vulnerable in the lowest room. He signaled to Scott that they should go back up to the room above. There they sat on a white linoleum floor, walls bright and shining. The mirrors gleamed even in the dark.

"I can't believe this is happening," Mike said. "How'd you meet these guys anyway?"

Scott shrugged. He seemed calm, even comfortable, in the midst of the madness.

"Edgar took me out to Hawk's trailer. You know, it's that place in the canyon, made up like a church, quotes from Revelations written all over the side."

"With the crosses in the yard? Jeez, that's Hawk? The guy who's supposed to save us?"

"He's like an ex-con, ex-biker, ex-everything. Edgar says he's rehabilitated, but I don't know. The people he hangs out with seem pretty wild. There's one guy, Stoner? Looks like a big blond caveman. I saw five guys ganging up on him, trying to drag him to the ground, but they couldn't do it till Hawk jumped in."

"And you really want to join this club?"

Scott chuckled. "To me, they make an interesting study in anthropology. The hierarchical structure, the messianic overtones . . ."

"Well . . . Edgar seems okay," Mike said doubtfully.

"He's intelligent enough, except for his obsession with ESP."

"You don't think it works?"

"The visualization stuff, it's meant to be psychological. It's a form of therapy, but I think he missed the point. It's all turned into mumbo-jumbo, psychic mush, in his head. I mean really, *ESP?"*

"I remember when *you* used to do black magic."

"That was an experiment. And at least I was drawing on some existing tradition. This is all old hippie bullshit people came up with after doing too many drugs. You know—peace, love and transactional analysis."

"Maybe Edgar's experimenting, too."

"Edgar's bored and desperate. Having a shrink for a mom has got him all twisted up. Last month he was into Transcendental Meditation and Eckankar. Next month, who knows?"

Mike sighed and banged his head back against the wall, feeling almost secure to be alone for a minute with his friend, with whom he had shared numerous moments that felt dangerous but turned out okay. Scott could keep him from going too far into fear—most effectively by ridiculing him, as he now derided Edgar.

"I should never have brought them all in here. I wish I never had . . ." His breath sucked back into his throat. He jumped to his feet. "The key!"

He dug stiff fingers into his pocket—his empty pocket. The other one was full of change. He turned it inside out and shook through a handful of coins, hoping one of the silver shapes would turn out to be something more valuable than a quarter.

"I don't believe it," he said. "Why is this happening to me?"

He headed for the stairs, slipped and banged his shins, kept going till he reached the top again, gasping for breath.

Up here, the other guys were talking in normal voices now, completely relaxed. Mike grabbed the doorknob, then hesitated, turning to Scott, who was just coming up the stairs.

"Go out on the balcony and look around, make sure no one's at the door."

Scott hurried to comply. "All clear," he called from the deck.

Mike was praying, trying to remain positive, as Edgar had suggested. He remembered putting the key in the lock, but he couldn't remember taking it out. He'd been so frightened and rushed during the chase that he had forgotten it completely until now.

Please let the key still be there. Let the key still be there, God. If there is a God.

No, that's wrong—think positive:

The key is there. The key is there. It's still in the lock where I left it. There is a God and the key is there. It has to be there. Visualize it. Use your fucking imagination!

He eased the door open half an inch, an inch. That was all the room he needed to see the brass knob shining in starlight. Polished brass and nothing more.

No matter how hard he tried to imagine it, he couldn't make out the faintest sign of any key.

Hawk could hardly hear Edgar on the phone. "Hold off a minute, would you?" He was talking to Edgar, but Maggie mistook him and left off chewing on his other ear. Saying nothing—but so expressively—she jumped down from the bed and walked the length of the trailer to where Stoner sat with his knees tucked up on the built-in couch, pretending to read *The Cross and the Switchblade,* an act he'd been faking ever since Hawk first shoved the book at him half a year ago. Maggie dropped down next to Stoner, took a swig of beer from his bottle, and let it dangle by the neck. She wouldn't even look at Hawk.

"Hey, Maggie, what's this word?" Stoner said, pushing the book under her nose.

"Fuckface," she said, and Hawk didn't know who she was talking to.

"Say again, Edgar," Hawk said. "I'm getting a lot of interference here."

Edgar was out of breath, his words stumbling all over each other. Just when Hawk thought he was getting the drift, the whole trailer began to roar. Hawk jumped up and hammered on the wall, but he could hardly hear himself pounding.

"Stoner! Tell Dusty to lay off a minute, would you?"

"Sure, Hawk." Stoner looked relieved at having an excuse to put down the book. He was wearing his usual big dumb grin, which got bigger and dumber when Maggie said, "I suppose you want me to move?"

"Naw." He picked her up as if she were a rag doll, got off the couch, and set her back down in his place. Stoner went outside and shouted at Dusty, his voice louder than the power tools. Everything turned quiet except the Saturday night traffic on Old Creek Road.

"Back up, Edgar. Where are you now?"

"My house."

"Meet me out front, then. Ten minutes."

Hawk hung up and got out of bed. Maggie stared at him.

"You ain't going nowhere," she said. "Not again—not tonight."

"Patience, my sweet Magdalene." He chucked her chin as he passed, and she made as if to bite his finger. "My tiny flock's in peril. Didn't you hear them bleating on the phone?"

"Are you trying to be an asshole, or does it just come natural?"

He winced and put his head out the door. "Stoner!"

The cars whizzing past sent crucifix shadows sweeping over the cluttered yard. The smell of motor oil was still strong after the hot day. Stoner was on his knees halfway into Dusty's van, the crack of his ass above his belt as dark as the gates of Hell. He backed out with a puzzled yet hopeful expression, holding a caged lightbulb on a clamp. Faithful as a dog, Hawk thought. There was a smudge of grease on Stoner's forehead, just below his curly blond locks.

"Hold it steady, dude!" Dusty said from inside the van.

"Turn it *off*," Hawk said. "We're making a cavalry run."

Dusty backed out of the driver's side holding a wrench. He was short and wiry with snarled black curly hair. In his ripped-up, oily jeans and tank top he looked like a real mechanic. Only his friends knew otherwise. When Dusty had finished with the engine, it might never work again. He had a tendency of working on things when he was dusted, as he was right now. That was how he got himself "motivated." His eyes sat on shelves of bone above pits so deep and dark that the flesh might have been scooped out with a grapefruit spoon; skin seemed to have been applied sparingly to his bony head, laid onto the skull like gold leaf. His shoulders and pectorals were covered with tattoos of hollow, tubular waves—surfers' wet-dream pipelines, with little Vaughn Bodē guys crouched down low at the tips of rakish boards, all ten toes gripping the tapered noses as they shot the tubes on tropical-sunset fantasy beaches. Hawk had never known Dusty to so much as wade barefoot in a tide pool.

"Whatta those little fuckups get themselves into this time?" he said.

"The fag on the hill has a posse out after them."

"Man, I'm sick of bailing those skinny-ass punks out of their messes. This is the last time, man. The last time. I got my own troubles."

Stoner said, "I'm not going near that place. That motherfucker Sal tried to kiss me once."

"Shut up and get the shotgun."

"Awlriiiiight!" Dusty said. "That sounds more like it."

Stoner pounded up the makeshift wooden steps of the trailer; he'd destroyed the original metal stairs by coming down hard on them on the same drunken night Hawk invited him to stay until he found another place. Months ago, that had been. Another source of friction with Maggie.

"Come on, Dusty, we'll take the jeep."

Dusty nodded. "That's good, 'cause this mother won't start."

"Somehow I had that impression."

Stoner clambered back down the steps, swinging the shotgun in one hand, clutching something shiny in the other. Hawk took the gun and grabbed his other wrist. Stoner flinched, twisting away, trying to hide what he had.

"Give it, you oaf. You want to get us all killed?"

Stoner hid his hand behind his back, looking sheepish at having been caught.

"Come on, come on."

Stoner put out his hand. The grenade looked about the size of a grape on his broad palm.

Hawk jumped back a step. "Jesus! Didn't I fuckin' tell you to put those somewhere safe? Somewhere if they blew up, they wouldn't take out half the town?"

"They're safe, Hawk. They're all in their crate except a few loose ones I got padded in socks."

"In socks?"

"Hey," Dusty said, "them dirty ones are like cast iron. Safer than a lead trunk."

"Just go put it away, would you? And *not* back in the trailer! Jesus!"

Stoner took a walk up the hillside.

Maggie stood at the door, staring down at Hawk. "I won't be here when you get back." She withdrew and slammed the door.

"Wouldn't be the first time," Dusty said, and turned away grinning.

Hawk stared after her a minute, tracing the lines of the big black cross painted on the door. Thank you, Edgar.

In the splash of floodlights mounted near the edges of the lot, the lines from the Book of Revelations looked wet, still dripping down the sides of the trailer. He tried to find one to calm himself, to give him focus before his mission, but they were all somewhat more intense than he felt he needed.

Have to put some Psalms up there soon. This whole apocalyptic thing was a bit too much for the day-to-day.

Dusty and Stoner settled into the jeep. Hawk joined them and fired it up, thinking of Maggie. The row of glowing plastic Saviors on the dashboard soothed him only slightly. As a man of action, he hated leaving things unfinished. Maggie in her moods was harder to interpret than Elijah's rant. He finally achieved a one-pointed clarity by focusing on the hood ornament, a polished chrome crucifix that gleamed like liquid silver as they passed under a streetlight on their way out of the lot. He screeched onto Old Creek Road, cutting through a narrow gap in traffic. Stoner howled in delight at the near miss, yet another brush with the oaf's imminent death. It was for exactly this reason that Hawk treasured the big clod's company. Stoner knew instinctively how thin the line was between Here and Hereafter. Most who walked that line so boldly had deluded themselves into forgetting the fact that they were essentially disposable. But Stoner knew it—reveled in the fact. Or else he was utterly ignorant of it. Hawk could never be sure which.

Dusty was in his own little world, his fishbowl full of dust, hunched over in the back of the jeep.

Old Creek was dangerous enough at midday; at night it was a constant string of dead man's curves. He loved to drive it fast, but traffic was too thick.

Crawling along with the summer tourist cars, Hawk wondered if the boys had pushed Sal too far this time. Edgar said he'd dispatched karate assassins, Sal's personal bodyguards. It seemed unlikely, but one never knew. Hawk believed that under the right circumstances, anyone was capable of anything. You couldn't always read it in their eyes. What were eyes anyway but a couple of cameras? Forget all that talk about the windows of the soul. Eyes were more like two-way mirrors, and the soul hung out behind them, watching you like a department store detective.

(Have to remember this for next Saturday, he thought. Some good riffs building here.)

No, there were no shortcuts to understanding people. You couldn't judge from one conversation, or even from a week's worth of talk. The only way to understand a man was through study over time. Some people had good years the way most people had bad days, years when everything flowed right to them without the smallest hitch; and in such times they appeared perfect saints, wise and compassionate and easygoing. If you were stupid enough to judge them by those fat times, you might be inclined to fit them with a halo. But the next year could start with a flood, followed by famine and drought . . . and suddenly your saint would be devouring women and children to keep his belly soft and fat.

As for Sal, Hawk hadn't yet made up his mind. There were so many unpredictable elements involved. A lot of complications.

The guy was a faggot, you had to take that for granted. If you let him, he'd tell you all about it, making everything real clear. He didn't care if anyone thought it was a sin; he wasn't apologetic or guilty or shameful, and he didn't show remorse. He was honest about it. Hawk respected that—no matter what other preachers said.

The thing Hawk didn't really trust—and the reason he still waited to see how things turned out, waited to judge—was the way Sal surrounded himself with boys. Hawk had known some of Sal's "students" over the years. Wild and mixed up, most of them—though what boys weren't? A few had hung out with Hawk at first, trying to be part of the One-Way Gang; but they had never really fit in. There was something in them he just couldn't reach. After drifting away from Hawk, they had hooked up with Sal and suddenly started to pull themselves together. He hadn't liked some of the changes they went through—the faggy accents, the bangles and makeup and all that superficial shit—but at least they'd managed to get their heads straightened out in some essential way. Sometimes this meant they finally faced up to their parents and moved out on their own, which Hawk had been telling them to do anyway. Randy was like that. A good kid from a fucked-up home. Sometimes they bleached their hair, like Martin Schwinn, who called himself Marilyn now.

When Hawk asked them how they were doing, they spoke of Sal in reverent tones: he was a great teacher, a good friend, a wonderful this and that. What Hawk could never figure out was if Sal was really doing all of this for them, or if he was doing it for himself.

With the older boys, it didn't matter. They'd fuck a gopher

hole if they got horny enough. Fine. But the younger ones were a stew of hormones, more desperate than the older kids. All their juices were flowing, but they'd had no time to learn control or discrimination. They were nothing but jailbait with balls. And there were a few like that hanging around Sal's place, taking tai chi lessons, selling his bad paintings, even slapping them out assembly-line fashion on the floor of Sal's garage. Hawk wasn't sure how much more than lessons was involved.

So the jury was still out on the matter of Sal. It might never come in. But better that than snap judgments. Better that than to make up his mind too quickly—and incorrectly—one way or the other.

The jeep lurched to a stop in front of Edgar's house. Edgar was waiting on the curb. He hopped in back and said breathlessly, "They're over there!"

"What kind of mess have you got me into, Edgar?"

"Sal did it, not me."

"All by himself? He's chasing you around for no reason, saying he's gonna kick your ass just because you showed up in one of his wet dreams?"

Stoner chortled and poked Dusty in the shoulder.

"I swear to God, Hawk, you know what kind of a dangerous faggot he is."

"All I got is your word for that. I sure don't see no army. Where do we go?"

Edgar pointed out one dark house among many. It was silent, unremarkable, the carport empty. Hawk didn't pull into it, but set the emergency brake on the hill and left the engine idling.

"Watch the car," he told the men, then followed Edgar to the door.

"Where's the trouble?"

Edgar looked over the edge of the porch, into the dark space between the houses. "They must have gone back to Sal's."

"I noticed. Can we go in or what? My patience is very short tonight. I had something important going on."

Edgar turned to him with a pleading look. "We needed you,

Hawk. We *needed* you. You always say if we get in trouble, if we really need you, we can call. You always say that, man."

"Yeah, yeah." Hawk shoved him toward the door, half fooling now. This wasn't quite what he'd expected. He felt like an idiot for bringing the shotgun, but what the hell. It didn't hurt to put on a show for the boys every once in a while. That was the stuff legends were made of. They'd grow up talking about this night for the rest of their lives, weaving him into their futures, telling their children about him. And maybe they would learn something from it, pass a useful lesson down through the years.

He raised his fist and pounded on the door. "Okay, assholes!" he shouted. "Open up in there!"

He heard excited whispering beyond the door, then a voice he didn't know: "They're back, you guys! And they have my key. They can get in without—"

Kurtis Tyre said, "Open the door, you fuckin' pussy. That's Hawk out there."

The door opened and Hawk saw a cluster of boys standing around in the dark.

"What is this," he said, stepping in, "a slumber party?"

He recognized Mad-Dog Murphy by his chattering laugh. He wasn't sure about the others. It was too dark.

"We didn't want them to know we were in here," Craig Frost said.

"That's all over now. You can stop hiding."

Someone turned on a light. Hawk saw blank walls, unfurnished rooms.

"Jesus, what'd you do, break into an empty house?"

"It's his place," Kurtis said, jerking his thumb toward a kid Hawk had never seen before. A smallish boy with horn-rimmed glasses was standing next to Edgar's new pal, the ironical Scott Gillette.

"They took my key," the kid with glasses said, as if Hawk was his big brother or his dad or something. "It got stuck in the lock and they grabbed it."

"You practically gave it to them," Kurtis said.

"Mike let us hide here, Hawk," said Edgar.

"I've got to get it back or my mom will kill me! This is a new house! I can't tell her we have to change the locks already."

"Why not?" said Hawk, enjoying the slow terror that consumed the kid's features. He probably deserved whatever fear he felt.

"Okay, relax," he said a moment later. "We're going up to visit Sal."

"All right!" said Edgar.

"Not you twerps. Dusty and Stoner and me. We're going to talk, not squabble. Can't have you kids hanging off my butt."

"Talk," Howard Lean said, head bobbing. *"Riiiiight."*

"Stay here," Hawk told them, " 'cause when I'm through with Sal, I'm coming back for you."

"You'll get the key?" Mike asked.

"Yeah, yeah, the key."

Hawk went back to the car, leaving the door open, a spill of light and voices following him to the street. He got behind the wheel and shook his head, aiming the chrome cross at the night, as if for target practice.

It took only seconds to reach Sal's house. Hawk shut off the engine and coasted to a stop at the curb. Music and the sounds of a party came from inside. Maybe a victory party.

"Dusty, you got the gun. Stoner, give him some camouflage. Not too subtle, though."

He climbed out of the jeep and strolled slowly up the driveway, past Sal's sleek black van, which looked a million times better kept than Dusty's. From the doorstep, he glanced back at the jeep. Stoner was leaning against the bed of the truck, grinning. The shotgun barrel poked out from under his armpit.

Hawk rang the bell, heard chimes inside the house. A few seconds later the door opened a few inches and Sal looked out.

Hawk said, "I need to talk to you."

"Is that so?"

"I heard my boys have been giving you some trouble."

"They tell you everything or just the parts they think you'll like?"

"That's what I'm here to find out. I don't have a gripe with you, Sal. I'd just as soon we never had call to see each other. So can we iron this out right now?"

"You alone?"

"Not exactly. But I left my friends at the car."

Sal leaned out and peered around the door. Stoner raised his arm to wave, revealing Dusty crouched in back with the shotgun.

Sal stiffened and started to withdraw, but Hawk caught him by the arm—or thought he had. Before his fingers could close on Sal's arm, it snaked up inside his reach and swept him back. Hawk stumbled on the edge of the stoop and nearly fell on his ass. Off balance, he threw himself at the door before Sal could shut it. Sal must have stood aside at the last instant because his plunge carried him into the house, meeting no resistance till he banged into the wall, bruising his shoulder. Straightening up, he found himself surrounded.

He was in the middle of a party. All the guests were male, most of them fairly young. They didn't look particularly menacing.

Except, possibly, for Sal, who waited by the door. He looked more relaxed now that Hawk was inside, on his territory.

"What it comes down to, Hawk, is that my friends and I don't like being called names. Names don't *hurt* us, we just don't like them. I don't see why we should put up with that shit. Would you?"

"What kind of names are you talking about?"

Sal grinned. "They didn't tell you that part, did they? You want me to repeat them?"

"No, I can imagine. Look . . . on their behalf, I apologize. They're a bunch of smartasses, we both know that. You know how kids think. They don't know shit."

"I just want to be left in peace, Hawk. I want to be able to have my friends over without the local chapter of the KKK, like your cute little 'S.S.' boys, coming around my door—and then running away when we put up a little fight."

"I don't even mind the names," said Randy, who stood in the door to the kitchen, wearing rubber gloves and holding a sponge. "What gets me is this mess."

He pointed to a wet green stain on the wall opposite the door. He wiped at it with the sponge, but apparently he had removed all he could. The plaster had sucked it up.

"Who did that? What is it?"

"One of your boys—with an avocado. I'm going to have to *paint.*"

Hawk reached for his wallet, but Sal stopped him.

"Forget it, Hawk. You want to make peace, I'll accept that. But can you make your goons stick to it?"

"I can tell them that any more trouble they get themselves into with you . . . I won't be bailing them out."

"Anyway," said Marilyn, inspecting his nails, "we wouldn't have hurt them, even if we caught them. It was enough to see them run."

A ripple of laughter went through the room.

"That's good to hear," Hawk said. "I thought maybe it was something like that. But you know, these little games you play . . . some people don't necessarily take it as lightly as you'd think. Sometimes the game goes too far. You know what I'm saying?"

The record that had been playing ended suddenly. Hawk was surrounded by silence; his words hung there in the middle of the room. Everyone watched him.

"I'm talking about the key," Hawk said.

The silence stretched on.

"The key?" Hawk repeated.

Sal shrugged. "So you said. What key?"

"You know what key. The one that got left in the lock. Now, the kid it belongs to isn't one of my boys, and he's shitting bricks right now, thinking his mother is going to find out what he was up to."

When nobody answered, Sal took a stab. "Okay, boys, we're

looking for a little peace here. Cooperation. If one of you has this kid's key . . ."

Someone nosed the needle back onto the album, pumping the room full of noise.

"Take it off!" Sal shouted. The speakers screeched. The silence was more tense than before.

Hawk looked around. There were faces he knew, but more he didn't. A few older men were mixed in with the younger; Sal must have been entertaining some of his customers tonight.

"Who has it?" Sal said.

"We didn't see any key," said Randy. "Someone would have said if they'd found it."

"Hey, Sal," said a kid Hawk didn't know. "What about your brother? He was there."

"Lupe?" Sal looked puzzled. "Yeah, where is he?"

"He didn't come back with us, but he hit that house first. Like, he was tracking Hawk's boys without us. If there was a key, he's the one would have seen it."

"So where is this guy, this Lupe?" Hawk asked, though it already seemed clear from what they'd been saying.

Nobody knew.

=8=

The painted moon was pretty but it gave no light. Mike sat in the dark, listening to feet pounding up and down the stairs. Mad-Dog's howls echoed through the empty rooms. He sighed and sank his head between his knees. After trying to keep everything under control, warning the others about smudging the white walls, he had finally given up and sought what peace he could in solitude.

The door opened suddenly. The light switched on. Mad-Dog stood in the doorway. "Hey, guy. Heard there's avocados somewhere around here."

Mike gestured toward the walk-in closet. "Help yourself."

Mad-Dog went out with an armful of avocados, already peeling the woody skin of one with his snaggle teeth. He left the door wide open. After a moment Scott came in and dropped down heavily in a corner, followed by Edgar, who sat cross-legged in the center of the room.

"Don't worry about your key," said Edgar. "Hawk'll take care of it."

Just then, the doorbell rang. By the time they got upstairs, Kurtis was opening the front door. Craig and Howard rushed in laughing.

"So what happened?" Kurtis said.

"Man, he just murdered Sal!" Howard said.

"Murdered him?" Mike repeated.

"You guys missed the fight of the century!"

They congregated in the living room. Craig nodded his agreement to Howard's breathless account: "We got there right as Hawk was going up to the door. Man, you should have seen it. Dusty was back in the jeep with a shotgun—"

"A shotgun?" Kurtis said.

"Yeah! Him and Stoner standing there grinning, Hawk goes up to the door and *bam-bam-bam!* Wails on it! Sal opens the door, just an inch, and he's like—'Please don't hurt me, Mister Hawk!' "

"Scared shitless," Craig concurred.

"But Hawk whips around, snags him, *wham!,* he's pulling him out of the house, then *bang!,* he barrels back inside with him and slams the door. You could hear all these guys howling inside, glass breaking—"

"So what are Dusty and Stoner doing all this time?" Kurtis asked. "Standing around?"

"No way! Dusty's got a gun, remember? They run to the door, Stoner kicks it in, and they crash inside. There's two shots, *blam-blam,* just like that."

Cold rushed through Mike. "They shot somebody?"

"Naw, just scared 'em, I think. But you could hear the place turning upside down. Stoner's laughing like—like Mad-Dog. All of a sudden someone comes flying through the glass upstairs, spinning right over the balcony, and lands on the sidewalk. It was Sal, man. Hawk threw him right into the street!"

"Sal?"

"You shoulda been there, man, it was infuckingcredible!"

"Liked it, huh?" said Hawk.

They turned around suddenly. Hawk was standing in the front door; he had come in quietly while Howard was jabbering.

"Uh, yeah, Hawk," Howard said. "I was just telling them how you took care of Sal."

"How I threw him through a window?" Hawk took a few

steps into the house. "I appreciate the legends, Howie, really I do. But I think the truth has more staying power."

If Howard had had a tail he would have tucked it between his legs.

Two men came in after Hawk. One was dark and bony in a grubby sleeveless T-shirt, with tattooed arms and a few gold teeth. The other was built like a refrigerator, so tall he had to stoop in the doorway.

Mike held back from Hawk. He was anxious to get his key, but Hawk seemed unpredictable. Better to wait until he offered it.

"All right, fellows, gather round," Hawk said. "It's time we had a little man-to-man."

Hawk gestured toward the dining room with its small square of gold carpet, and everybody slowly flocked toward it. Mike sensed a scolding in the air, at which his mood soured further. Who was this guy anyway, to chew them out? He wasn't their father, for God's sake.

Hawk stood in the middle of the thick yellow carpet as if he were taking center stage. The boys sat down in a loose ring around him, leaning back against the mirrored wall or the counter that divided them from the kitchen. Mad-Dog started wolfing down another avocado, green sludge showing whenever he grinned. Hawk's two cronies crossed their arms and took posts near the door, like bodyguards.

Hawk smiled, narrowing his eyes, looking down at them. "Okay. We're all cool here, right? We're all so fucking cool ice won't melt on our tongues."

Mike thought he looked a bit like a wolf, the Big Bad one, leering at them with some secret knowledge hidden behind his slit eyes.

"Yeah. We're a bunch of hip, dangerous dudes, so don't mess with us." Hawk began to imitate a strut, swaggering in place down an imaginary street. "Yeah, yeah, yeah. Keep on trucking. Cool, ain't it? Cool, cool, cool."

Howard and Craig glanced at each other and shrugged.

"Yeah, Hawk," Howard said, "we're cool."

Hawk let his mask slip; underneath it was nothing but disgust. "Not cool," he said. *"Fools* is what you are, trucking your way straight to Hell. That's another one-way trip, boys. One-way in the wrong direction."

He jabbed a finger at the carpet.

"You know what I mean? The ground cracks open, fire licks up, and down you plunge. Sound okay to you? Think your cool is gonna matter when you're down there? You think you can stay cool when everything else is on fire?"

"Snowball in hell," the big blond Neanderthal said, and guffawed.

Hawk turned around and stared at him. "Thanks, Stoner, for that brilliant and original comparison. That is pure poetry."

Stoner fell silent, hiding his smirk while Hawk shook his head.

"Sometimes I think you guys don't hear a word I say. I don't know why you bother hanging around me, let alone why I put up with you. Am I fooling myself thinking I can make a difference in your lives? Is it totally asinine to think I can teach you anything from my experience, or steer you away from the mistakes I made? Am I wasting my time with you guys?"

Edgar spoke up. "Uh, maybe, Hawk . . . maybe we think that, you know, if we want to be like you, we gotta go through the shit that made you what you are. It's sort of like a paradox, right?"

Hawk looked surprised and then disappointed by this logic. Suddenly Mike saw Hawk as another typical adult saying the same old stuff: *I'm so disappointed in you kids . . .* It was the same speech he got from his mother when he'd done something wrong, now that he was too old to whack with a hairbrush. But at least she had a right to say what she wanted, being his mother and all. But now here was this Hawk, this nobody, trying to make Mike listen to everything he had to say, trying to shake him up. And at the end of the lecture, when Mike was supposed to be limp and grateful for Hawk's assistance, philosophical and otherwise, Hawk would finally hand over the key.

Recognizing the routine sapped it of all possible impact. The boys weren't just trying to be like Hawk—he was trying to be like one of them. Mike saw it all the time: teachers indulging in the latest slang, pretending to be "one of the gang," as if that would earn them kids' respect. It was the kind of hypocrisy that drove him nuts. *You're not one of us!* he wanted to shout at Hawk.

Instead he stifled a yawn and gave his mind permission to wander. Hawk seemed to have no straight answer to Edgar's question. It was cleverly posed, Mike thought. Chalk one up for the boys.

Mad-Dog finished one avocado and began gnawing on the pit, eyes rapt on Hawk. Shreds of whitish matter dribbled from his mouth and onto the floor, next to a pile of green skin. Mike would have to go over the whole house later, cleaning up after these guys, hiding their tracks. Hawk's boots were crusted with dirt; crumbs of it speckled the bright, freshly shampooed carpet. His mother would think he'd led an army in here. Which was closer to the truth than he wanted her to know.

"I've told you my story," Hawk said. "You know I understand you guys. I went through the same shit you did, walked the same fucking streets, all right? Take it from me, I know where the road you're on leads. I did the drugs, the crimes, all that shit, same as you. The drugs burned my brain, made me stupid, and the crime just got me into jail. One leads to the other, men. And I'm not just talking about jail. I'm talking about Hell. That's where you're headed. So you keep right on truckin'!"

Behind Hawk, Dusty and Stoner exchanged glances. They were laughing, it seemed, but silently.

Somehow Hawk heard them. He spun around.

"You think what I'm saying is funny, Stoner?"

"No, Hawk! No . . . It's just, well, you're always preaching."

"Is that all I do? Talk? You think I don't set any good examples by my action?"

"I didn't say that."

"Hallelujah," Scott whispered.

"What kind of examples do you set, Stoner? What're you going to tell Saint Peter when you get to the pearly gates? What's your great achievement in this lifetime? What're you gonna tell him? 'Well, uh, uh, lemme see . . . duh . . . I dunno, I . . . I swiped a crate of hand grenades from Camp Pendleton!' "

Everyone, including Stoner, laughed at Hawk's Stoner imitation.

"And what about you, Dusty?" Hawk said.

Dusty stiffened. "I'm not one of your baby boys, Hawk, that you can talk to me like that. I don't need no preacher-man on my ass. Plenty of shitwipes sitting in jail figure they can get out faster if they start whacking off to the Bible 'stead of beaver magazines. Keep on thumpin' that ol' black book, Hawk, I don't care. But leave me out of it. I'm a good Catholic, man, and you don't know nothing about us. I got my own road to Heaven."

Hawk turned away from him. "I'm glad you do, Dusty, because you sure need it. But these boys here are different. They need role models, especially the primo example of that righteous dude who lived and died for them two thousand years ago. I'm not talking about some magic man who turned water into wine and brought the dead to life; I'm talking about the real guy those stories are based on. I'm talking about the real life of the straight-talkin', woman-lovin', two-fisted fightin' Jesus."

"Hey, Hawk," Edgar said suddenly, "do you think Jesus had ESP?"

Hawk said nothing for a minute. He stared at Edgar, and shook his head. That disappointed look again. "Edgar . . ."

"It would explain some things, wouldn't it? Maybe he made people think he was doing miracles without actually doing them. I mean, getting inside their heads and making them see what he saw. That would still be pretty miraculous, wouldn't it?"

"Edgar . . ."

"Walking on water, and that stuff with Lazarus, I mean maybe he was in like a catatonic state and Jesus just—"

"Edgar!"

Edgar fell silent.

Hawk looked exasperated after yelling; he collected himself, taking a breath before speaking again. Mike was afraid he might go on all night, and he would never get the place cleaned up. The only way they were going to get out of here was if they all pretended to take his lessons to heart. And if that was all it took, it would be worth it. Out-hypocrisy the old hypocrite.

"I think that's really, really true," he said to the other boys. "What Hawk's been saying."

He could see Hawk's eyes brighten, snapping toward him.

"We should all learn a lesson from this," Mike said.

"Okay, finally, someone's hearing me," Hawk said. "What is this, all you guys tired of listening to me? Only makes sense to someone who's never heard it before?"

"I'll bet they get it," Mike said. "Don't you, guys?"

Around the room, warming to his method as if by a closed-circuit telepathy from which Hawk was excluded, the others began to nod. "Yeah, really, Hawk. It'll never happen again."

"Right on."

"Yeah, man, we see what you're saying."

"Leave Sal alone," Hawk said.

"Sure, man."

"Whatever you say."

"What he does is between him and Heaven, all right? You guys aren't the ones to pass judgment on him. You should be worried about the judgment someone's sure as shit going to pass on you."

"Amen to that," said Scott.

They all struggled to their feet, realizing that the worst had passed.

"Can we get a ride, Hawk?" Howard said.

With a surge of relief, Mike realized that everyone was finally leaving. The house was intact. He'd had a scare, but that was all. It wasn't going to get any worse. He never had to see any of these guys again. Monday he'd go back to Glantz Appliances and doodle in the storeroom, hang out with Scott, figure out how he was going to get laid. Everything would be the same as before.

He followed them outside, switching on the carport light. Hawk's Jeep was a sight, with a huge chrome-plated cross for a hood ornament, a row of glowing Jesus figurines on the dashboard, and verse from the Bible painted all over the sides. He was embarrassed just seeing it on the same block where he lived.

Howard and Craig clambered into the back, squeezing in beside Stoner. Dusty took the front seat. Hawk slipped into the jeep and the motor roared to life, deafening Mike.

"Hey!" he shouted. "What about my key?"

Hawk sucked in his cheeks a little, giving Mike a look he couldn't quite read. Maybe he knew Mike had been fooling when he pretended to agree with the sermonette; maybe Hawk wanted him to barbecue a few minutes longer over the coals of a slow, hellish fire, which was what his dread felt like.

"Hey, sorry," Hawk said, "I almost forgot."

Mike put his hand out.

Hawk shrugged at the open palm. "What's your name? Mike? I'm sorry, Mike, somebody else has it now. Guy named Lupe, I think. You know him?"

=9=

Mike pushed a piece of English muffin around his plate in a smear of egg yolk and hollandaise sauce. Everything glistened sickeningly in the morning sun, bouncing off utensils and the silver coffee pot a waitress had left on their table. His eyes ached, his head throbbed. For about a year after the divorce, when his mother had moved down to Bohemia Bay, he'd had frequent migraines. He'd taught himself to relieve them with the aid of a cheap self-hypnosis manual. Now he felt another coming on, the first in ages, like a hot needle jabbing deep into his right eye. Scott said the brain had no nerve endings in it, but something in there *hurt*.

"Are you going to answer me?" his mother asked.

He avoided her eyes under the pretext of shading his face. Their table, on the patio of the Dumas Père restaurant, sat in direct sunlight.

"I already said I'm sorry," he replied.

"You're *sorry?* That's just great. We give you a little responsi-bility . . ."

"We have extra keys," Jack interjected. Mike looked up at him sharply, surprised to receive any support, least of all from Jack.

"That's not the point," his mother said.

"What is the point?" Mike said, sounding shrill and false in his own ears. "It fell out of my pocket! What's so irresponsible about that? I looked for it, but we were hiking around in the hills. It could be anywhere."

"Boys get into these things," Jack said. "Why don't we just finish enjoying brunch before we get back to packing. We already did a lot last night and this morning, Mike. You and Ryan missed the worst of it."

His mother looked at him steadily, as if to say, This isn't over. "Did you remember to tell Mr. Glantz you need tomorrow off to help us move?"

He stiffened, because he had forgotten.

"Mike?"

"Yes!" he said.

"Don't you dare crab at me. You've gotten out of plenty of work already. I know you have a job now, but so do we. Jack and I only have so much time to get this done—we can't loaf around all summer like you kids. What's the problem, anyway? Didn't you get any sleep last night?"

"I slept fine," he said. "There's nothing wrong. I've just got sort of a headache."

She looked dubious, as if she somehow suspected the real story. But there was no way she could know—would ever know—unless he told her. Which he never would.

He and Scott had slept on the floor of the moon room, in sleeping bags borrowed from Edgar. Or rather, Scott had slept and Mike had lain there restless and unsleeping, thinking of the key, of the gang that had chased them through the dark streets, of how close they had come to disaster—how he'd thought it averted, only to find it crashing down on him again. Hawk's failure, his own mistake. Stupid, stupid, stupid. He'd wondered all night—worn himself out agonizing over—what his mother would say, and what he would tell her. Instead of dreaming, he had cooked up false but acceptable versions of reality.

He realized with relief that the scenario for which he'd steeled himself was even now passing. The worst was over.

Mike drained his orange juice and looked away from the table, knowing his mother would need time to cool off. If he managed not to talk back, things would return to normal by the time they got home. He stared out over the patio's low cement-block wall, at Central Beach below. The Dumas Père sat on the very brink of an ocean cliff. Beneath the patio, ice-plant slopes spilled down to the sand, cut by asphalt trails where tourists and the local senior citizens, in brightly colored sun hats, strolled. The Coast Highway was clogged with traffic; suspended exhaust fumes and heat haze made everything look insubstantial.

"What's that?" Jack said.

It occurred to Mike that he'd been dimly aware of sirens for some time; but suddenly they were all he heard. Down at the traffic light, where Old Creek Road ended at Central Beach, several police cars were turning off the street, driving down the lifeguard road toward the boardwalk and the beach.

The volleyball courts, busy all day every day in the summer, were deserted now; players and watchers had crowded toward the police, spectators at another sort of event.

A bright yellow lifeguard Jeep was parked on the sand. The crowd surrounded it, though Mike could see the cops and a few lifeguards pushing back, warning them away. Their shouts came to him seconds after their mouths moved, disjointed by distance. The sirens died with a whoop as the last police car arrived. Far off he heard a fainter alarm. South down the highway, beyond the fancy beach hotels, he caught a flicker of colored lights—hard to distinguish in the overall glare of full noon—and spied an ambulance creeping through the heavy traffic.

"Looks like a drowning," Jack said.

"Oh, how terrible," said Mrs. James. "I hope it's not a child."

"I'm gonna go see," Mike said.

"I don't think that's such a good idea," she said. "Especially with all the work you've got to do."

"There's a lot of packing left," Jack put in, siding with her now, though Mike had the distinct impression that Jack himself would have liked to go down for a closer look, excitement being such a rarity in Bohemia Bay.

Mike hopped the low wall, landing in a bed of ice plant. "I'll see you at home," he called over his shoulder. "Probably beat you there!"

His mother cried out once, but weakly. He tumbled down the hillside and sprang onto a path, startling an old woman at an easel. She had been painting the most familiar, timeless seascape in Bohemia Bay, only to have it spoiled by cop cars, crowds, and a hint of mortality. Like last night's first whiff of danger, Mike found the scene irresistible; but an old woman might see such things differently. Incipient migraine forgotten, he rushed down the trails and plunged into the hot sand, his tennis shoes squeaking as he ran toward the crowd.

He hated his shoes filling up with sand—it was too much like walking in a nightmare—so he made his way to the boardwalk as soon as he could. Joining the crowd, he heard police and lifeguard radios crackling. Most of the onlookers were down on the sand, gathered around the perpetual pool of brackish salt water that dribbled from the Old Creek storm drain. They stood in the muddy sand amid puffs of scummy foam and twists of colored nylon rope and fly-pestered heaps of rotting kelp.

Mike found a spot on the boardwalk, right above the storm drain. Dropping to all fours, he leaned over the edge of the planks. Voices echoed in the tunnel. A radio hissed, turned down low. Ripples spread out into the murky pool from the tunnel's mouth, carrying changes of color. Someone in the drain said, "Jesus." Red clouds fanned from the opening, shot through with darker veins and richer clots of color.

The people at the water's edge made sounds of horror and backed up onto dry sand, fearing contact with the water. Mike stared down at a young man's face, impossibly white, the eyes bulging behind glass. The crowd grew stealthily more silent and began to pass away. His reflection dwindled into darkness. Everyone must have heard his heartbeat. And then the world turned gray, as if he and the sun had both gone behind a cloud.

Sometime later, opening his eyes, he saw blue sky. He was flat on his back. Hot sand burned his arms and people stood over him, staring down. Closest, kneeling, was a lifeguard, her nose painted white with zinc oxide.

"Okay, buddy, lie still for a minute. Can you tell me your name?"

She was taking his pulse, he realized. She laid her palm on Mike's forehead, probed his neck with strong fingers. Mike's skin felt clammy, feverish in the heat, but he didn't feel so bad that he wasn't already admiring her gleaming tan shoulders, the way sweat beaded and dripped toward her freckled cleavage. She was so close. If only she would lean closer and give him mouth-to-mouth . . .

"Can you hear me?" she said.

"Mike James," he blurted, feeling stupid on top of everything else.

"How many fingers do you see, Mike?"

"Three?"

"Okay. You pass with flying colors. You live around here?"

"Not far. A few blocks. What happened?"

"You fainted."

"Really?" He tried to sit up, but a wave of weakness washed through him. As it passed, he remembered blood surging into the briny pool, and then clouds closing in.

Blood. Oh God.

He twisted around and barfed convulsively in the sand, eyes squinched shut, humiliated to think of the volleyball crowd standing there watching him. It was worse to think that a second ago he'd been wanting to taste the lifeguard's tongue in his mouth. Now all he felt was nausea.

When he opened his eyes again, the crowd had turned away, but the woman was still studying him. There was some activity around the mouth of the tunnel, which was only a few feet away. He turned his head to avoid seeing whatever it was.

"Feeling better?" the lifeguard asked.

Mike nodded. "Yeah. Was I out long?"

"Nah, less than a minute. I was coming out of the tunnel, looked up and saw you falling. Nearly scared me to death."

"You caught me? Now I'm really embarrassed."

"Don't be." She kicked sand over what looked remotely like Hollandaise sauce. "You saw more than you could handle, that's all."

"I'm an artist," he said impulsively, light-headed but still wanting to impress her. "I should be able to look at anything."

"Well, we all have our limits. Maybe you should stick to seascapes."

He stuck out his tongue. "Bleah."

"Are you going to be okay?" She was starting to look impatient.

"I guess so." Mike got up, brushing sand from his clothes. He felt clammy but steady enough. "Is— Could I ask what you found in there?"

"At the risk of making you faint again, it looks like someone was hurt in the pipe. A dog found him, cut up pretty bad."

"Hurt? You mean—killed?"

"Well, the police are keeping us out of there, so I'd say that's a possibility."

"Wow," Mike said. "Murder."

"I better get back to work," she said, and grinned. "Keeping people like you from seeing more than they want to."

"Thanks for, uh, catching me."

"No sweat."

She padded away down the sandy bank, back toward the pipe. Fortunately, the people were clustered so thickly around the mouth of the tunnel that Mike couldn't really see much of anything. He watched her legs and ass instead as she walked away through the crowd.

Things could have been worse. He could have landed in the bloody water, right in front of everybody!

As he headed for the boardwalk, he saw a familiar figure running toward him across the highway, causing the stranded tourist cars to blurt their horns.

It was Hawk. He looked winded, messed up, as if he'd run all the way down Old Creek Road from his weird little trailer. Hawk crossed the grass and the boardwalk, running straight to the spot where Mike had knelt and fallen in.

He stopped at the edge of the planks and shouted down: "Where is he?"

Hawk didn't wait for an answer. He jumped, landing with a splash that made the crowd recoil. Hawk thrashed around, struggling to free himself from the mud, dragging toward the storm drain opening; he was spattered with grime and slimy kelp. Before he could reach the pipe, a man came rushing out to meet him.

It was a police officer, his trousers wet to the knees. He grabbed Hawk by the shoulders and held him back.

"Lemme go," Hawk said. "A lifeguard radioed. I know you've got one of my boys in there."

"It doesn't matter who's in there. It's none of your—"

Hawk threw off the officer's hands and tried to get past him. Stopping him required a full body-block. The cop shoved Hawk up against the curved concrete wall just inside the mouth of the pipe, and pinned him there to the crust of dead algae.

"You can't go messing around in there, God damn it!"

Hawk sank back, blinking out at the beach, seeing for the first time that he was the center of a mob's attention. A few of the lifeguards came to help hold him. He shook them off, looking past the cop into the dark core of the tunnel.

"Who is it?" he said. "Which one?"

Mike's fever intensified. One of Hawk's boys . . . one of the One-Way Gang. He wanted to be far away from here now, far from last night or any knowledge of Hawk. But his legs wouldn't carry him. It was all he could do to climb back onto the boardwalk and find the nearest bench.

A minute later, Hawk hauled himself up from the pool onto the boardwalk and shook like a wet dog, sprinkling bystanders with mud and brine. He paced back and forth, his heavy wet boots loud on the planks, muttering, until he noticed Mike watching. Then he strode over and dropped down on the bench beside him.

"What do you know?" he said.

Mike tried to speak, but his mouth was as dry as the beach. He spread his empty hands.

Hawk gazed at him, then shook his head in surrender. "Ah, fuckin' cops." After a moment he looked at Mike again, as if finally recognizing him. "What're you doing here, anyway?"

"I was up . . . there." He gestured feebly toward the cliffs, the Dumas Père.

Hawk lurched to his feet and strode over to the edge of the boardwalk again; he peered down at the tunnel, then stormed back. This time he stared over Mike's head, at the highway.

Mike twisted around. A stocky man was hurrying through the crosswalk from the gas station. He wore the station uniform, a blue cap and a blue workshirt. He was greasy up to his elbows. When he saw Hawk, he changed direction slightly, ambling toward him. He took a cigarette from his mouth and cocked his head in a casual nod.

"Hawk. What's up?"

"Alec. Something real fucked."

"A murder," Mike blurted.

"No shit? I been watching for a few minutes, but it's hard to get a chance to come look. Craig peeled out early today, left me fuckin' stranded over there."

"Craig?" Hawk said suddenly. "Where'd he go?"

Alec shrugged. "Said he was taking a break for a smoke. I saw him head over to the beach—and then he must've just cleared out, the shit. He knows it's just him and me Sunday morning. Usually he's reliable. I was hoping you might know if anything was up with him, girl trouble or something."

Mike said, "Craig . . . Frost?"

Hawk grabbed Alec by the arm, wrenching him around, marching him toward the tunnel. "When was this?"

"Shit, what's wrong? Early—you know how early he comes

on. Takes his first break around seven-thirty. Watch it, Hawk, you're gouging me!"

"Hey!" Hawk yelled again, holding Alec as if he might thrust him over the edge. "Come out here!"

"Tell that fuck to go away," came a hollow, echoing voice. "Just tell me one thing. Is it Frost? Craig Frost?"

The same cop came out of the tunnel and squinted up at them, shading his eyes. "I talk to the parents, Hawk. Not you. You're nobody."

Hawk let go of Alec, who staggered backward, windmilling his arms for balance.

"Hey," Alec said. "Craig? You mean—? Are you—is this serious?"

Hawk spun him toward the highway. "Let's go."

"What's happening? Go where?"

Mike, almost in spite of himself, fell in behind the men, as if to miss this would be to miss everything. He couldn't resist gathering any possible scrap of explanation. Craig Frost had for months been a familiar sight early in the morning, at the pumps. To think that last night they'd been hiding in Mike's house together, Craig swearing and laughing and dreaming up stupid schemes, and now . . .

Behind them, the cop was shouting: "Bring him back here, you bastard!"

"I guess they want to talk to you," Hawk said smugly.

"Why?" Alec asked.

"Because it's Craig in there, and they just figured out you're probably the last one who saw him. But I get first shot at you, don't I? *Don't I, Alec?*"

"First shot at— Oh Jesus, Hawk, what are you saying? What happened to Craig?"

They reached the street. For once, the traffic was moving, Sunday drivers flying by, so close that Mike could have reached out and touched the chrome trim of the Cadillacs, or whacked a sideview mirror so hard it would take off his hand. Hawk glanced back. Mike looked, too, and saw the cop struggling up onto the boardwalk.

"I'm going to let go of you, Alec," Hawk said. "When I do, I want you to get in your truck and drive out to my place. Then we're going to have a talk, all right?"

"But I can't leave the station now, it's—"

"Alec, you just had a death in the company. For Craig you can shut down."

"Oh. Yeah." Alec looked numb; but Hawk looked as if he had been switched on, as if he had always carried inside him all kinds of strange, dark, quiescent machines waiting to be thrown into life . . . and now they were finally running. "For Craig," Alec said.

"I'll meet you there."

Cars slowed, stopped for a light, leaving the crosswalk clear. Alec rushed into it, heading for the gas station. There was another kid over there, in the blue shirt and cap. Mike could hear Alec yelling at him: "We're closing up!"

Hawk made as if to follow. Then, as if he were totally aware of everything Mike had seen and heard and thought, he glanced down at him and said, "Go home, kid. Remember what I said last night? You don't want any part of this."

Mike kept his mouth shut, but he was thinking: *Yes I do!* Wanting it with a hot, desperate energy, as if he'd been charged up somehow, as if there was something in him the equal of anything in Hawk. His veins felt flooded with fear and electricity—in short, with life.

Hawk crossed the street an instant before the light turned red. By the time the cop finally reached the sidewalk, everything on his belt clanking heavily, the cars were pouring past. He looked red and swollen and sweaty in his dark, heavy uniform. He gave Mike a look of utter disgust and irritation, as if he were the cause of all the cop's woes.

"What are you looking at?" he snapped.

Mike took off running.

=10=

After leaving the storm drain, early, Lupe walked south along the shore. There was such a warm glow in his belly that he hardly felt the chill of the ocean air. Except for footprints of daybreak joggers and beachcombers, the sands were bare of humanity. Although he was confident he had left the pipe without being seen, it wasn't till he had strolled around several juts of the shore cliffs, hands thrust deep in his army jacket, that he felt he could relax.

In a tortured snarl of sea rocks, where the waves rushed gurgling through pockets in the slick brown stone, he crouched down out of sight of the apartment buildings that covered the cliffsides and washed his hands in a tide pool. He peeled away the film of drying blood. He cleaned beneath his nails. Wishing for a mirror, he splashed his face with seawater in case any blood had spattered there. An oceanic taste filled his mouth, both salty and sweet. The power of the sea, of all nature, was spreading through him; he relished the surge of new strength. He opened the switchblade and started to wash that as well, until he remembered that salt water might rust the spring. Contenting himself with scraping off the flecks of tissue before they scabbed over, he watched sea anemones groping at the sifting rain of small fleshy particles that drizzled into their pools, seizing the tidbits and plunging them into their soft gullets; tiny crabs darted out from under rocks, fighting over the fragments.

The initiation of the Pump Jockey had gone very well, he thought. The boy was right for his collection.

The Pump Jockey had been easily lured with the promise of a climax to yesterday's confrontation. Lupe had discreetly let himself be seen from across the Coast Highway, and then retreated as if in terror. When the boy followed him into the pipe, he had run as far as the branching tunnels before stopping in pretended confusion, though he had explored the sewer in darkness and knew that both routes joined again not far ahead. There, beneath the manhole cover, he had let the boy catch up with him.

The Pump Jockey's laughter, his low threats of "faggot," had long since faded from the world, but in Lupe's ears they were nearly as loud as the waves. Nearly as loud as the shrieks that had come while cars rushed overhead, while church bells rang in the distance and gulls screamed on the beach.

Now, hearing a scrabbling sound like something digging up from the rocks, Lupe shoved the knife into his pocket. A big Irish setter came running over the rocks, bounding toward him. He hurried away before the dog's owner followed.

As the air warmed, he stripped out of his jacket and stuffed it into his pack. His eyes constantly roved the cliffside for shelter, dark places. Although the shadow of the cliff was still long and cool, nearly touching the tideline, he knew the heat was on its way. Where not completely covered by buildings, the cliffs were so overgrown with ice plant that they looked like freeway embankments and offered as little shelter. He needed a hole, and there were no overpasses or bridges here to hide him.

Far down the beach he saw a yellow lifeguard jeep approaching. A flight of stairs ran up between two houses that seemed to float above the sand on enormous cement columns. Lupe started up the stairs, heading for the highway. Halfway up, he spied a dark recess beneath one of the houses, less substantial than a crawl space, but large enough for a boy or a small man. He scuttled into it, grateful for the cool and dark, suddenly conscious of his exhaustion. He had been up all night, wandering the streets, making his way back to the beach and the tunnel, sometimes fingering the knife he planned to use that morning, sometimes tracing the edges of the key, whose time would come later.

He had taken out and studied the key many times since the night before, wondering what it meant, where it fit in. Silver, gleaming like a fallen piece of the moon, it was an unmistakable invitation—a promise for some future date. For now it lay buried deep in a pocket, safe and sleeping.

The crawl space was cramped, littered with rusted plumbing, clogged with spiderwebs. He turned around several times like a dog settling down to clear itself a bed. From here, daylight was only a narrow band of glare. He turned his back on it, curling up in the deepest corner of the cave, head pillowed on his pack. Dreams were not long in coming. Neither were the boys.

Long after nightfall, the boy found himself on a road he didn't know, beneath shattered streetlamps, above a huddle of dark apartment buildings. The smog-shrouded valleys of Los Angeles lay below; above him rose a dark crest, hunched like the back of a sleeping dog. A huge loom of black metal stood atop the hill, soaring into clouds whose bellies held a smutty reflected light. The night felt charged with energy and stank like a leaking battery. Snapping sparks fell from the power lines that swept up to the tower from the horizon. The hairs along his arms and spine stood on end. He thought he heard laughter in the wires, but when he turned to go back the way he'd come, he discovered that the laughter was behind him. It was real.

The boys came up from the houses, or flocked out of nowhere, silent as shadows, surrounding him. But shadows could not have grabbed him so forcefully; shadows could not have pushed him up the hill and into the cave.

That was the First Cave. All he'd seen or could remember of it—fragments.

Sandstone walls appeared in leaping bursts of bluish light that came with a roar and then faded, like the flame of revelation in a nightmare which shows a monster's grin for only an instant, then shuts off and strands you in darkness.

This was a darkness full of laughter, full of fingers digging into his flesh, pinning him to the ground.

When the light flared again, he saw a blue tongue of flame licking from the nozzle of a blowtorch. Hissing and spitting, it kissed his cheeks, singed his eyebrows, then went away somewhere out of sight.

Someone said, "Get his pants."

He couldn't believe where the flame went next, roaring over his crotch, kissing him with fire. It was more pain than a soul could bear—though a body might. He fled from that place the only way he knew, escaping into darkness with nothing but his mind and imagination to carry him. His spirit was a thing of pure agony, neither awake nor asleep, alive nor dead, but suspended somewhere in between—somewhere he had never dreamed of finding.

Skin shriveled, sizzled. Blood-rich tissue swelled, popped, burst. Thanks to the torch, his wounds were instantly cauterized.

He dreamed that he was floating in the sky, a god inhaling burnt offerings, his own flesh the sacrifice.

That dream never ended.

The boy spent months in white rooms, surrounded by white people. His soul was likewise bare and antiseptic—cauterized. Sometimes he felt blindingly white, as if the fire that purged him still burned somewhere inside. Sometimes he only *burned,* without reason, and he fled the light, fled the world again. The sun was a blowtorch burning holes in the walls where he hid, trying to get at him. The doctors were agents of the fire, boring into him in their own way. They brought him food on trays, chunks of meat, the smell of which sent him reeling back into memories and left him vomiting. They stopped feeding him anything that had ever been able to bleed.

But the doctors, determined that he should return to the world at any cost, remained ignorant of what they were sending forth. Something had hatched in the First Cave, a remote, detached divinity that inhabited his altered body, taking up residence in all the empty places the original Lupe had left behind.

His chief therapist was a long-haired, bearded young man who considered himself streetwise. Dr. Brownhouse was flush of face and shiny white, his eyes gleaming with all the new wisdom he had to dispense, things he claimed could heal the boy through and through. This eager young fellow, with psychedelic posters on the walls of his clinic, had been through countless seminars of the new school, and he had learned a bold language of holism.

Whatever happened to you, Lupe, you're young enough to get past it. You have to tell yourself that you will get over it. You have allies within. I want you to claim them, seek their help. I want you to see them clearly, call them to you. Visualize them—draw their power into you. Bring yourself together. You're an artist, I've seen your sketches, I know you can make these pictures in your mind. So use that power. Make them as strong as you can.

Some of Lupe's sketches were tacked to Dr. Brownhouse's walls, but they were old work, childish fantasies from all the time Lupe had spent confined and dreaming in his Aunt Theresa's house, in the small room where she locked him so he'd be "safe." Her worst threats of what might happen to him if he left the house had not come close to matching the reality. As if stunned by how thoroughly life had shamed his imagination, Lupe had not touched so much as a crayon since the incident.

He kept busy, though, putting the doctor's words to work: *Face what you fear.*

It was sound advice, and once he was able, he followed it.

He was afraid of the dark as he had never been before, afraid of caves and holes, so that was the first fear he forced himself to face. He shut himself into dark rooms, closed himself into closets, found windowless basements and huddled in the blindest corners until terror seeped away and the dark became an ally.

Eventually he found his way back to the First Cave. He watched it till nightfall, staring into the empty socket as if an eye might emerge to stare back at him. When nothing came, he knew that he had conquered his fear completely, though he was not ready to reenter that particular place. Not yet.

Miguel was his first initiate. He took him in an ivy-choked, abandoned tunnel not far from the First Cave, luring him with a tale of a suitcase he'd found filled with hundred-dollar bills, maybe the stash from a bank heist.

In darkness he claimed that first life. It was a bloody initiation, no less for himself than for Miguel. He consumed the boy's power, literally absorbed his vitality, and afterward stood in the dark imagining Miguel as he had been in life, in full flower. Opening his eyes, he saw the soul-shadow standing before him.

And Miguel remained. Because he was the first, and the source of so much inspiration, Lupe allowed him to keep his name. Small, thin-boned, a fierce but silent companion, Miguel had followed Lupe east out of L.A., as if eager to join in the search for companions.

They crossed the country, hitching rides in empty trucks and crowded cars, through parched farmlands and plains wracked by thunderstorms. Often, when the company of people seemed unbearable, they went on foot.

Lupe found initiates wherever he went.

They were drawn to him from all over the lands through which he traveled. He won their trust easily, because he was—or looked—so young, so innocent, simply another boy like themselves, traveling alone. The Hopi had sullen eyes but a quick smile; he could not believe Lupe had come all the way from Los Angeles to the colored deserts of the Southwest. He showed Lupe a wind-carved notch high in a sandstone bluff where they sat drinking whiskey and smoking weed while the sun went down behind a distant butte. At the moment the first star appeared, Lupe introduced the Hopi to Miguel, and the second boy's strength warmed him all through a cold desert night. Falling snow melted when it touched him. He was a flame among the stones. He found a road and followed it till daybreak, when the two boys (friends now, closer than they'd ever be to Lupe) disappeared.

Gradually the desert sun had come to seem too bright. Facing his fear of the fire had always been harder than facing the dark. He knew this was a weakness, but was helpless. Fire could not be endured in the same way as darkness. The stars shone like white flames; even the moon threatened to scorch him. Seeking shelter, he traveled east over broad lands whose flatness frightened him, since no secrets could be kept there. He traveled as quickly as possible, sometimes wishing he had remained in the desert, with its canyons and eroded walls and ancient sculpted stone. But soon he found himself in rich countryside like none he'd ever seen, among other kinds of shadows: shadows of woods, shadows of mountains, shadows of caves. This land was fertile with darkness.

Virginia, Tennessee, Kentucky, the Carolinas. Limestone caverns had gnawed and wormholed away the underside of every surface. There were big caves like subterranean Disneylands, full of lurid lights and guided tours, offering ridiculous souvenirs. He knew he could never be comfortable in these places, though he always looked with longing at the unlit side tunnels, the regions no one had mapped. Once he slipped away from a tour and lost himself for days in the dark, living on icy water and imagining himself a slippery blind thing that had dwelt there forever.

He met the Cherokee in the Appalachians. The land was full of runaways. Together they hitchhiked and camped for several nights in the national parks, until Lupe convinced the other to take him to a sacred cave, a place of his ancestors, where they planned to eat mescaline. Lupe always pretended to carry a rich supply of psychedelics, a lure to most of his companions on the road.

Sometimes sex was the bait. Certain fellow travelers warmed to Lupe's hints of things that could best be done in deep darkness. He would always remember how the Virginian had grinned and said, "We could do those things in any old motel."

Lupe said, "Not *these* things."

The Virginian had picked him up in a battered truck, heading north through the Shenandoah Valley. Lupe steered the talk to caves, which was easy enough with signs advertising them every few miles. "Forget about them ones on the map. I know a better one. No ticket price, either." As they turned onto a rough narrow road among pines, Lupe glanced at the bed of the truck and saw Miguel, the Hopi and the Cherokee crouched down in back.

That night, when he retraced his route along the same road, four shadows rode in the bed.

Over a year later, hitching south on the same stretch of highway, he accepted a ride from a young Marine on his way home to Charlotte on leave. Lupe described the Virginian's cave as the hideout of old distillers, and said there was supposed to be a cache still hidden there. It was late by the time they found the place. The Marine was tall, strong, and recently trained in fighting; but all his advantages went for nothing in the dark.

The cave states were the most fruitful by far. Somehow he wasted more than a year in New York City, which he feared at times he would never escape. He'd thought that with its subways and cavernous buildings he would make many friends; but he never found comfort there. The city, which should have been a collector's dream, made him doubt himself; consequently, few trusted him. He sponged off older men who held no attraction for him, since few had the sort of vitality he sought in his initiates. They were only useful alive. He did learn things in this period, however; he learned to read; he learned how to mold himself according to the desires of others, how to talk like them and act like them, to blend into each little world in which he found himself. He had started some of this with Dr. Brownhouse, spending time in a place and among people so different from those he'd always known. But New York allowed him to hone his skills, as he ranged between ruined tenements and penthouse suites.

He added but one boy to his gang in all that time, a wasted, scrawny addict whose initiation was less an act of desire than of self-defense. It had been so long—he needed *someone*. Absorbing his power, Lupe felt such a violent jolt of sickness that he instantly regretted his decision; but it was too late. The Junkie was his forever, polluting the purity of his collection.

Once back in the country, he initiated the Marine almost immediately. Then came the young black Musician, who never played a single note for Lupe either before or after his initiation, though the long drawn-out wail of a freight train's whistle was music enough in the dark, onrushing boxcar where he met the other boys.

After that, Lupe's thoughts began to turn toward home.

Toward Sal.

It was because of Sal he had ended up in the First Cave, powerless and vulnerable. Sal had stunted him—shattered his life. So it was Sal he thought of, now that he had made himself whole. Now that he had allies.

When he returned to Los Angeles after years of wandering, after dozens of other lesser caves, he felt ready at last to master the First Cave. It took him days to gather the courage, and when he finally visited the place he found the hump-backed hill covered with new buildings, the rock itself leveled or gouged away. The cave was buried or destroyed—there was no way of telling which. He shrugged off his disappointment that there would be no showdown, knowing it had been a childish wish. The true First Cave was inside him now, where it would remain unchanging, bottomless, a pit that could never be filled in or covered over. None of the outer caves could have been any darker or deeper than the one within; and in facing that one, he knew he had mastered them all. He was ready now. He was whole.

It was time to find his brother.

* * *

His boys woke him, crawling in around him like baby rats nudging up against their mother to nurse. He opened his eyes and saw the Pump Jockey, respect and remorse in his expression, apologizing silently for every slur he'd shouted before his initiation.

Lupe stirred, feeling claustrophobic. Golden light shone on the dirt wall next to him. Twisting around in the nest, he saw the sun just touching the horizon, seeming to melt on the water. With the sight came a pang of anticipation, again the recurrent sense that tonight, finally, something crucial would happen, some indescribable change would come over him and blow away everything that had grown old and stale. With the Pump Jockey's power still fresh inside him, he felt a welcome renewal of hope. The feeling faded as night came on. Nothing would ever change, he realized again. Not for him. His stomach felt bottomless.

He waited until the sun had vanished, stirring violet into the orange clouds. The boys had faded with the sun, though he had hoped they would stay and keep him company.

He crawled out alone, feeling exposed on the cliffside and on the stairs, but no one gave him much notice. The beach was lightly populated, though it showed signs of having been crowded. People were shaking out towels, folding huge umbrellas, dragging coolers over the sand toward flights of stairs. Beer cans and broken sand toys littered the beach. As Lupe walked, continuing south, his stomach growled, reminding him that he hadn't eaten much more than a handful of nuts since yesterday. There was money in his pocket, including a few bucks he'd taken from the Pump Jockey.

A glimmer of neon atop the cliffs caught his eye. FOOD & SPIRITS. Broad windows overlooked the sea. The stairs that scaled the cliff below the restaurant were lined with men, most of them sitting and staring down at the waves, a few talking.

As soon as he saw them, he knew what he was looking at. Their style of dress, the trimmed mustaches and close-cut hair,

the predominance of black leather, only confirmed a more visceral knowledge, a tense anticipation.

Many eyes played on Lupe as he walked toward the stairs. He
pretended to ignore them, but he felt his body vibrate like a
drum skin with the attention. As he took the first step, the young
man sitting there gave him a slight nod and smile. Others said
hello as he climbed past. Lupe did not acknowledge their greet-
ings. At the top of the stairs, he found himself at the edge of the
restaurant's patio. He spied a bar inside the place, and heard the
sizzling of meat on a grill. Repelled, he sought a table outside
near the cliff's edge, where all he could smell was the sea. A few
of the men on the stairs had tracked his progress, and now gazed
up at him speculatively. He looked away as a waiter appeared
and dropped a menu on his table. It showed a pair of lobster
claws waving out of a dark hole—tiny beady eyes above a grin.

"Welcome to the Rock Lobster. Can I get you a drink?"
When Lupe looked up, the waiter's expression grew pinched
and nervous.

"I'm sorry," he said in a soft, confidential voice, leaning
nearer. "You're going to have to show me some I.D."

"For a garden salad?" Lupe asked, keeping his voice light,
pleasant.

"Oh, well . . . that's no problem." The waiter smiled and
winked. "But I wouldn't try the bar, if I were you."

"I'm old enough if I wanted to."

"Maybe you are at that."

The waiter walked back inside. Lupe followed his progress
through the crowd around the dark interior bar. Heavy disco
music pulsed out into the evening. Out here, it was much
calmer; couples sat talking quietly, sipping drinks. At the small
outdoor bar, separated by several stools, two men sat drinking
alone. One was young and trim; he kept glancing at his watch.
Lupe studied the other. Late forties, thinning colorless hair,
paunchy, wearing thick plastic flesh-tone glasses.

He thanked the waiter for his salad in a loud, friendly voice
and was gratified to see the object of his study take a casual look

in his direction. The look lengthened. As Lupe lifted a fork to his mouth he pretended to notice the man at the bar for the first time. The other glanced away quickly, then looked back more slowly. Lupe returned the gaze steadily, holding eye contact for a meaningful length of time. Then he turned slightly to gaze back down at the stairs.

As he was eating, he heard another chair at his table scrape on the patio bricks. He turned, smile at the ready.

"Hi." It was the man from the bar. "Mind if I join you?"

"Free country," Lupe said.

Doubt crossed the man's face. He started to run a hand through his hair. "Just kidding," Lupe said. "Have a seat."

The man's look of gratitude was pathetic. He dropped down quickly. "Can—can I buy you a drink?"

"No thanks. I'm Rico, by the way." Lupe put out his hand and the other shook it, his hand plump and sweaty.

"Rico, hi. Pleasure to meet you. My name's Raymond."

"Rico and Raymond," Lupe said musically, still grinning. Raymond blinked hugely behind his thick lenses, confused by hope.

"You're not . . . from around here, are you, Rico?"

"No, I—"

"Excuse me." Raymond put up a finger, hesitant, as the waiter approached. "Could I have another margarita please? Can I get you anything, Rico? Coke? Mineral water?"

"Sure, I'll take a Coke."

The waiter winked at Raymond. "Coming right up."

"I'm sorry, you were saying?"

"I'm just . . . passing through."

"Oh really? Heading anywhere in particular? Or from any-where?"

Lupe shrugged. "Away."

"So . . . you're not in town for long?"

"Maybe a night or two. Depends."

"On . . . ?"

"If I can find a place to stay. You know."

"You don't have any friends in town? You're not visiting anyone here?"

Lupe looked down at his nearly empty plate, sighed. Allowed himself to shake his head minutely.

"I don't mean to press, Rico. I mean, we only just met and all, but . . . if it's not too bold of me, can I tell you what I think?"

Lupe shrugged.

"You're running from something, aren't you?"

Lupe looked up sharply.

Raymond smiled gently, with understanding. "Or some*one?* Parents? People who don't understand you? Won't accept who you are?"

Lupe looked away, clenching his jaws.

"It's all right, Rico. You're safe here. You're lucky you came. This is the right place for you."

"I've been places like this before," Lupe said.

"Well, of course you have. You know who you are, even if other people don't."

"That's right," Lupe said. "I have my pride."

"Yes! Rico . . . what you've done is very brave. I know that may not mean much coming from me. We're strangers, after all. But I feel as if I know you already; and I do—I really do know your situation. If you knew me better, I hope what I'm saying would give you confidence that you're doing the right thing. A lot of boys like you lack confidence. But I'm here to tell you that you're right. You can trust your impulses. Whatever you decide, that's what's best for you."

Lupe said, "I wish I did know you better."

Raymond reached out, put a hand lightly on his wrist, almost unable to hide his eagerness, as if he were the only one doing the manipulating. "Can I offer you a place to stay?"

Lupe let himself smile. "Really?"

The waiter returned at that moment with their drinks and the tab for Lupe's salad. "I'll pay for this too, Tyler," Raymond told the waiter, handing him a bill. Lupe watched him return to the bar that was now no darker than the night. Something caught his eye, moving through the shifting crowd of faces, lit by an angular flash of strobe light.

Lupe jumped up, grabbing his pack. Raymond lurched to his feet. "What is it? Did I say something—?"

"Can we go right now?" he said. He put his hand on Raymond's arm and rushed him toward the patio gate.

"What's your hurry?"

"This place is too noisy, too many people. I can't handle it right now."

"Oh, of course, I'm sorry. You poor thing, you must be exhausted. When was the last time you slept in a bed?"

From the street, Lupe glanced back through a hedge that encircled the patio. Through a break in the branches, he saw his brother standing in the doorway of the bar, staring at the table Lupe had just fled.

He saw me, Lupe realized. For only an instant, but it was enough.

"My car's right here," Raymond said. He stopped by a white Porsche and unlocked the door for Lupe. "There you go."

"I didn't mean to rush you," Lupe said as he slipped in. "You didn't even get your change back."

"Oh, that's all right. Tyler knows me. I'm in there almost every night, waiting for my luck to change."

He looked down daringly at Lupe, and slammed the door.

Lupe didn't expect to know where they were headed, in a town that was still so new to him; but when the Porsche began to climb up a steep hill street, he thought he knew where he was. Seeing the bare scrub at the edges of the headlights, lining the curvy road, he thought they were returning to Sal's neighborhood. He envisioned the map of Bohemia Bay; he tried to remember the name of the place.

"Is this Shangri-La?" he asked.

"No, that's a little south of here, over the hills. I'm in what they call Rim of the World. How do you know about Shangri-La?"

"I heard somebody talking about good neighborhoods."

"Not exactly beachfront property, I'm afraid, but I love it up here."

Lupe relaxed. In such a small town, he'd be close to Sal wherever he settled, but he wanted to keep some distance between them for now.

They came out on winding streets among trimmed lawns, rock gardens, juniper hedges. Housing tracts from the Sixties. It was a warm summer night in the suburbs. Kids were everywhere, riding bikes off the curbs, skateboarding down driveways under floodlights, building up speed for leaps off plywood ramps.

"You like it up here?" Lupe asked, his first genuine question of the evening.

"Sure, it's . . . regular. I like the noise, the feeling of people all around. I don't believe in isolating myself, hiding out in some colony away from the rest of the world. Bohemia Bay is isolated enough as it is."

They turned into a court, a short cul-de-sac. A sunken garage door yawned ahead of them, opening as they approached. Raymond drove down into a tidy garage with a spotless concrete floor. The Porsche's drippings were caught in a shallow aluminum sheet. Through a door at the back of the garage, they went into a fair-sized kitchen. Wooden counters, wood paneling, cupboards, racks of wine and knives. Beyond that were a dining room and living room.

"You live alone?" Lupe asked.

"Sadly, yes. For now."

"I only meant—it looks like you could fit a big family in here."

Or several families, Lupe thought, remembering how he and Sal and Aunt Theresa (not to mention her men) had crammed themselves into a small two-room apartment, in a crowded, noisy building where they counted themselves fortunate because others lived with six or eight people in the same amount of space.

"I suppose you could. Four bedrooms, two baths. But this, for me, is the main attraction."

Raymond walked through the dining room to a sliding glass door, and slid it open. Lupe followed him out onto a balcony that ran the length of the house.

Darkness below, and the scent of the hills, sagebrush and horehound and anise. A breeze full of rich earthy smells came up from the earth, where Lupe could see only shadows. Bamboo clattered in the wind. There were no lights visible anywhere except for the neighboring houses in line with Raymond's on the verge of the hills. Starlight imparted the sense of a canyon below them, a deep valley with ridges running down into it. Lupe began to guess at the secrets among those folds of earth, in hidden places marked by animal tracks, with no people anywhere.

He closed his eyes, leaning on the balcony rail, and breathed in the smell of earth, imagining that it had blown out of caves, dreaming that the ground here fell away forever into an endless pit, with tiny trails that only he could discern spiraling down into it. He was down in the darkness with his boys, moving by touch and smell, sure-footed in a sightless world.

Raymond's hand startled him. "Wait till you see the sunrise from this deck." The hand stayed on his shoulder, massaging slightly.

Lupe turned to face him. "I'd like to sleep in, if that's okay. Lately it's been, you know, park benches, always getting rousted by cops."

Raymond pulled back, his disappointment quickly veiled. "Well, and so you shall. You've had a rough time of it, I'm sure. I should let you get to sleep now. There's plenty of time to watch a sunrise or two."

"Where do I bed down?"

"There's a spare bed made up, don't worry about that. Can I get you anything? More to eat? Do you want to take a shower?"

"I'd just like to sleep."

"Whatever you want, Rico, is fine with me. Any way you want it. Just—just think of my house as your house, for as long as you care to stay."

Lupe must have given Raymond an odd look. He wished he could have seen his own face, to be sure what thoughts he might have betrayed.

"I really mean that," Raymond said emphatically.

"I know you do."

And because some sacrifices were necessary at times to keep things running smoothly, he leaned forward and put his hands behind Raymond's neck and pulled the older man slowly forward—not that Raymond was resisting.

"You're a very special man, Ray," he said, and kissed him on the mouth.

$=11=$

"You guys are formally deputized," Hawk told the gang gathered behind his trailer that night. Their lone lantern exaggerated everything from the whiteness of their skin to the pitchy black of the night. It was easy to imagine they were facing an enemy of utter evil, waging a campaign of goodness and light. But the faces of his boys held plenty of fear and less noble emotions.

"Fuckin' A," said Kurtis Tyre. "Now we're a real posse. Let's beat that fag-ass queer into the ground."

Hawk loped down to face Kurtis, whose eyes all evening had been hot with anger and sneering rage, as if this were the occasion he'd been waiting for to vent the considerable poisons gathering inside him. Kurtis was his wickedest, his most challenging project. Abused, probably; sadistic, certainly. For that reason, Hawk wanted him in the forefront of his deputies. He thought Kurtis had more than a little of the black streak in him, and might even think like Craig's murderer. Given the benefit of Kurtis's sick insights, Hawk hoped he might anticipate the killer's next moves. But it was not important that Kurtis know this. It was more important that he fear Hawk and stay in line, and be wary of transgressing their spontaneous, unspoken code.

"We are on the side of Law," Hawk said to him, knowing that the others would take the words as if addressed to them personally. "Not *the* law, which wears the face of our old friends in blue—"

"Fuckin' pigs," Kurtis said.

"—but Law itself. The cosmic principle of right action. That which is right because it is righteous, and not because a bunch of paid-off judges got together and agreed on the best way to protect the interests of the politicos who put them on the bench. Now sometimes, Kurtis—though it seems incredible—this Law, this righteousness, overlaps with the law of the police and the courts. And one of those ways is in not judging things too soon, not jumping to conclusions. If Sal's responsible for this, we'll find that out in time. But if you take it for granted that he's guilty, and then you turn out to be wrong, you'll be staring at him so hard you'll miss the real clues in the corner of your eye. You are not judge, jury and executioner, Kurtis. Neither is any one of us. What you are right now is *my* eyes, *my* ears, *my* hands."

"So what does that make you?"

Hawk cuffed him lightly on the side of the head and sat down next to him on a log stump, hands clasped between his knees, looking from face to face. Howard's eyes were red, his face pale and streaked with grime. Some of the others looked equally bad. He saw in them the realization that Craig's death could have come to any one of them—might in fact still be on its way. It didn't matter that they were only fourteen, sixteen, eighteen years old. They could have been dead since this morning, slashed to ribbons in a storm drain, fixed forever at their present age.

"I can't move around freely right now, not the way I'd like to. The cops are gonna be watching me. They'll be watching some of you, too. I figure they think you guys are just as likely as not to off one another."

Kurtis kicked a bootheel at the dust. "Why is it whenever there's trouble, we always get the blame?"

Hawk's grin felt to him like a nervous tic, pulling his whole face sideways. "That's just the kind of people we are. If we weren't, would we be sitting here right now?"

"What are we supposed to be looking for?" Edgar asked.

"I can't tell you that. You won't know till you see it."

"You mean there's no clues at all?"

"Alec didn't see anybody around. Craig went off for a smoke by the water. It was early. That was the last he saw, and that's all he saw. If Craig was killed in the pipe, which seems likely, then somebody had to get him in there first. And it must have been somebody he knew. I can't see anybody dragging Craig in if he didn't want to go."

"He might've ducked in to smoke a doob."

"No," Howard said. "He was dry last night. We haven't had weed in a week. Uh . . . sorry, Hawk."

"So maybe somebody had something he wanted," Edgar said. "Like a lid."

"Coulda been a girl," someone else said. "I mean, Craig, he'd let a rattlesnake suck his dick."

A loud thumping from down the hillside carried to them. A huge figure approached from the trailer, carrying a massive box. As Stoner walked into the circle of light, Hawk jumped up and gave a disgusted cry. The stupid oaf! His boys froze when they saw the word PENDLETON stenciled across the side of the crate.

Hawk would have struck him, but he was too afraid of upsetting Stoner. Instead, with all the diplomacy he could muster, he said very quietly, almost whispering, "What's wrong with you, Stoner?"

"I was just gonna ask where you want me to put 'em, since you said we should hide any shit that could get us in trouble."

Hawk was expecting visits from the police. The matter of Stoner's grenade stash had somehow slipped his mind until now. He had to wonder where the box had been hiding.

"Just—just set that thing down," he said calmly, with a soft, patting gesture, to demonstrate how it should be done.

"Really," said one of the boys. "Stoner, man, you are massively fucked!"

Stoner chuckled, stooped over, and set the box on the dirt, none too gently. Hawk relaxed slightly.

"I know a good place for that," Edgar said.

Hawk gave him a nod. "Can we do it tonight? I don't want this hanging around."

"Whenever you're ready."

Hawk nodded to Stoner. "Put that thing in the jeep. Wrap it in foam or something first. Shit."

Edgar started down the hill, and the others got up to follow him. Hawk stopped them with a word.

"I don't want anybody in on this except Stoner and Edgar. The less of you know where this stuff is stashed, the safer we'll all be. Not that I don't trust you like my own little lambs."

A few of them made bleating sounds.

Thirty minutes later—Hawk driving at unaccustomed speed, slowing to a crawl for every turn, braking whenever the headlights suggested a bump or crack in the street ahead—they drove past Edgar's house to the end of Shoreview Road. He gave fervent thanks that he'd installed new shocks in the Jeep three months ago; even so, the ride had never seemed so jolting. They parked by a padlocked fence. Beyond was a private dirt road so deeply rutted that in places it looked like a stream bed. Even if he'd had a key to the gate, Hawk would not have driven a box of hand grenades over that road for any price.

He stood back while Stoner unloaded the crate, wrapped in a piece of foam mattress. He winced when Stoner tossed the box onto his shoulder and held it there one-handed.

"Would you mind keeping both hands on that?" he said. "Edgar, you lead the way. I want you to give Stoner plenty of light to see where he's stepping. And Stoner, please, don't trip."

"Shit, Hawk, I'm light on my feet."

"Uh-huh."

For a while, the flashlight glittered on broken bottle-glass and corroded cans, burst tires, pulped and desiccated newspaper; the ruts in the road looked like canyons. Stoner avoided most of this without having to be warned. But then Edgar set off through weeds and brush. They passed a TV with its guts blown out, a bullet-riddled tin can stuck on a stick, spent cartridges. All Hawk could see was the moving spot of light leading them on; the rest of the world was a blank. They moved through a dense patch of thistles that had blanketed the ground with white down. Stoner cursed as the spines of the fierce bushy plants stabbed him. If there had ever been a trail here, it hadn't been used in years.

"Couldn't you find an easier way, Edgar?" Hawk said.

"Yeah, watch out here, it's kind of slippery. There's like a cliff."

Stoner grunted and stepped onto bare dirt. Dust smoked from his heels. Hawk followed in dimmer light, and felt the ground crumble. His feet nearly went out from under him. He crouched down for balance, cursing, and heard Stoner laugh. "You okay back there, Hawk? Better give him more light, Edgar—whoa!"

"This is the worst part," Edgar said.

At that moment, the flashlight went dead. "Shit!"

"Don't move!" Hawk yelled.

"Jesus," said Stoner, somewhere ahead of him, "I can't see a thing."

The light came on again, weaker but still alive. Edgar was shaking the flashlight, which made everything jump. He was below them, shining the light up at Stoner's feet. "You make it down okay?"

"Coming," Stoner grunted, and crouched to skid and slide down the steep hillside, without any hands for balance. Hawk swallowed the ball in his throat. At the bottom, next to Edgar, Stoner rose up chuckling. "Used to do that all the time when I was a kid."

"You may not live to be an adult if you keep it up," Hawk said. "Look out." Then he slid, too, and joined them at the bottom, coughing at the dust he'd raised.

Edgar went on across flat, unmarked, weedy ground, shaking

the flashlight repeatedly to keep it alive. Hawk saw a dark ridge above them, it could have been five feet away or five hundred.

"Around here somewhere," Edgar said, and started scuffing at the dirt with a toe.

"Can I put this down?" Stoner asked.

"Gently."

"Here it is," Edgar said. He knelt near a juniper bush, one hand tugging at what looked like a bit of gnarled root. He pulled it and dirt sifted free of a big piece of board. He leaned the trapdoor against the bush and leaned over, looking down into the large square pit he'd uncovered.

"It goes in a few feet," he said. "Leo and I dug it, you know, as a hideout. Took us a week."

"I'll get down there first," Hawk said. "Then you hand it to me."

He edged past Edgar and lowered himself in. Touching bottom, he could just rest his elbows on the edge of the pit. Stoner appeared above him, already hefting the crate. Hawk tensed to receive it. The fucker was even heavier than he'd remembered. He crouched down awkwardly, cramped in the hole, straining to keep the box steady. When he had it down on the earth, he asked for the flashlight and aimed it deeper into the hole.

A tunnel went back about six feet, into a chamber with another sheet of plywood for a ceiling. Hawk pushed the crate into the far end of the burrow till it butted up against the earthen wall. He crouched there with it for a moment, smelling the close, confining dirt, studying the den's features, imagining how a couple of boys might hide out here in a world of secrets, thinking of how little kids pulled blankets over chairs and tables to fabricate caves and tunnels, how darkness held such power over humankind because it had reigned over the imagination since the beginning of life. Were children ever taught to fear the dark, or was such fear instinctive? Darkness, he thought, is so much a part of us that we never know where to begin doing battle with it . . . if indeed that's the proper response.

Stuff for a sermon, here.

There were little shelves gouged into the walls, holding candle stubs, books of matches. A roll of magazines was stuffed in another niche. Hawk picked up one of them, expecting motorcycles or hot rods. He was disappointed to see the raunchiest sort of porn, Danish stuff, closeups of gaping cavities, lots of slime and wet pink mattress-meat. He supposed he should be grateful for an absence of donkey dicks and shit-eaters, but it was hard to keep his perspective in the clammy little burrow. The walls exuded a moldy stink he hadn't noticed at first.

"What's that?" Stoner said suddenly, startling him. He'd dropped down into the hole. Hawk shoved the magazine back onto the crude shelf and backed out, pushing Stoner ahead of him, glad for fresh air. "Nothing, go on, let's cover this up."

When they had camouflaged the trap again, and were hiking back uphill, Hawk said, "So Edgar, you come here often?"

"Naw," Edgar said. "Not since Leo moved away. Used to play here a lot, but that was, you know . . . I sort of grew out of it. It's more of a little kid's thing."

Just then, the light went out completely. It had been dying for so long that it made little difference; their eyes were already used to the dark. They shuffled along through the dust, hardly speaking, until Stoner said, "Is it true what I heard about Craig, Hawk?"

Hawk tensed, knowing what he meant, but not wanting it to get around. He didn't want Edgar to hear, for some reason; not that Edgar's ears were tender. He had to admit that he couldn't protect the boys from everything—or from anything, really.

"I don't know," he said awkwardly. "It's just a rumor."

"What is?" Edgar asked.

Hawk wasn't about to say it himself, but he couldn't stop Stoner from speaking.

"The killer cut his balls off," Stoner said. "And took 'em along wherever he went."

PART TWO

ESP

=12=

Midway through the summer, with no warning, Scott Gillette called Mike to announce that he was moving.

"It's fuckin' Walter," Scott said. "Shit-eatin' bastard psycho fuckhead. He's known for weeks, but he kept it from us. Even from my goddamn mother."

"Knew what? Where are you going?"

Scott groaned into the phone. "Can you come down here?"

"It'll take awhile."

"I'm not going anywhere. Not till I go to Texas."

"Texas? Jeez! Okay, I'm coming."

He dropped the phone and ran downstairs, through Ryan's room, its white walls now covered with sports posters and pennants, the visible portions scuffed by sneakers and imprinted with the pentagonal patterns of a soccer ball Ryan kicked around when no adults were home. TV sounds blasted up the spiral steps. Mike yelled down the stairwell: "Ryan! I'm going to Scott's! Tell Mom!"

A muted yell answered him. He hurried back upstairs, ducking into his room for his skateboard, his backpack and a windbreaker. Outside, he climbed steep streets toward the highest ridge in Shangri-La, passing the vacant lot where he'd hid in the grass his first night up here, then a huge round water storage tank he hadn't noticed in the dark that night, and which he hardly noticed now. He was already accustomed to the neighborhood. How had that happened? The long, quiet streets were home now—as familiar as the beaches. When he wasn't with Scott or Edgar, he sat in his room under the painted moon and drew. He had plenty of time for it. The Glantz sisters had found his clipboard in the storeroom, legions of gory monsters and naked barbarian women parading around under the light-bulb inventory lists. On Tuesday following the move, Mr. Glantz had greeted him with the clipboard and a handful of torn-up illustrations. "Now I see what you are, boy."

Even though his days were free again, Mike stayed up in Shangri-La unless he had reason to leave it. He liked the isolation, the silent streets, the absence of crowds. The only thing he didn't like was the utter lack of girls. There were *none* up here as far as he could tell—hardly any families at all. Two men shared the house next door to them, a homosexual couple—"gays," his mother called them. Sal was apparently one of a community up here. Not that Mike saw much of his neighbors. Jack had built him a desk inside the walk-in closet, and sometimes he sat there six hours at a stretch with his pens and pencils and oil pastels, drawing dragons and armored gunmen, barbarian warriors with blood-drenched broadswords, skeleton things, spaceships and sleek cars, lithe half-naked women clinging to the legs of brawny soldiers. Creatures from his imagination were all that interested him. The rest of the world was so quiet and boring in its day-to-day sameness. Even this neighborhood had divulged but one night of excitement; then, as if spent, all its mysteries exhausted, it had shut up so tight that it seemed a different neighborhood entirely. It was hard to believe he had ever been afraid here—that the house where he lived, packed full of furniture and his mother's flowers, was the same empty shell in which he had sought shelter from Sal's gang.

Right now the nearness of Sal's house made him recall the events of that night, but as he stepped on the board and kicked away from the curb, thoughts of the key vanished again for a while.

He had new troubles staring him in the face. Scott was moving to Texas?

It seemed impossible, not yet a real threat. He and Scott would undoubtedly come up with a scheme to upset the whole plan and keep the move from happening. There was plenty of time to outwit Walter.

From the south end of Shangri-La, a long twisting street went down through the hills, past cliff-perched houses that seemed to be made mostly out of glass.

Mike hesitated at the top of the descent, looking down at the ocean hundreds of feet below, wishing he had the guts and the balance to step on the board and gather all the speed he could, cutting those dangerous curves with skill and precision.

Edgar had given him the skateboard and a few riding lessons, but Mike had finally begun to admit he didn't have the necessary reckless confidence for the sport—not to mention the balance. He hated lugging the board around and could never stay on for long. He was wary of tumbling and scraping up his hands and knees, banging on the hard cement.

Still, it was faster than walking down the long hills. So few people lived this high up that hitchhiking was unreliable.

Compromising, he sat down on the board, grabbed the sides, and raised his feet.

It was speedy transportation, even sitting. Several times cars came down behind him and honked. He banked way over to the side of the road—there were no sidewalks or shoulders here—and let them pass. He wobbled and fell frequently; but braking with his feet, he kept his speed well under control, and none of his spills were painful. When he ran out of hill, he tucked the board under his arm, walked to the Coast Highway, and stuck out his thumb. It took only two minutes to get a ride, there were so many cars.

Scott lived in South Bohemia, up a shady hill street. There

were no crowds south of town, since the beaches were private and restricted to residents—some of them nudists. The warm hush suited the depression Mike felt stealing over him. Gloom gave way to shock when he saw Scott's house. The front deck was heaped with cardboard boxes.

Scott's stepfather appeared at the picture window, making Mike flinch into the shadow of a hedge. Walter unnerved him. This latest action—abrupt and unexpected coming from anyone else—was completely in character. When Walter turned away from the window, Mike hurried down the driveway. He could hear voices yelling inside the house, as something heavy slammed down, or shut, or into something else.

Scott lived in a room Walter had built for him by running a partition down the center of the garage and dropping in a ceiling. When Mike knocked, Scott pulled the warped door open, scraping it over the cement floor of his room, which was littered with moldy, mismatched shag-carpet remnants. Scott blinked out at the day, his eyes looking small, red and puffy. It was dark in the long, narrow room where one little desk lamp burned. It smelled of the oily engine parts stored in the other half of the garage. Scott hauled the door shut behind Mike and threw a heavy crossbar latch across it.

Mike was at least half a foot shorter than Scott, but the ceiling was so low it brushed his hair when he walked. Scott was forced to stoop continuously. He went to the bed at the far end of the room and sat down heavily. The place was a worse mess than ever. Usually Scott's books, if nothing else, were neatly organized, running along the walls in alphabetical order. Today they lay in collapsing heaps, sliding over the bare floor, some thrown haphazardly into boxes.

On the bed beside Scott were various weapons, including saber, foil and epée. It was the fully loaded—and cocked—speargun that caught Mike's eye. He stepped aside when he saw the barbed tip aimed right at his crotch.

Scott noticed, and picked up the gun. "If Walter comes in, I'm shooting him. You can be my witness."

"Watch out with that," Mike said.

Scott grinned and pulled the trigger. The bolt flew past Mike and buried itself with a splintering thunk in the door.

"Jesus!"

Scott got up, hunched over as always, and stomped across the room. He worked the spear out of the door as violently as possible, ripping it free along with several jagged shards of wood. When he was finished, a second small source of light pierced the gloom.

Mike glanced over at Scott's desk, where piles of typing paper were stacked. Scott was writing a book about "Rupert Giles," a boy genius who continually devised ways of slowly killing his evil stepfather, "Wally": domestic warfare not so loosely based on Scott's own life. In the latest installments, Rupert had hired a Mafia hit man to castrate "Wally" with a steam iron. The book was called *Seascape, With Dead Stepfather*.

"So . . ." Mike said. "How's the book?"

"It's finished. I mean, we're moving to Texas. There's no seascape where we're going."

"You could put that in. It would be sort of funny."

"What, *Panhandle, With Dead Stepfather*?"

"It couldn't be any weirder than the rest of it." He was trying desperately to find some bright spot in all this.

Scott reloaded the speargun. "I may never write again. Fucking Texas, day after tomorrow. It's all worked out, Mike. There's nothing I can do about it."

"But—but, why?"

"Walter got a job. My mom's been after him for fucking years to get a job, and when he finally does, it's in Texas! The shitty thing is, he probably won't keep it more than a week. We'll get out there and something will happen, he'll flip out again with one of his Vietnam flashbacks, attack a state trooper instead of a beach parking-lot attendant, and that'll be it. Since my mom doesn't have a job there, and they probably don't need more teachers, we'll be stranded forever. In Texas! I can't believe it!"

Mike dropped into the desk chair.

A fit of screaming broke the prolonged silence. Voices came from the house. Then they heard the crashing of glass.

"One less lamp to pack," Scott said.

Ms. Gillette's voice rose high and shrill, the words unintelligible. Walter's response was pitched ominously low.

"She says she's not going. Her own job and all. But she will. She's already giving in . . ."

"You're really going to stop writing your book?"

"My book? It doesn't mean anything now. It was my escape from this place. I'll have to find something else for Texas."

"What if—what if I did drawings for it? We always wanted to do a collaboration. How about that?"

Scott actually smiled for a moment. "Oh . . . okay . . . yeah. That would be great. I'll leave you the story and you can go ahead and start."

They heard a desperate bleating from one side of the garage. Scott's only window was draped with a thick beach towel. He pulled it away as if drawing the curtain on a small, hot stage.

The window was level with a scruffy patch of dirt yard scattered with Walter's collection of junk: auto parts, a cast-iron wood stove with no door, and a pyramid made out of two-by-fours and plastic sheeting, inside of which a heap of metal scrap was turning orange. The pyramid's metaphysical properties (Walter claimed it could sharpen razor blades and garbage disposal units) apparently could not stop the advance of simple rust. Chickens pecked at the burr-clover.

In a far corner of the yard, raising dust, Walter was wrestling with the goat he'd bought a few months ago. A coil of rope was slung over his shoulder. They watched him drag the goat over to the bushy lemon tree whose branches shaded the whole yard, and without which it would have been unbearably bleak. He pressed the animal to the trunk, pinning it in place with the weight of his body. Walter looked grim and determined; teeth bared, he was talking to the goat—or to himself—in a growling voice. He knelt to tie the goat's hind legs together, cinching them tight.

"What's he doing?" Mike asked.

"Lightening the load."

Walter slung the free end of the rope over the lowest, thickest limb of the lemon tree and yanked hard. The goat swung upside down into the air, screaming like a child. Walter tied the rope to the trunk, and then moved between the goat and the window, reaching for his belt. Mike went cold when he saw Walter unsheathe his hunting knife.

What Walter did next, his body hid from view; all he knew for sure was that the goat stopped screaming even as *he* wanted to start. Walter jumped back so he wouldn't get sprayed, and Mike found himself staring at the goat, hanging limp, its jaws drenched in blood that poured out and pooled in the dirt. Walter turned toward the window, blood in his beard, and came rushing at them. Mike let out a yell, but Walter was only chasing a chicken. He snatched it up and turned away, busy with the knife.

Mike backed up and sat on Scott's bed, numb, dizzy and cold. He closed his eyes and let the grayness close over him. It felt like a familiar friend.

When he came back to himself, Scott was shoving magazines in his face. Slick ones, with an odd musty smell. The pictures flashing from the pages made Mike come suddenly awake.

"Here," Scott said. "I'm bequeathing these to you."

It was hardcore pornography, some Danish magazines Scott had been hoarding.

"Wh-what?"

"Go on. I can always swipe more from Walter. It's a crime you don't have any decent stroke-books."

Mike blushed, staggering to his feet and pushing them away. "Get out of here."

"Go on, take 'em."

"No, I don't want—"

"Sure you do." Scott shoved them into his hands.

At that moment, someone pounded on the door. Walter shouted, "Scott!"

-= 129 =-

Heart pounding, Mike jumped up to hide the magazines in his backpack.

"What do you want?" Scott said sourly, a challenge in his voice.

"Open this fuckin' door before I kick it down."

"Go ahead," Scott said under his breath, but he crossed the room slowly all the same. He unlatched the door, leaving Walter the work of opening it.

Walter was even taller than Scott, so he didn't bother entering the room. Bent, he peered in at them, grinning when he saw Mike.

"James the man. Helping out the Scooter-Pie?"

"A little," Mike said. Walter was scariest in his jolly moods.

"Far out. Work up an appetite and stay for dinner. Think we're gonna barbecue tonight. Have us a bon voyage party."

"That sounds good," Mike ventured.

"You bet it is. Ever eat goat before?"

Mike glanced out the window. The goat still swung from the lemon tree. Flies were circling.

"I—I don't know if I can stay," he said. "My mom, ah . . ."

"Suit yourself," Walter said and walked off chuckling. "Scott, I'm gonna need a hand butchering this baby, so when you two are through . . ."

"I'm going to do him like that goat," Scott whispered, kicking the door shut again. "There's lots of places to hide a body in Texas."

It struck Mike then with terrible finality that Scott was really leaving, and nothing the two of them did, no harebrained plot they hatched, was going to change a thing. As long as Scott was a minor, Walter controlled his fate. Scott, his best friend, whom he'd assumed he would know for the rest of his life—or at least throughout high school—was leaving. He was practically gone.

"I'll kill him if it's the last thing I do," Scott swore.

Three days later, he *was* gone.

=13=

The windows of Raymond's Porsche were tinted so dark that Lupe could almost convince himself it was evening rather than noon, but the illusion was spoiled by exhausted tourists shambling past in swimtrunks and sandals, looking beaten by the sun. Their children slouched by, dragging plastic sand shovels. The spear-point eucalyptus leaves along the avenue dangled straight down without stirring. He kept the air conditioner turned all the way up.

Finally the door of Bohemia Travel, Raymond's agency, flew open. Raymond came grinning toward the car, tipping up his sunshades to peer in at Lupe. He carried piles of bright brochures.

Lupe leaned over to unlock the driver's door.

"Aloha!" Raymond said, slipping in.

He dropped the brochures in Lupe's lap, letting his hand rest on Lupe's thigh a moment before drawing it slowly away.

"Do you know how long it's been since I've had a week's vacation—let alone a month? You'd think a travel agent would get away more often. But the place doesn't run itself. I hope I can forget about it long enough to relax."

Lupe leafed through the pamphlets, repelled by photographs of leafy green tropical forests, exploding volcanoes, snowy mountain peaks, sunny beaches. He'd had all he could stand of beaches and sunshine. Bohemia Bay was bad enough. If he'd thought they might actually make it to Hawaii, he would have been itchy with dread.

"The condo reservations are all squared away, everything's set. Are you as excited as I am?" After a moment, Raymond looked over and caught Lupe gazing at the sidewalk where a tall tan boy was striding past, swim fins hooked on a finger. "Rico?"

Lupe nodded slightly.

"Rico . . . what's wrong *now?*"

Lupe shrugged. He was thinking of all he had yet to accomplish before their "trip" could begin. He had convinced Raymond to take a whole day packing and setting last-minute things in order so they wouldn't have to rush for the plane. The flight didn't leave until tomorrow evening; he had until then to finalize his plans.

"If you're getting in one of your moods again, let me warn you: *Don't.* I won't put up with them today—they're inappropriate. We should be celebrating! When I see you like this, I start to doubt everything. I mean, if you're going to sulk for the whole trip, I'd just as soon stay home and work. At least there I feel useful."

"I'm not sulking," Lupe said. "I'm thinking about how much fun we're going to have."

"I hate it when you lie to me. And you're so blatant about it!"

"Don't tell me you know what I'm thinking, Ray. You're not a mind reader."

Raymond twisted the key; the car roared to life then settled down to a purr. "We need gas." They backed out of the space. A station wagon idled behind them, waiting for the spot. "I mean, if you would only communicate a little more—make an effort to tell me what you're thinking, instead of playing these moody guessing games. You can't blame me for expecting the worst. Sometimes all I do is open my mouth and you're out the door, running off into the hills. What you do out there for hours at a time, I can't imagine. How do you think that makes me feel?"

"I told you, I need time to myself. I need my own space."

"I leave you alone all day! There's nothing you have to do, you've got a room of your own, and I never bother you even when I *am* home! I mean Christ, Rico, I give you everything you could need or want. I'd give you so much *more* if you would only trust me. . . ."

He must have sensed Lupe's tension winding tighter now. They had been down this path before. If they'd been at home, Lupe would be heading for the door now; as it was, his hand kept straying to the handle.

"Not that I mean to pressure you," Raymond added quickly. "I have too much respect for you to . . . to impose on you. But I can't help feeling, sometimes, just the slightest bit, that you're—you're using me. I mean, if you only showed a little appreciation once in a while. But instead, with you, it's just nothing. Nothing!"

The Porsche had pulled into a gas station. Raymond shut off the engine at the pumps. His words were becoming too much to stand: the whining in his voice, his subtle hints of how everything could be better between them if only Lupe would give himself away. For a moment he felt that it wasn't worth it, that this whole routine was nothing but trouble. He could do without Raymond's house if he had to. He had no intention of initiating the man, bringing him into the gang. His death would therefore be needless, wasteful, and Lupe hated waste. He should get out now, before the luxuries of life with Ray made him totally soft and indecisive.

Go on, he told himself. Do it alone, the hard way, like you always have before. It's cleaner. Less mess.

He put his hand on the door and opened it.

"Where are you going?"

"This isn't working out."

Raymond's face went white. "No, Rico, wait, I'm sorry. I'm

sorry!" He stretched across the car, grabbing at Lupe's arm. "Please don't go. I didn't mean anything, I didn't mean it. Just sit down, please. Stay!"

Half out of the car, Lupe hesitated. It was hard to give up everything he'd been constructing for these past few weeks. The security of a house with fully stocked cupboards, conveniently located in the hills. And a stretch of at least one month ahead of him, free and clear, during which he would have the whole place to himself, and no one would come nosing around since everyone knew that Raymond was away . . .

He could give it all up; it was only a plan. Still, he was proud of the situation because, after all, it was his creation. He had invented Rico for Raymond to fall in love with. Rico had coaxed Raymond into planning a month-long Hawaiian retreat for the two of them, hinting that in Hawaii Rico might finally let go of his inhibiting fear and mistrust—might finally give himself to a man who had done so much for him, and received so little in return.

Raymond was desperate to receive his reward. He was utterly in Rico's power.

Yes, it was hard to let go of that. Very hard.

Yet . . . wasn't it better alone, living by his own resources, close to the edge of things?

Lupe wondered if he was going to have to pry Raymond's fingers from his arm. The long nails were digging into his flesh.

Hoping for an omen, some sign of his own mind, he looked up and saw where he was.

It was the same gas station he had visited his first morning in town. There was the phone booth where the Pump Jockey had seen him ripping out a page. And here came another station attendant, dressed just like the Pump Jockey, in the same blue uniform and cap. For an instant he thought it *was* the Pump Jockey, appearing without warning in the full light of day.

The realization that it was an older man, a living man, did little to calm his racing heart. The thought of the Pump Jockey had already shaken his determination. Things were never completely in control, no matter what he thought. It could all get out of hand if he wasn't careful.

That was why he should hold on to Raymond's house and stick to his plans for the month ahead. Nature guaranteed nothing, apart from what he could scavenge for himself. His whole life was proof of that. He needed something to fall back on.

The man came right up to him, stared him in the face. For a cold moment, Lupe thought they recognized each other, though he could not say how. It was a fleeting impression, maddening.

"What can I get you?"

He turned away, stammering, and slid back into the car, pressing himself deep into the leather seat. He pulled the door shut. Raymond looked grateful, as if Lupe had just given him a gift. The attendant went around to the other side, where Raymond was holding a bill out the window. As the man leaned over to ask Raymond what he needed, his eyes reached into the dark interior, glancing again at Lupe. Yes, there was recognition there. Something to be feared. Something unpredictable.

Lupe sank deeper into the seat, knowing he should never have let Raymond talk him out of leaving the house. He shouldn't be seen in public at all for a while.

It was weak of him, he realized, to hold on so desperately to Raymond's things. He was becoming as weak as Raymond; such was the older man's influence.

Well, it wouldn't matter after tomorrow. Raymond's house, without him in it, was no threat. Lupe would rule there, restored to himself, alone except for his boys.

And even if the man in the blue uniform had recognized him, what could he possibly do?

Hawk and Alec sat in the cramped space of the trailer, in stifling afternoon heat that drew the smell of gasoline out of Alec's stained blue uniform. The sixth can of a sixpack stood on the Formica table between them. It sat unopened, and Hawk kept staring at it, waiting for Alec to make his move. Alec had drained the other five himself. Somehow Hawk's restraint seemed to trouble him, since he couldn't convince Hawk to drink. Hawk was not even tempted. Alec's cigarette, though . . . He had quit a year ago, but they were always a temptation. Especially when the trailer was chokingly full of the smoke, and there seemed nothing left to say. It would have been easy to occupy his mouth with a cigarette, reverting to idle chatter. But he had asked Alec to stop spouting and wait, asked him to hold it and keep the picture fresh in his mind while they waited for their guest. They had been waiting for almost an hour. It was nearly dusk, but sometimes the trailer stayed hot until late at night. The sea breezes didn't seem to cool this year.

At last Hawk heard a car pulling into the lot. It could have been anyone—people were dropping in on him all the time— but he got up and swung open the door, and it was Randy all right. He got out of his pickup truck and stood looking at the trailer. He wore a Stetson, blue jeans, polished Western boots, and a red bandanna around his neck.

When he saw Hawk, Randy came loping forward, his hand out. "Hawk," he said. His smile was a bit suspicious, but he had no real reason to doubt Hawk. Nothing had ever gone bad between them; Randy had simply moved on.

Hawk shook his hand and led him into the trailer. When Randy saw Alec, he hesitated on the threshold.

"Saved this one for you," Alec said generously, lifting the final can.

"Uh, no—no thanks." Randy stepped inside and pulled the door shut. His Stetson bumped the ceiling. He took it off, casting Hawk a quizzical glance.

"Have a seat, Randy," Hawk said. "How've you been?"

Randy looked at the choice of seats. Apart from the unoc-cupied bench opposite Alec, there were two unmade beds at opposite ends of the trailer; one was Hawk's, the other Stoner's "temporary" heap on the couch. Randy leaned against the wall instead.

"Good enough," he said.

Hawk nodded. "Listen, I called you—well, I had a feeling I should talk to you instead of Sal."

"What about Sal?" Randy said, moving off the wall, taking a subtly defensive stance.

"It's just—I think I have better rapport with you. I don't know how Sal would take this."

"Take what?" Randy looked at Alec, who flicked a look at Hawk. Hawk nodded for him speak.

"I saw a guy at the station today," Alec said. His voice was slurred and phlegmy. "A kid, really—sort of Mexican looking, real young but built. Pretty memorable, now that I think of it. But somehow I never remembered him till then."

Randy looked curious. "Remembered him from when?"

Alec popped the beer for himself, and took a swallow. "The day before Craig Frost, you know . . ."

Randy apparently saw where this was leading. He moved closer to the table.

"See, I sort of remember Craig and this Mex kid—or somebody who looked damn like him—I remember them getting into a thing that morning."

"What kind of thing?"

"I'm not sure. The kid was over by the phone booth. I think maybe he ripped a page out of it; Craig never said. He'd gone over to scare him off, maybe hassle him a little. No big deal at the time. But it bothered me when I saw this kid all of a sudden today. Like, what was he still doing around? I only saw him right around the time Craig died. Thing is, I sort of remember him going to the beach that morning, down by the storm drain. . . . It's kind of unclear. But I told Hawk I'd tell him if I thought of anything, you know, that bothered me. And the more I think about it, the more I wonder if I might have seen that kid the next day, like on the morning Craig died. On the beach or the boardwalk or somewhere, maybe just out the corner of my eye, like that. I'm sorry it's so confused."

It had been less confused a sixpack earlier, Hawk thought irritably. Alec had been sure of it then.

"And . . . so . . . what does this have to do with me? Or with Sal?"

"That was my idea," Hawk said. "Come on, I'll stand, you sit down."

"I'm fine, Hawk. I'm just choking in here."

"We could go outside, but when people see I'm home, they tend to drop by."

Randy said, "You still give your sermons?"

"Sure," Hawk said. "On the mount."

"The hillside, you mean."

"That's the place."

"So let's go up there."

They made their way onto the hill behind the trailer, where Hawk could easily see anyone driving into the lot. There was shade, so they were cooler as well as more secluded. Hawk didn't like Alec drinking up here, or smoking. He didn't permit his boys to do either. But he wasn't about to say anything to Alec. Too late to be an influence there.

"So . . ." Randy said when they had settled down on stumps.

"Alec got me thinking," Hawk said. "Remember the night before Craig's murder?"

Randy's face was unreadable.

"You know, with that trouble up on the hill?"

Randy grinned suddenly. "Yeah, I remember." He chuckled. "Night of the avocado. Your tough little straight boys running from a gang of queens. That was quite a sight."

Hawk agreed that it must have been, but he suppressed his own smile.

"Took two coats to hide that guacamole stain."

"Yeah? What it started me thinking was—there was someone else around that night. Remember? I never saw him, but you did."

Randy's face grew serious again. "Sal's brother? Is that who you're after?"

"That's why I called you. I couldn't just go up and ask Sal

questions like this, make him think we're looking for his brother."

"You saw him today?" Randy asked Alec.

"I don't know who I saw. He was kind of unique looking, though, like I said. Memorable."

Hawk asked, "What did he look like, Randy?"

Randy's eyes drifted toward the trees. "He looked like a boy. Like a young boy. His face didn't match his body at all. Physically strong, kind of rugged, like he'd been around. It sure wasn't a kid's body."

"That sounds like the fella I saw," Alec said. "He ducked in and out of a white Porsche, this older guy I've seen before driving it. One of those downtown merchants or real estate agents. One of them flower-shop boys."

"Well, Sal's not—I mean, we only saw him that one time, if it is the same kid. Lupe, that was his name."

"Right," Hawk said. "Lupe."

"We figured he took off. He told Sal he'd been traveling all over the country, and we thought he'd gone back to it."

Randy sat for a moment, thinking, then looked up sharply at Hawk.

"You don't think Sal knows anything about Craig Frost, do you?"

"I didn't say that."

"Because I was with Sal all that morning, man, and other guys too. We were working out." Randy was on his feet again. "His brother never came around."

"Well, this was pretty damn early," Alec said, and belched.

"I spent the fucking night in his bed, all right?" Randy shouted.

Alec looked at the ground, his mouth clamped shut, plainly embarrassed.

"If you think he'd murder some jerk kid for throwing an avocado through his door—or for anything—you must be crazy."

"Hey, hey, calm down," Hawk said. "It's just shreds of evidence and nothing clues and a whole lot of suspicions. I'm not thinking anything in particular, except that I'd like to talk to the kid if he's around. Say, if he shows up at Sal's place, it'd be helpful to know."

Randy narrowed his eyes. "You mean if he shows up when I'm there?"

"I'm not asking you to do anything you're not comfortable with, Randy. Not like being a spy or a traitor or anything."

"Sal's my best friend, man."

"Right! So you ought to protect him."

"From what? Sal didn't do anything."

"I only mean that you should make sure the cops get the right guy."

"Why would they make a mistake?"

"You know Bohemia, Randy. We've got like three blacks, two spics, a Chinese family that runs an import shop . . . If anyone else says they saw a vaguely Cholo-looking dude on the beach around the time Craig was killed, they're gonna descend on Sal. By the time all you boys explain that you were sleeping in his bed and taking his lessons that morning, they'll have turned everything upside down and inside out. I'm talking about your whole life, Randy. They'll run you out of town—Marty, I mean Marilyn, and all the rest—once they've made an example of Sal. That's their job, man. They're bugging me constantly, me and my gang, and most of my boys are right up their alley, attitudewise."

Randy stared at the ground, Stetson hat pulled low over his eyes, mouth grim.

"And you know, Randy, I'm not even talking here about the real trouble Sal could get into. I'm not even mentioning his *art* sales."

Randy swallowed, turned away, paced toward the trees where the sun was setting. The rustling leaves made the sunlight seem to fracture and clash. He looked straight into the glare, then spun back toward Hawk.

"I can't do what you're asking," he said. "All I can do is tell him what you told me. Anything else, I'd be a snake."

Hawk put up his hands in frustration.

"No, no, just . . . just say you saw Lupe somewhere. Say you heard I suspect his brother or something. Don't tell him we've been talking, Randy. You don't know how he'll take that."

"Look, if there's a possibility that Lupe did kill Frost, I want Sal to know about it. If he's dangerous, people should know. They should be on their guard. All of us."

Hawk thought about this a moment. "But if he comes around, and Sal knows I'm looking for him, he's just gonna protect the guy."

"You don't know that."

"He's not gonna turn his own brother over to me."

"To you? I thought we were talking about the cops. No deal, man."

Hawk stood up, exasperated. "All right, forget it. I can't blame you, Randy. Maybe it does sound like betrayal."

"No, it sounds like a setup. I'm not joining your little conspiracy. I'm not gonna keep secrets from my best friend just to feed your little power trip."

"My power trip? Am I the one with a dozen boys running his . . . errands . . . ?" The words dried up in Hawk's mouth.

Randy gave him a sour, ironic smile. "See you 'round."

Hawk nodded, feeling flushed and stupid. He put out his hand. "Forget we talked, man. Do what you think is right."

Randy didn't take his hand. "I always do." He started down the hill.

"I just want you to know," Hawk called after him, "we're on the same side."

"Is that right?"

"And one more thing," Hawk said. "If you want evidence, stop by Alec's station, check the phone book. See if the page with 'Diaz' is missing."

Randy was getting into his truck. "Shit, Hawk, you could

have ripped it out yourself." He slammed the door, backed out of the lot, and tore away down Old Creek Road.

Hawk turned away, depressed. Another link of trust was broken. He looked to Alec for some support, however meager.

Alec sat slumped in the dirt, propped against the podium, eyes shut and snoring, beer can empty. A trail of drool glinted on his chin in the late afternoon light.

The Rock Lobster was packed, as Sal had expected on such a warm summer night. The men who drank and partied here did not have to worry about rising early; most were on vacation, living in summer homes. Bohemia Bay was sometimes known as Fire Island West. On weekends, gay tourists swelled the crowd past the bursting point, and men spilled out onto the patio, into the alley, and all along the stairs down to the beach.

Standing on the topmost step, Sal saw men packed together on the stairs, laughing and moaning. In the shadow of the cliff, below lampposts that were knocked out methodically each time the town replaced them—guests of the Rock Lobster taking turns with the official wrist-rocket—there was a more intimate but no more furtive seethe of activity. For those who desired it, something resembling privacy was available on the hillside, in caves cut away beneath the hedges.

Sal moved away from the steps, away from the cliff and the beach. This was no longer his scene, although in moments of extreme (usually drunken) horniness or loneliness he still turned to it, blending into the dark at the edge of the crowd, joining the strangers who waited there in perpetual anonymity. He imagined entering those shadows and switching on a flashlight, interrogating the startled, sweating couples. He had lurked in many such places himself at one time, before he had found other ways of making a living than with his cock and his mouth. He had lived in fear of the probing spotlight on a cop car.

Tonight he was the one searching the shadows, but he needn't beat the bushes for his prey. He wouldn't have been here at all if he hadn't known exactly what questions to ask, and of whom.

Sal Diaz, gay detective. He smiled at the thought.

He crossed the patio and sat at the outdoor bar, under a red floodlight that made a half-drunk beer on the counter look like a glass of blood. The bartender set down a napkin. Sal asked for a club soda.

As he drank it, he cast his mind back to the night he'd seen Lupe out here, an instant before his brother vanished. Had Lupe noticed him, or had his sudden departure been coincidental? Had Lupe sought out the Rock Lobster deliberately, because he felt comfortable there, or had he only stumbled across it, and not realized what kind of place it was until later? Maybe he had come thinking he might run into Sal, then panicked and fled when he spied his brother.

He had been with a man, though, and the man had departed just as hurriedly. So it seemed possible that Lupe had come here knowingly, and had left without seeing Sal. Had left with another man, because that was what he wanted.

Sal rarely visited the Rock Lobster more than once a week, but he had been coming a few nights weekly since then, hoping to spot Lupe or at least the man he'd left with. Sal felt sure the other man was a regular here, a lonely face familiar from many nights of hanging out here at this very bar. But neither Lupe nor his companion had reappeared since Sal had increased the frequency of his visits. And he'd had no reason to pursue the matter any further; Lupe was entitled to his privacy. If he was hiding from Sal for some reason, then perhaps he simply wasn't ready to be frank with him.

Or so Sal had told himself until tonight, after hearing Randy's story about Hawk. Suddenly he had good reason to find out what he could.

Tonight's outdoor bartender was new to the Rock Lobster. Sal watched the door to the interior for a minute, until the waiter he'd been looking for came out and set a couple of plates on a table. Sal waved to catch his eye.

"Tyler!" he said.

"Hey, Sal." Tyler glided over. "How are you?"

"Great. Can I talk to you a minute?"

"Sure, you want a menu?"

"No, I have a sort of personal question."

"Oh, really?" Tyler's eyebrows lifted humorously. "And I thought I was too old for you."

Sal laughed, and tilted his head so that Tyler would lean in closer. The man next to them got up, leaving them alone at the end of the bar. With the sound of disco music thudding out of the restaurant, he doubted anyone would overhear them.

"I know this is asking a lot, but do you remember a night a few weeks ago—"

"Oh, Jesus."

"No, really, you might remember. You were waiting that night; you were in and out from the patio."

"I know exactly the night you're talking about."

"Please. This is important."

"Sorry." Tyler bent closer, as if he had finally picked up on Sal's intent.

"There was a guy out here at a table. Latino. Looks a lot like me, in fact, but much younger. Baby-faced sort of kid. And there was someone with him, an older man—a regular, I think, because I used to see him all the time sitting right where I am now."

Tyler was already nodding. "Sure, I remember. I was going to card the kid, except he only wanted a salad."

"Yeah, he's a vegetarian."

"Well, sure, I remember him. But if it's a phone number you want, you're out of luck."

"It's not him I'm after."

"No? He seemed like just your type."

Sal let this slide. "The older guy, who would that have been?"

"Jealous, Sal?"

"Please . . ."

"Well, there's one regular inhabitant of this stool I haven't seen around here lately. I think he's finally got something going, a steady relationship, so there's no reason to sit here and troll every night. I'm glad for him, really. He was such a sad case. Nice man, but you know, not exactly Ganymede."

"Do you know his name? Where I might find him?"

"Sure, it's Raymond Mankiewitz. He owns a travel agency downtown. Bohemia Travel, I think. You should ask Miller—you know, the owner? Ray set up a whole Hawaiian package deal for him last year—condo, car, everything."

"This is great." Sal scribbled on a cocktail napkin, then pulled a roll of bills from his pocket. Tyler stopped his hand. "Please, don't insult me."

"I'm just paying for my drink."

"Oh. Well, next time I actually *serve* you, you can leave an extra big tip."

"I'll do that. Thanks again." He left a bill on the table and got up.

"Got to get back to work. That heat lamp will only keep a hamburger hot for so long."

"Oh, one more thing. Do you know what kind of car this guy drives? This Mankiewitz?"

"Do I ever. He usually parks it right out there in the alley when he comes around. It's only my *dream* car. A beautiful creamy white Porsche."

Tyler waved a goodnight and dived back into the restaurant.

Sal started toward the exit, then realized what time it was. He would do no more detecting tonight. He went back and sat down at the bar, just where Raymond Mankiewitz had always sat. When the bartender looked his way, he ordered a margarita.

He was no less alone than Raymond tonight, he supposed; most of his friends were too young to drink.

=14=

A strong smoky smell saturated the neighborhood. One of Raymond's neighbors was firing up a barbecue. Lupe fought the urge to gag, since there was nothing he could do about it. Fortunately, the warm wind coming up from the canyon kept the smells from overwhelming him; and indoors, in the guest bedroom, it wasn't too bad. These suburbanites were constantly burning meat. Why couldn't they just eat it raw?

Lupe owned almost nothing he would have needed in Hawaii, aside from clothes Raymond had bought for him. His knapsack, containing all his true possessions, was stashed in a small niche down in the canyons, where there was no chance of Raymond going through it. Still, to keep up with pretenses, he had been slowly stuffing a small duffel bag, while wondering how and when he would finally make his move. He had tried to work himself up to it the night before, but had found it impossible to concentrate. Raymond had had music going, lights on, was running around singing and dancing until late; when he had finally passed into a drunken sleep, it should have been very easy to finish him, but something held Lupe back. His own mild intoxication, perhaps. He wanted his mind to be crystal clear for the killing.

As it turned out, he was glad he'd held off. Since waking,

Raymond had kept remembering all sorts of things that needed doing, people who had to be called and reminded that he would be away, business that must be tied up so that nothing could go wrong in his absence. Lupe would not have been able to take care of all this alone; so now he was determined to wait until the last possible minute. When the car was packed and Raymond was making a last survey of the house to check on the locks and the lights, that would be the best time. He would be excited and hurried; he wouldn't notice what was coming.

Lupe did not imagine anyone would start to worry about Raymond for at least five weeks. The mail and newspaper deliveries had been stopped. Utilities were paid in advance. Raymond's affection for the suburbs apparently went unrequited, since his neighbors in the cul-de-sac had shown only squeamish hostility in the few interactions Lupe had witnessed. He supposed they would be the last ones to question Raymond's absence. As for himself, Lupe planned to sleep during the days. It was a more comfortable schedule for him; he had suffered the daylight for Raymond's sake, in order to promote his plan. Consequently, he had seen his boys rarely in the past weeks—no more than a few fleeting glimpses while he roamed the hills late at night.

Well, soon the house would be full of them.

At the thought, Lupe felt a quickening in his entire being— the promise of some great fulfillment or metamorphosis. It was like electricity in his soul; he could almost hear the humming. He closed his eyes, trying to prolong the sense of a door about to open. Just then, Raymond came into the room behind him.

He felt a soft touch on his back. "Are you excited, Rico?"

Lupe forced himself to respond, though his nerves were screaming for solitude. "Yes."

"It's going to be wonderful to have time alone together, away from all this craziness."

"Uh-huh."

"I thought . . . I'm all packed myself. I'm fixing lunch, and afterwards I thought maybe we could take a little nap."

"I'm not really tired."

Raymond sighed, looking down at Lupe's bag. He clutched Lupe's hand briefly, letting go when the pressure was not returned. He walked back into the hall. "Lunch'll be ready soon." Should he use the switchblade? He hadn't thought about that. Sal had given him the knife when he was getting out of the hospital. He had only used it for initiations, and Raymond was no one he wanted for his gang. Too old and . . . wrong. Worn out. He didn't have what Lupe wanted in a follower. The wrong sort of adulation filled his eyes, the kind that made Lupe uncomfortable no matter how long he endured it.

He zipped up the duffel bag. A kitchen knife would do just as well. The kitchen was probably the best room for it anyway. Linoleum tiles were easily mopped.

Out on the deck, Raymond was whistling. Lupe had started to whistle a few notes of his own, to no particular tune, when he heard a sizzling sound. Meat on a hot grill. It was too near to be a neighbor. He checked a scream, swallowed his bile, already heading for the living room.

He had warned Raymond—*warned him*—

Out on the deck, Raymond stood over a low hibachi grill, adjusting a seared steak with a long fork. Fat spat in the fire, hissing and burning, joined by the thick, rank smell of charred meat.

Lupe's head caved in, cutting off light and oxygen. He gasped out a suffocated shriek and rushed at the deck, seeing it as though through tinted glass.

Raymond saw him coming and leapt back with the fork dangling from his fingers by a leather cord. "Rico!"

As he stepped onto the deck the wind shifted, wrapping him in coils of sickening smoke, stuffing it down his throat, stinging his nose and eyes, bathing him in the stench of burning. Smothering him.

He lashed out at the source, kicking the hibachi across the deck. Hot coals went tumbling; the grill plates rattled away.

Lupe snatched the fork from Raymond's fingers, grabbed him

by the back of his neck, and forced him down on his hands and knees.

Raymond begged desperately, as if he had no idea what he'd done wrong. But he should have—must have—known. How many times had Lupe told him he couldn't stand meat, cooking meat, burning meat? How many times had he forbidden him to cook it, on threat of Lupe's instant departure?

"Please, Rico, please . . ."

He had pressed Raymond's cheek to within an inch of a heap of coals.

"I told you," Lupe raged. "I told you!"

"It was only for me, a little steak, I thought out in the air—"

"Shut up!"

He couldn't let go of Raymond's neck, or even ease off a fraction of an inch. The steak had stopped cooking but the smell was still overpowering. His fingers were locked in Raymond's flesh. He brought the fork with its three-inch tines right up to Raymond's gaping eye. Raymond struggled away from the fork. Lupe forced them steadily closer together.

"My god . . . my god . . ." Raymond blubbered. Weak. Pitiful. When the boys begged like this, it spurred him on; but Raymond's debasement gave him no pleasure. He only wanted to end it quickly. He rolled the fork in his hand, wondering at the best way.

Then the stink began again, far worse than before, because far more familiar.

Raymond's hair was fuming in the coals. Lupe loosened his grip, setting Raymond free. As Raymond groped for balance, his hand went down among the embers, his full weight pressing on the hot grill. Raymond screamed and flesh sizzled and hair continued to burn.

It was all too much. Lupe threw himself at the railings, spewing vomit. Behind him, even before his retching subsided, he heard the sliding glass door bang shut.

He turned, wiping his mouth, to see Raymond latching it, locking him out.

"What are you doing?" he asked miserably.

Raymond backed into the living room, holding his burned hand to his belly. One side of his face was blistered, hair singed from the temple.

Lupe threw himself at the glass.

"Stop it!" Raymond shrieked.

Lupe forced himself to smile. Relax, he told himself. Calm down.

"Raymond . . . please. I told you I couldn't stand you doing that. I warned you more than once. Didn't I?"

"That's no excuse," Raymond gasped hoarsely. "My God, look what you did!" He raised his scarred hand in recrimination. "What were you going to do to me?"

"It's not my fault. You have to believe me—it's uncontrollable. Just . . . please just let me in, and I'll explain."

"You would have killed me!"

No duh, Lupe thought, fighting down a grin. He was hysterical. The stink clung to his nostrils. How could he think through it?

"No," he said. "No, I—I wouldn't hurt you, Raymond. I— God, this is hard for me to say. It's so hard to believe that you—you don't want to hurt me. I've been hurt myself, Ray. I could never do that to anyone. I know what it's like and I'm sorry. I want to . . . to make it up. Please just let me apologize."

Raymond put a finger tenderly to his cheek. Bitterness and grief welled from his eyes. For an instant Lupe truly did regret what had happened—and all that was yet to come.

"Ray, I . . . I love you."

Through the depths of pain and fear, he saw that Raymond was still dragging along a deathless load of hope. It just might get him through the door. Raymond started tentatively forward, but then his hand or his face must have twinged, reminding him of what had just happened.

"Please, Ray. I feel terrible. It just comes over me, when— when I smell meat burning. I'll tell you why. I'll tell you what happened, if you'll just let me in. I've never told anyone, but I'll tell you. I trust you, Ray. I need you. You've done so much for me."

"The—the steak was for me," Raymond said faintly, weakening though he hadn't realized it yet. "I know you don't eat meat. I know that, Rico. I was going to make vegetables for you, a shishkebab, that's all. I thought it was okay to make a steak for myself."

"It's all my fault," Lupe said. "It's a huge misunderstanding."

The fork still dangled from his fingers, hanging out of sight behind his leg.

"Please," he said again.

Raymond came forward.

In his eagerness, Lupe moved rapidly to meet him and saw another, stronger look of dread pass over Raymond's face as the fork swung into sight from behind Lupe's leg. Lupe jerked his hand to hide it again, but that guilty movement betrayed him further.

Stupid!

Raymond took his hands from the latch.

"Fuck," Lupe said. "Come on, Goddamn it. Open the fucking glass!"

At that moment, the doorbell rang. Lupe froze. Raymond turned and stared across the living room, in disbelief.

"Open the door," Lupe hissed. "If you love me . . ."

But Raymond was turning away, grateful for the interruption. The fucking cavalry had arrived. Lupe banged on the glass but Raymond ignored him, walking down the hall to the front door. He backed away from the glass, not wanting to be seen out here, telling himself that it must be the mailman or a paper boy. Once they went away he would still be out here, waiting for Raymond, cooler and more convincing than before. Yeah . . .

The door was hidden from his sight, but he saw light flood the hall when it opened. Raymond spoke loudly, for his benefit: "Please come in."

Someone else said, "Thanks very much. I don't mean to intrude, but—"

Without a thought, Lupe sprang in a single fluid motion over the nearest end of the balcony. He hit the hillside rolling, got to his feet, and ran downhill, abandoning in that instant of panic everything he'd planned, everything he'd created by sheer will. Maybe it was better this way. Heading for the safety of the deep canyons, that voice echoing in his ears, he felt a giddy eagerness, as if some great event was just about to occur.

Maybe, down there, he would finally find the cave of his dreams, the cave he could smell when the evening winds shifted. How had he ever fooled himself into thinking any other life was worthy of him?

While Raymond Mankiewitz was staring at Lupe's photograph, Sal looked past him into the dark house. He could have sworn he'd heard Lupe's voice as he was walking down the driveway. He was tensed for confrontation.

Raymond looked up at Sal, worried, then he too glanced back quickly into the house. He said loudly, "Please come in."

"Thanks very much," Sal said. "I don't mean to intrude, but I have reason to think you know him, or did."

"I have to—to get a better look at this." He moved toward a table lamp and switched it on, holding the photograph under the light. "Yes, this is Rico, but . . . much younger."

"His real name is Lupe. Guadalupe Diaz."

"Lupe?" Raymond spun toward the deck. Outside, through the sliding glass doors, Sal saw a distant range of mountains through the summer haze; nearer were lines of hills, far ridges of the same Greenbelt canyons that ran behind Shangri-La.

Raymond rushed toward the glass and pressed up against the pane as if trying to see around the corners of the house without opening the door. "Where . . . where did he go?"

"Was he here?" Sal said, not quite believing it.

"He called himself Rico . . ."

Raymond's voice trailed off as he unlatched the door and slid it open. Sal joined him on the deck. Together they looked down on tangles of dense brush, islands of bamboo, clumps of cactus edging the bluffs and outcroppings of worn sandstone that dropped away into the deeper canyons. The hot wind shook every shrub, making it seem as if someone was crawling away under the landscape.

Smelling smoke, Sal looked down at the deck. Scattered coals smoldered on the redwood planks; a piece of dirty steak lay folded in one corner like a discarded rag. He tried to imagine the scene he had interrupted.

"Gone," Raymond whispered. He started to drag a hand across his face, then hissed and pulled it away.

Sal glanced over at him. "Jesus!" He hadn't noticed in the dark house, but one side of Raymond's face was a mass of blistered, cracked and oozing skin; his hair had been singed so recently that shiny blobs still clung to the ends of the brittle, damaged strands. His hand was scored with a grid of fierce red lines, patterned on the hibachi's grill.

Sal took him by the shoulders and drew him back into the house, leading him to a sofa. "Where's your burn cream?"

"In the bathroom," Raymond gasped, weeping openly now. "He lied about his name. Lied about . . . everything, I guess."

"Don't worry about that right now. My car's outside. We'd better get you to the hospital."

In the bathroom, Sal found a huge aloe plant thriving in the filtered light from a frosted window. He broke off a thick green tendril and carried it back to the sofa, along with a bottle of aspirin. Cool syrup dripped from the broken frond, pooling in his palm. He smeared the gel gently over Raymond's burned face and hand. Raymond shut his eyes and sobbed, but without further tears.

"Who are you?" he said.

"I'm Sal Diaz. Lupe's brother."

Raymond opened his eyes. Stared for a moment, examining his face, then nodded. "You look like him, a little. But I recognize you. And your name's . . . familiar."

"I got your name from Tyler at the Rock Lobster; you've probably seen me there. Your office told me you were going away. I'm glad I caught you before you left."

"I won't be going anywhere now. Rico—I mean, Lupe and I—were traveling together. He's your brother, then. I—I was desperate when you rang. I didn't want to be alone with him. I didn't want to leave the house, though, with him out there. I might have called the police. He did this to me!" Raymond gestured at his face with his burned hand, now cramping from the pain.

Sal went to the kitchen for a glass of water, which he offered to Raymond with several aspirin. "Take these. You're probably in shock right now, but the pain is only going to get worse. When you're ready, I'll drive you."

Raymond nodded, choking down the aspirin. "Thank you. Why were you looking for him?"

"Because I was afraid he might hurt someone. If he hadn't already."

Raymond shook his head, then took a huge breath. He pushed himself upright, staggering slightly so that Sal had to support him. "All right," he said. "I'm ready for anything now."

Sal had never been in such a quiet emergency room. South Bay Hospital seemed deserted at midday. There was sand on the floor, and trails of water where a surfer had come in right behind Sal and Raymond, still in his dripping wetsuit, his hair matted with blood. The nurses had literally pushed Raymond aside to reach the surfer. When the one nurse remaining at the desk finally returned her attention to Raymond, she informed them that they would have to wait for treatment of such minor injuries. There was only one doctor on duty, and he was busy. Yet, as they waited, more emergency patients came in—a vomiting child, a man with a sprained ankle, a girl with a bloody toe—and each was whisked away out of the waiting room while Sal and Raymond were left to wait. Raymond kept an ice pack pressed to his face, but Sal couldn't believe it was cold anymore; he could hear it slosh without the crunching sound of ice.

He noticed that the nurse kept glancing at them, as if wishing they would give up and go away. Her eyes said, *Faggots.*

"Let me tell you about Lupe," he said after a while.

"Yes . . ."

"We grew up in L.A., in a building that should have been condemned. I spent most of my early life in the same apartment; I guess that was some sort of stability. It was cramped and falling apart, and there were always men visiting my Aunt Theresa. Our mother died right after Lupe was born; Theresa took us in, not too willingly. I'm not sure why she didn't abandon us right off. She didn't have what it takes to raise children. Things might have turned out better if she had dumped us.

"Lupe never knew any other way of life. But I was always angry—at my mother for leaving us, at my aunt for taking us in, at the world for being the way it is. I was always fighting and running away, hanging out with a gang. Theresa couldn't complain; as a role model, she left a lot to be desired. I guess I was following her example when I got into hustling myself.

"I had, I guess you might say, an aptitude. I used to spy on her pimp, peeking through the door to see him naked, strutting around proud. Even at a young age, it excited me. One day the pimp came over while Theresa was out. He talked me into letting him in. I was thirteen. I can still remember his mouth and the smell of booze, the way he looked at me when he decided what he was going to do—knowing I couldn't stop him. Anyway, I wasn't sure I wanted to. It was violent, but not so different from my fantasies. You'd be surprised. I had practical knowledge, you know, from watching him with Theresa; I already knew he was rough. The real thing turned out to be pretty close to some of the scenes I'd been carrying around in my head, you know, in that desperate way a horny adolescent wishes for someone to touch him, no matter who."

"Adolescent?" Raymond said wearily. "I still feel that way."

"After that, it was like all the chains just snapped. I figured out I could make it on my own, and make money, too. Even save it, since I never cared about doing drugs.

"I'd sleep with whoever would take me in for a night, or even a few hours. Lupe was my only tie with home. He was at Theresa's mercy. Once I ran away for good, she became even more protective, she started locking him up in her room. She'd padlock it from the outside, so if there'd been a fire or something he would have been trapped. Maybe because he didn't know any better, Lupe never seemed to mind. He was an artist from early on; as soon as he could hold a crayon he was drawing. Good, too—he had natural talent. He could draw anything, things he'd only seen on TV. At least I guess that's where he got them from. He certainly wasn't drawing from life. He'd never been out to see anything.

"I used to go crazy, thinking about him locked up like an animal in a kennel. Sometimes, when I knew Theresa was out, I would break in and take him out and around with me, my little brother."

"How'd you get him out?"

"My aunt would leave the key in the front room—less chance of losing it there, I guess. Anyway, Lupe looked up to me. I took him places where I was known, where I had a few friends. Not my old gang, though. I stayed away from them once I started hustling—which I only did where I wasn't known. Even so, word got around of what I was up to. Things got dangerous for me.

"One day we came home and Theresa was there. We got in a huge fight about how she treated him. Then her pimp came in. He'd been waiting on her and since I was slowing her down, he beat the shit out of me. I could barely crawl away. He said he was moving in with Theresa and threatened to kill me if I came around again.

"The next day I stole a gun and went back for Lupe. I had this idea I was going to set up house for the two of us, away from Theresa. I found her pimp alone in the apartment, and pulled the gun on him. But Lupe wasn't there. He said Lupe was in the hospital and Theresa was with him. That news maybe saved his life. I had really wanted to kill the guy.

"By the time I found the right hospital, Lupe was in stable but critical condition. Lupe had broken out and come looking for me. But the poor kid—he didn't know the neighborhoods where he would be safe. He didn't know shit, only that he had to get away and I was always the one who said I'd protect him. I sort of pieced together from my aunt that the guy had gone after Lupe the night before, after he'd warmed up on me. So he just wandered around looking for places I'd shown him, looking for people who knew me . . . and from what I finally figured out, he finally went up to a gang of boys—you know, I mean a *gang*—and asked them if they knew me.

"You can imagine how they took this. Plenty of them knew *of* me. Even my own old gang wanted to kill me. I'd been chased a couple of times. Probably would have been killed if they'd caught me. I was learning some martial arts from an old guy in the park—karate, white crane, and then tai chi—but the main thing I'd learned was to keep away from trouble. Lupe walked right into it.

"Someone found him in the morning. I went up to look at the place, for clues, gang-signs, to figure out who'd done it to him. It was this big hill covered with garbage; on the peak was a huge metal pylon where the powerlines came through. You could hear them buzzing and crackling up there. Cactus everywhere, flies and shit, stripped cars. Down under the pylon was a big sandstone cave, so much broken glass on the ground it was like pebbles on the beach. Pretty deep, too. That was where they'd taken Lupe. In the back I found an old ripped-up mattress, stained with blood. And an acetylene torch. That was the worst part.

"You know, they . . . they wounded him. And cauterized him with the torch, so he wouldn't bleed to death. There were burn streaks like whiplash scars all over his legs and butt. But they'd held it a good long time between his legs."

Raymond sat with his head between his knees, just listening, not responding. Sal was grateful for the silence. They continued to wait for medical attention, but the looks from the staff at the counter suggested that no one was in a rush to help a couple of queers.

Sal cleared his throat and continued.

"He got better, slowly. Real slowly. But how can you ever get over something like that?

"He lived with me for a while, when he got out. I made him follow through with his therapy, and there was a lot of it. But it was like the whole experience pushed him over some edge I could never really understand. He all of a sudden seemed much older than me, in a weird way. More independent. It's hard to explain.

"I sat in on some of his counseling sessions, and I could see him taking to them, working them around to suit him. The doctors kept working on Lupe to . . . to not let anything stop him. To face his fears, that was the main thing. To get power from the things that terrified him. They gave him visualizations, you know, like meditations to do. Imagining himself whole again, and healthy, and strong. I sometimes think he took these things too seriously. I know he stopped drawing, period. I tried to convince him to keep at it, as therapy, but he had stopped listening to me. I always felt he sort of blamed me. Because, you know, I wasn't there for him.

"It wasn't long before he left my place. He lived like I had for a while, on the street, among strangers. But he wasn't afraid of anything. The worst had already happened. I tried to help him when I could, but he rejected my help. He didn't need me anymore; and in some strange way, I felt he didn't trust me.

"I ran into him less and less . . . and eventually, my own life got to be more than enough for me to deal with. I was working hard to get myself together, onto a path of strength and healing. I tried to stop hustling, tried to make money at a few other shitty jobs—though that was hard, since the pay was nothing. But one

of them, an art sales job, led to something more rewarding.
. . . And that eventually let me get away, let me come down
here. I hadn't seen Lupe at all for years, until a few weeks ago.
Then I saw him for only a few hours, and he vanished again. Or
I thought he had."

"My God," Raymond said. "The poor boy. What he went
through . . ."

"I know," Sal said, "but that only goes so far. We can't blame
him for what happened when he was younger. But we have to
protect ourselves from whatever it is he's become."

"Then you don't trust him either?"

"A boy died a few weeks ago, I don't know if you remember."

"You mean the one at Central Beach?"

Sal nodded.

"And you think . . ."

"I have reason to think Lupe and that boy had a run-in."

Raymond suddenly went pale. "That was the night I met
him. I remember they were talking about it at the bar."

"The night I saw you together," Sal said.

Raymond suddenly bolted from his seat, stumbling toward
the reception desk. The nurse rose, white-faced. "What's
wrong?"

Raymond barely made it to the trash can near the desk; he
bent over it, heaving, his whole body racked by spasms.

"Oh dear," the nurse was saying. "I thought it was only a
burn."

Sal hurried to put his hands on Raymond's head and back,
offering what comfort he could. "We've been waiting almost an
hour!" he said while he held on to the other man. "Even if it
was only a burn, don't you think he needs care?"

She gave him an embarrassed look, and set off down the hall.
The things one had to do to get attention; you had to make a
lot of trouble.

Sal looked down at Raymond, who relaxed and sank back on

his knees, panting for breath. Sal patted his head and left his hand there. It was sort of absurd to be the one comforting Raymond.

"My God, my God," Raymond moaned.

Imagine how I feel, Sal thought. He's my brother.

=15=

"Come on, Dusty," Stoner kept pleading as they played cards in the van. "Crack a window, woncha? It's an oven in here."

"I see you know fuck-all about surveillance," Dusty said. "Our only advantage is this tinted glass. We crack a window, anybody going in or out of Sal's place can look over and see your big dumb face grinning at 'em. You might as well stand on his lawn, watch him through the fucking picture window."

They sat in the dark rear of Dusty's van, a dim grotto stinking of motor oil and spilled beer. They were parked on the wilderness side of the street, where the windshield gave them a poor view of Sal's house, about a block away. Sweat covered Stoner like suntan lotion; his T-shirt was drenched in it. If the playing cards hadn't been waxed, they would have swollen up like sponges, sopping sweat from his hands.

Stoner threw down his cards.

"I'm dying, man!" he choked. "Hawk wouldn't do this to a fucking dog!"

Dusty slowly put down his own cards.

"You gotta learn patience—bide your time. You ever watch the surfers, man, sitting out there all day waiting for that perfect wave? It's transcendental, Stoner. You gotta transcend."

"Don't talk about the ocean, Dusty. It's bad enough already."

"No? You don't like me to talk about the cool, wet, refreshing ocean? Those nice icy waves, frosty as a big glass of beer? Just salty enough to quench your thirst?"

"Dusty!"

"Come on, be a man."

Stoner set his hands on his knees and pushed himself to his feet with painful effort, like a clawhammer pulling an old bent spike from hard wood. He staggered toward the door, making the whole van tip like a boat about to capsize.

"Where you going?"

"I need air."

He opened the side door, stepping into the dead grass at the embankment.

"Jesus Christ," Dusty swore.

Stoner hesitated, then reached back in and pulled a wad of Kleenex from a box on the floor.

"What's that for?"

"Not that it's any of your business, but I have to take a shit."

"Oh, great. Why don't you ask Sal if you can use his toilet?"

"Plenty of bushes in the hills, asshole."

"Just hurry it up."

"What do you think I'll do?"

"I seen you spend half the afternoon in the trailer's little shitter, and you hardly fit in there. I can't imagine what you'll do when you got the whole outdoors."

"Fuck you." He started to slam the door, then remembered to ease it shut.

"If Lupe comes around . . ." Dusty said.

"That'd be just my luck."

He shut the door and heard it latch, but not before Dusty called, "Remember to light a match!"

There was no one in sight, not even at Sal's place, but he tried to keep between bushes as he scrambled toward the ridge. A couple guys had come out Sal's front door fifteen minutes ago, lugging a big black painting that looked like Venice: canals, lights, those canoes with the big fruity curves at one end, the kind you rowed with a pole. He couldn't imagine who liked that crap, until he remembered how he saw them all the time in restaurants, motels, bars. The paintings were a good front. Just about anyone might have reason to buy the ugly things.

He wondered if Sal had any black velvet bullfight pictures. Stoner kind of liked those. Or dice and cobras, that real Mexican stuff. Or maybe one of those big burly Aztec dudes in a feather headdress carrying some native chick up the steps of a pyramid like he was about to sacrifice or maybe rape her. That was the kind of thing he'd hang on his wall, if he had a wall to hang things on. He knew Hawk wouldn't want stuff like that in the trailer, even if there was room.

Jesus on black velvet, that was more Hawk's speed. Yeah!

He reached the top of the slope and stood figuring out how to get through the barbed wire. The fence was a joke: three rusted strands strung between bug-eaten posts. Flimsy, but it was still more than Stoner could slip through easily. He found the rottenest post and kicked till it cracked and snapped at the base, spewing dust and termites. He walked down the post, over the wires, and into the Greenbelt.

On the far side of a thick growth of sage, he came out in a cactus patch. Deer trails, marked with pellets and paw prints, suggested an easier path. He sauntered through the late afternoon; it felt cool and breezy after hours in the stinking van. It was useless, staking out Sal's house. Lupe was probably in Mexico or Canada by now. He'd have seen Alec, known they were after him, and split town.

Looking back, all he saw of Shangri-La were the tips of poles and the wires they held up. He cut north through the brush until he found the fire road they'd followed the night they'd hid the grenades.

He quickened his stride, looking for thistles. The stickers had worked their way through his boots for days afterward. He was still finding them in his socks, weeks later. If he forgot every other landmark, he would remember the field of thistles.

Everything was different by daylight, but Stoner knew the

hills from years of hiking and riding dirt bikes up here. He used to live in Rim of the World, before he failed so miserably at school so many times that he'd had to drop out, causing his father to kick him out of the house since any kid old enough to leave school was old enough to leave home, as the old man said. *When I was your age, I was working fifteen hours a day blah blah blah* . . . But Stoner had never held a job for long. He couldn't concentrate; it was the same problem he'd had in school. He did odd jobs, helped out here and there (a car theft here, fence some stolen weapons there), with no steady friends till Hawk came along.

Hawk had set him up with jobs and places to stay, but always put him up again and again when things didn't work out. Hawk put up with a lot. Stoner owed him more favors than he could count. He felt obliged to wait in the van and watch Sal when Hawk asked him to. Still, that didn't mean he had to do everything Dusty said. He could take a break every once in a while.

As the vast field of thistles appeared ahead, he grinned. He cut off the road, kicking up clouds of bristly down, anticipation quickening his steps. Sitting in the van with Dusty, he had thought of a way to relieve his boredom with a little walk—and a lot of privacy. Oh, it had looked like good stuff, way better than the cheesy crap he usually got ahold of. He wondered if he could smuggle it into the van without Dusty noticing. If he didn't hide it, Dusty would lay claim to the stuff, and then so much for privacy. Besides, getting caught with the stuff would be embarrassing. Dusty would know why he'd taken so long, and tease him about it for days, or forever, like those stickers that were even now working back into his boots. And what if Hawk found out? Would he kick him out of the trailer?

A huge shape bounded out of some bushes. Stoner's heart nearly stopped. He was mortified, as if he'd been thinking aloud.

But it was only a deer, a big buck with sprawling antlers startled by his approach. It leapt away from him, springing over a ridge, and was gone.

He laughed with relief, but he could could feel his cheeks burning.

Fucking deer! Why was he ashamed? What did an animal care? It was thoughts of Hawk that made him feel guilty.

He kept hearing the deer for some time, crackling through the underbrush. It seemed to circle back behind him, sometimes loud and close at hand, then cutting out abruptly. Echoes were weird in the hills. It all made him feel even more apprehensive. The thought occurred to him that Dusty might be following. But why would Dusty want to watch him take a crap? And Dusty was dedicated. He'd be watching that house twice as hard now that Stoner was gone. Playing solitaire.

Stoner went slipping down a dusty slope and found himself in a little canyon. The sandstone walls were pitted and pocked with caves, the biggest of them hardly enough to shelter a dog from the rain. Years ago, he and some neighbor kids had scouted the whole Greenbelt—the name was new back then—looking for caves. The only decent one in the whole region made up for all the measly little pockets. It was enormous. They dubbed it the "Forty Thieves" cave because it was the sort of place you could imagine Ali Baba hiding treasure chests and pots of gold. The Forty Thieves was a steep tunnel that went upward fifty feet or more into the rock, on a dusty slope. At the end of the climb was a high round chamber. An owl lived way up inside it; you could see the hole it nested in, and its pellets were scattered all over. Stoner hadn't thought about that cave for years, but the memories were amazingly clear. Forty Thieves: little wads of bone and fur; the taste of the dust every movement stirred up; how good it felt to enter cool shade after toiling over hot, dry trails.

He would like to see it again sometime, but he couldn't remember where it was anymore. All the gulleys and canyons in the Greenbelt looked alike. He'd have to set up an expedition with Edgar. Edgar knew the Greenbelt real well. He probably knew the Forty Thieves cave, though only Stoner and his friends had called it that, and sworn themselves to secrecy. All the kids who roamed these hills and canyons probably found that cave and thought themselves the first to discover it.

Skulking through manzanita and juniper bushes, Stoner wondered if he'd passed the place. Suddenly the ground beneath his feet let out a splintering sound and began to sag. He threw himself back, barely in time. He'd stepped on the plywood trapdoor, nearly broken right through.

After the cracking sound, he heard branches breaking softly nearby. That deer was still banging around. He looked for antlers briefly, but saw nothing. He couldn't see how it had gotten down the slope, but it probably wasn't the same beast anyway. There were other animals in the hills, even wildcats—or so they said. In all his years of roaming the Greenbelt, Stoner had never seen anything worse than a rattlesnake.

He got down quietly, not wanting even animals to see him now, and swept at the dirt with his hands, uncovering the rope handle. As he pulled the trap open, earth sifted into the hole. He leaned the door against the juniper tree, then lowered himself into the pit.

He had to get on hands and knees to move deeper into the hideout. He could see the trunk full of grenades on the foam pad, exactly where Hawk had left it. His pride and joy, souvenir of the best night of his life, a raid on Camp Pendleton that he'd made with some pals (all of them now in jail for other crimes) just to prove the U.S. Army was no match for a handful of wild boys. Stoner had walked off with the biggest box he could carry; the other guys had left with a few guns and small demolition bombs that looked like nine-volt batteries. The crate was his baby, and he was happy to pay it a visit, just to see that it was safe. Hawk always complained it was too dangerous to have around, but Stoner held onto the thing. You never knew when it might come in handy.

He waited for his eyes to adjust, then looked around for the shelves he remembered. First he saw candle stubs, but he wouldn't be staying down here.

Ah. There they were. Hawk had shoved them back on a shelf,

out of sight. Grinning, Stoner squeezed in a few more feet. The ceiling scraped his back; dirt grated down his pants and made him cough. He felt like Winnie the Pooh, stuck in Rabbit's hole, as he reached for the stack of porno magazines.

They were cool to the touch. Slick paper. Good stuff. He was almost unbearably excited. He considered going ahead and lighting one of the candles, sitting down to look them over in the dark, where it was nice and cool. But the place was built for boys, and too tight for him. Reluctantly he backed out, dirt falling in his face and gritting up his eyes. He crouched on his knees in the sun, coughing and wiping his hands on his shirt, then trying to wipe his eyes with some shirt cloth from his shoulders.

Brush crackled behind him. He dropped the magazines instinctively. He'd seen a shadow move over the sun, and it didn't have antlers. He opened his eyes before they were quite clean; dirt chafed his eyeballs.

"Dusty?" he said, though he could see right away that it wasn't. It was some kid he didn't think he knew, though it was hard to tell because he was standing right over the hole, silhouetted against the sun.

"Uh," Stoner said, dropping his gaze for a second, finger in his eye. The magazines had fallen open on the dirt floor, showing everything. His face was burning.

When he looked up again, the kid moved out of the sun's way, blinding him. Squinting, painful tears in his eyes, Stoner could see that the kid was holding a chunk of rock so big it made his arms bulge and tremble with the strain of raising it over his head. Stoner was so embarrassed that although he saw the rock, its meaning just didn't register.

He started to rise, propping his weight on the edge of the pit. "These aren't," he said, awkwardly.

Then the rock came down like a hammer, nailing him into the ground.

=16=

"Close your eyes," Edgar said. "Imagine a blank movie screen."

Mike's eyes were already closed. He tried to see the screen as brilliant white, as if the film had snapped and the bare bulb was glaring on the surface. He discovered that his imagination produced a scene far more detailed than Edgar suggested. He had an impression of empty seats around him, a lofty ornate ceiling decorated with chandeliers and baroque plaster moldings, as if he were sitting in an old fancy theater. Maybe it was a memory of someplace he'd seen as a child.

"Keep your mind empty," Edgar said. "See only that screen. Now . . . pictures are going to start appearing on it. They'll just sort of pop into view. That's what you draw. And keep your eyes closed if you can."

"Draw with my eyes shut?"

"Sh . . ."

His grip tightened on the pencil; the tip rested lightly on the sketch pad he held.

What should he draw? The seats? The chandeliers? No, the exercise hadn't started yet. He was supposed to clear his mind.

He tried by force of will to make everything vanish except the screen, so of course that was the first thing to go. Alone in the dark theater, he called it back again. When it finally returned, it was no longer very bright. His head felt full of swirling gray mist.

"Relax. Concentrate."

Easier said than done.

No, I'm not even supposed to think that. I'm supposed to keep my mind a blank. But every time I think about making my mind a blank, I have to think something, and then it's not blank. I have to think without thinking, somehow. Without words.

Maybe if I could think in pictures, that would do it.

"Now I'm going to try sending you a thought," Edgar said. He didn't feel at all ready to receive it. Suddenly the carpeted floor of his room felt hard as granite; the shag strands scratched his ankles. But he couldn't tell Edgar he wasn't ready, not without further disrupting his concentration. Scott had said ESP was a waste of time, but Scott wasn't around to suggest anything better. By default, because they lived a block apart, he and Edgar were becoming best friends.

"I'm going to project it right on the screen," Edgar said. "So you draw whatever you see."

Mike's eyes fluttered open involuntarily. He had an instant's glimpse of his bedroom. Edgar sat against the wall, under the painted moon, a clipboard propped on his knees; he was sketching. Mike looked down at the blank tablet in his lap, closed his eyes again.

Now behind his eyes he saw a blank sheet of paper. It was greenish, turning red, then purple. No, he thought. Turn white! But the image, when he forced it, turned black.

"Relax," Edgar said.

Mike must have been visibly squirming.

"Come on, Mike, ESP happens when you're not trying. As soon as you pay too much attention to it, it runs off like a skittish cat."

So what's the point, he wondered, of exercises like this one? Wouldn't *trying* to develop telepathy make you certain to destroy it?

Try not to try. . . .

According to Edgar, everyone was linked through their subconscious minds. Humanity shared the same thoughts, but everyone was so busy listening to themselves talking that they never heard the greater murmur. If he could only be quiet, he might hear Edgar's thoughts instead of his own. He might break through the barrier that separated them.

Edgar's reason for his ESP exercises was to create an entire gang with psychic powers—a group of kids who never spoke, but knew each other's minds instantaneously. They would move as one entity, a single mind with a dozen bodies, working in perfect silence. Think of the crimes they could commit!

Oh, shut up, he thought. Edgar is nuts. And so am I for listening. Scott told me so already.

A pang went through him. He missed Scott the way an amputee misses a severed limb. He had a ghostly friend where before he'd had a real one. For years he had been able to pick up the phone and Scott was there; he could hop on a bike or a bus, or hitch a ride to Scott's house. Scott had been his chief ally in school. Next year, everything would change. Edgar was okay, but he was no genius. Mike sensed that he would never have another friend like Scott, and with that knowledge came a feeling of desolation.

This was useless.

"Edgar, I can't—"

"Sh! Keep trying!"

Sigh . . .

Blank screen, blank page, white screen, window, empty house.

Blank, blank, my mind is a—

Wait, now what was that? A house? Do I draw that? Was that a picture from Edgar's mind?

Stop thinking and draw. What have you got to lose?

He peeked at the paper and sketched a sloppy house, a square with a triangle on top of it for a roof. He drew a round window like a porthole with cross-bars in it, then closed his eyes again.

He hadn't drawn a house that badly since he was using crayons. But artistic skill wasn't the point of the exercise.

More pictures came unbidden, tumbling after the first. It was as if, inside him, a gate had opened. Dream images, too many and too fast to identify, flickered in the dark behind his eyes and were just as quickly gone. A cat, a car, a flower pot. He had taken hold of one picture, tugged on it, and found a dozen more attached, like a magician's trick with scarves. He sketched quickly, hardly opening his eyes.

Mountains, cities, the moon. He wondered if all he really saw was his imagination at work. Was he simply staring coldly at the processes of his mind? Was there nothing mysterious about it after all? It didn't feel all that different from the way he normally dreamt up things to draw—dragons and demons and damsels. . . .

And here came a rush of *them*.

Women, starkly posed, pictures of photographic clarity—in fact, most were straight out of the magazines Scott had given him as a going-away present. So much for the chivalric images of knights and ladies he'd once pictured in his dreams. These noble folk were *going at it* in the most ferocious ways imaginable. They were, frankly, unimaginable—except for the fact that he had photographic evidence. The pictures wheeled past, not quite as clear as those in the magazines, shadowy at the edges. He knew these were not Edgar's thoughts, so there was no point in drawing them. He was afraid to sit here with his eyes closed in front of Edgar. Afraid because he could feel a lump growing in his pants, and once it got going he would be helpless to dispel it.

He slapped down the tablet deliberately and opened his eyes. "I can't," he said.

Edgar was staring intently at his own clipboard. He had rolled a sheet of paper into a cone and was looking at his picture through it, to hone his concentration. It took him a second to come out of his trance; he looked up and let the cone unfurl.

"What? You haven't—did you draw anything?"

Mike shrugged and handed over his tablet, tangled with figures bearing little relation to the things he had seen behind his eyes. As sketches they were embarrassing; he would have to explain each one.

Edgar looked confused and somewhat disappointed, but then he brightened.

"Hey, you got one!"

"What? I did?"

Edgar laid his clipboard on the carpet, revealing a painstakingly but poorly drawn hot-rod with huge rear tires, a long tapering body, and tiny spoked front wheels. The driver's compartment was a distorted bubble with a stick-figure cramped inside.

Mike hadn't imagined—or drawn—anything remotely resembling a car. None of his sketches even had wheels.

"See?" Edgar said. "It's amazing."

Edgar was pointing at the porthole Mike had drawn in his crude house. There was a fanatic's gleam in his eyes.

"That's a window," Mike said.

"But see? It looks exactly like this tire." He touched the spoked front tire of his drag car.

"Edgar, you drew a car and I drew a house. They're totally different!"

"Don't be so literal. These little spontaneous things, that's where it really happens. You'll see."

"I doubt it."

"Anyway, if it's confused, it's 'cause we haven't practiced much. My mind kept wandering, I mean." He grinned slyly. "I, uh, kept thinking about sex!"

At that moment, someone knocked on the door. Ryan stuck his head inside. "Come here, you guys!"

Edgar jumped up. "What's going on?"

"I think somebody's watching the house."

"What?"

Ryan led them down the hall into their mother's room. The

bedroom was dim, the light from outside filtered through dozens of orchids that grew inside and out on the deck, some in hanging pots, spilling falls of flowers, delicate petals that looked like spiders or dancing dolls or gaping lips; others were bare leaves and stalks now at some colorless phase of their slow life-cycles. Some stood in pots, others grew from lumps of wood. They were Ms. James's passion—her Epidendrum and Brassia, Odontoglossum and Dracula orchids. Clustered pseudobulbs bulged from the pots like grapes; rootlets and creepers probed the air, brushing the boys as they went through sliding glass doors onto the deck. There, behind the shade of a bamboo curtain, Ryan stopped and pointed down into the hilly canyon.

"I was on the deck in my room but it's too easy for them to see us there."

"Who?"

"I don't know. First I thought it was a deer, but I swear it ducked down when it saw me looking. Deers don't do that."

Edgar and Mike peered through the blinds, scanning the shrubs in the canyon below. The sun was touching the houses on the far side of the gulch, so it was dark and getting darker down there. Plenty of trails ran through the bushes, including the one Edgar had taken the night Sal's gang cornered them. He had seen kids from houses across the canyon playing war games in the bushes, battling for possession of the slope below Shoreview Road. But this evening he saw nothing.

Ryan said, "I don't see him. I don't even know for sure where he was. He could have gotten away by now."

"If it was anyone at all," Mike said.

"It was! There was someone there!"

"Better lay off the hard stuff," Edgar said.

"What's that supposed to mean?"

Edgar laughed. "If you have to ask, you wouldn't understand."

"Yes I would. Drugs, right?"

Edgar laughed again.

Mike meanwhile was thinking unwillingly back to the night

of terror, wondering if any of Sal's gang might drop by every now and then to check the house. They might still be waiting for their chance to use the key. . . .

The key was never very far from Mike's thoughts. It cropped up a few times daily, without fail. Every time anything made him nervous or insecure, he remembered it and felt a little worse, a bit more fearful. He supposed that eventually, when nothing came of it, he would forget. Sal's brother, if he was the one who'd taken the key, had probably forgotten all about it. He was an adult, after all. He had better things to do than pick on kids. Yes, the key would fade away like everything that had bothered or frightened him, things that seemed so desperately important one moment but were later harder to recall than the details of a fever dream.

But for now, the night he'd lost the key was still fresh in his mind. As it might be in the mind of whoever had taken it. Sal's brother or not. . . .

Of course, he couldn't say any of this to Ryan. Or even Edgar for that matter.

"It's no one," he said. "Don't be scared."

"I'm not scared."

"No?" Edgar said. "Even though your folks aren't getting home till late tonight?"

"No," Ryan said. "I'm going to Dirk's house anyway."

"Oh . . ." Edgar smiled. "So your boyfriend can protect you, huh?"

Ryan lashed a kick at Edgar's shins, which meant more than it might have since he was wearing soccer cleats.

"Oh ho!" Edgar cried, leaping back.

"I'm not a faggot, you faggot! You ortho diplo!" Ryan lurched at him, knocking down a pot as he did. The orchid hit the deck and the pot cracked, spilling bark chips and gravel.

"Shit!" Mike cried. "Stop it! Mom's orchids!"

Ryan and Edgar stopped abruptly. The three of them knelt, sweeping up the potting soil and dumping it into the pot. Despite the sound of its fall, the pot was only chipped. They tried to rebalance the plant—a flowerless clump of broad leaves—and set it back on its post.

"Let's get out of here," Mike said, brushing the last of the soil across the deck so it fell through the boards onto Ryan's deck below. "You're lucky you didn't hurt the orchid, Ryan."

"You're lucky I didn't hurt you!" Ryan shouted at Edgar, who was at least a foot taller, but not quite as muscular. "You quay diplo-docus!"

"Come on, Mike, I don't have time for this pipsqueak."

Ryan stomped out of the room and down the stairs.

"So what do you want to do tonight?" Mike asked.

Edgar looked at him for a guarded moment, as if considering something interesting. Then the look went away, and he shook his head slightly.

"What?" Mike said.

"Nothing."

"Nothing? My mom left me money for dinner. You want to go down to Taco Bell?"

"Taco Bell? *Awlriiiiight!*"

=17=

"Don't look now," Edgar whispered, "but I think we're being followed."

Mike went cold. "Followed?"

"Look in this window, you can check out the reflection."

They were passing a real estate office whose display showed nothing of any possible interest to two teenage boys. Mike feigned enthusiasm for floor plans. Meanwhile, in the dark glass, he could see a large van cruising slowly down the street behind them. It was inky black, streetlights sliding slick upon it.

"Sal," Edgar whispered.

Mike choked, wishing he could crouch down and vanish, drip away into the gutters and through the storm drains, into invisibility. Sal, whose wall he had smeared with avocado, whose brother had the key, stalking him . . .

The van pulled to a stop, rumbling right behind them. Mike grabbed Edgar's arm.

"If we run downhill, it'll have to make a U-turn," he said. "Then we can cut between houses, hide in bushes."

"I'll count to three," Edgar said, in instant agreement.

At that moment, he heard the side door opening. In the window he saw figures stepping down, coming toward them. White faces swam in the black glass.

"Forget about counting," Mike whispered. "Just run!"

As they turned to make their escape, feet rushed toward them, slapping on the pavement. Mike darted sideways as a hand snagged on his sleeve.

He screamed and hurled himself down the street, desperately trying to remember every shortcut, every driveway, any little niche where he could crawl and hide. Behind him, insane laughter. He glanced back because he couldn't hear Edgar at his heels. Had they caught him?

Up the block, a cluster of people stood on the sidewalk by the realtor's office. Edgar was among them, waving. "Mike, wait up! I was joking!"

"Chicken-shit!" came another voice, also familiar, followed by the high-pitched, hysterical laughter of Mad-Dog.

"Jeez." He thudded to a stop and swung around, panting. Mildly humiliated, he headed slowly up the hill. He was glad they couldn't see him blushing in the dark. The van looked just like Sal's.

"Come on," Edgar said, urging him in, "let's go for a ride."

"I don't know," Mike said, trying to see into the van. It was tomb-dark inside. "I haven't been to church since I was seven."

"No, Hawk's not here. It's Dusty's van."

"Oh . . ."

Mike climbed in after Edgar, and pulled the door shut. Inside, it was crowded and dark. Bodies cut off most of the light coming through the windshield. The air was full of pungent smoke that made him cough; it smelled like burning lawn-trimmings. There weren't any seats. He tripped over something soft but bony, stumbling against a carpeted wall. "Get off my leg," said a girl's voice.

Mike recoiled, wishing he could see. A girl! There were no windows, though, on the sides or at the rear. When his eyes adjusted a little bit, he saw the back of Dusty's head. He was driving. Edgar climbed up between the two front seats and started rummaging through a box of eight-track tapes. There was a thin pale woman with bleached white hair sitting in the passenger seat. In profile, her eyes looked like crystal balls with streetlight beams bending through them. A small, twisted cigarette fumed in her fingers. He suddenly realized what he must be smelling.

"All right, Dusty!" Edgar said, and shoved a tape into the player. Music boomed through the van, heavy bass and drums, a shrieking flute. Edgar grinned at Mike. "He loves to drive when he's dusted."

"This ain't strictly a joy-ride," Dusty said. "Tonight we're *gonna* find Stoner. Just like the dude to go out for a shit and never come back."

The van hit a bump, hurling Mike backward. He landed among bodies; Mad-Dog shoved him away, snarling. He lay where he had fallen, anonymous in the darkness, melting into it. He felt almost ecstatic to be so hidden.

"Come on, baby," said a voice in the corner nearest him. It had to be Kurtis Tyre. "Come on." He heard a girl's muffled laugh, choked noises. Kurtis said, "Mm-hm. Yeah." They were kissing, he thought, though it seemed too loud for that. Slurping sounds. "Yeah, man," Kurtis said. "Yeah." There was nothing in *his* mouth.

"Here, have a drink." Edgar was suddenly next to Mike, silhouetted against the windshield, his extended arm a faint blur. The bottle was shiny and half full.

He took the bottle without thinking, as if the earlier ESP exercises had finally taken hold. As he uncapped the bottle, the vapors stung his nose; his tongue seemed to swell and plug his throat. He'd stolen swigs of liquor from Jack's bottles and it had never hurt him before.

"Don't let him drink that," Mad-Dog said in his raspy little voice, putting his hand on the bottle. "He's a wimp. He'll puke on everything."

"You only want it all for yourself," Edgar said defensively. "Mike's tough. He won't barf."

Mike managed to wrestle the bottle away from Mad-Dog, and after winning the half-hearted struggle there was no question of refusing the drink. While the first swallow was eating its way through his guts like Liquid-Plumr, he chased it with another. The liquor left lumps on his tongue, like balls of lint or wet paper. He washed away the residue with a third swallow.

"Give it," Mad-Dog said, jerking on the neck of the bottle.

"Wait!"

"Yeah, Mike, not too much," said Edgar. "That's powerful stuff."

"It's not the whiskey that'll get you," said a voice Mike recognized as Howard's. "It's the acid."

"Acid?" Mike let go of the bottle. "What do you mean, acid?"

"As in lysergic," said Edgar.

"Isn't that . . . LSD?"

"It's spiked all right!" Howard whooped. At that instant, someone started making strangling noises in the corner; Kurtis was going, "Oh, yeaaaaah."

"If he spews, Edgar, you're cleaning it up," Mad-Dog said.

"Spewin' sputum!" someone sang.

"How—how much did I take?"

"No way to tell," said Edgar. "Kurtis makes it pretty strong."

"Soaked a quarter sheet of blotter in there till it fell apart," Kurtis said. "Hey, don't kiss me with jizz in your mouth, baby. Think I'm a faggot, I wanna taste that? Fuckin' *rinse* first."

Mike swallowed and swallowed again, flexing his tongue, feeling the paper shreds coagulating in the deep folds of his mouth, behind the molars. Acid. LSD. What was it anyway? Was it the stuff that replaced bone tissue so you had to have constant doses to stay alive, or was that heroin? His knowledge of drugs came mainly from a film he'd seen during a school field trip to the Museum of Science and Industry in L.A. All he remembered of the movie was needles going into wormlike festering veins, followed by pictures of scary sugar cubes and whirling spirals with grinning skulls zooming past in a storm of black and white pills and capsules, against a background of insane laughter something like what Mad-Dog was doing now. He also remembered a skinny kid puking in a wastebasket, a miserable image which had obliterated any desire to experience the exciting, Halloween-like thrills of spirals and skulls. LSD was the hallucination drug, responsible for acid trips, psychedelic art, and hippies.

Psychedelic art, he thought. Wow . . . like the Yellow Submarine!

I might have a hallucination! I might see things that don't exist, with my eyes wide open. Is it like dreaming when you're awake?

I'm going to find out.

He could feel his heart pounding harder than ever, keeping time with the thoughts ripping through him. He listened carefully, straining his eyes in the dimness. There was very little to see so far. He supposed that almost anything might appear in the darkness, and it wouldn't be as impressive as hallucinations in broad daylight. He hoped it would be something better than skulls and needles. He liked skulls well enough, and drew them all the time, but needles were another matter. Maybe he would see something he could draw or paint. He'd never done much in color, or with paint, but this could be the thing that sparked him. He could be the next Peter Max! A whole line of Day-Glo posters and notebooks and decals and lunchboxes unreeled before his eyes. Maybe he should ask Dusty to drive by his house so he could pick up a tablet and a pen. But it was too dark in here, and jostling. He couldn't possibly draw. What was he thinking?

He wished again that Scott were here. This was the sort of thing they should have done together, in case it got too weird. He wasn't sure exactly how much he trusted Edgar.

On the other hand, if Scott had been here, they might have talked each other out of drinking; together, they might have dared less. Then he probably never would have tried LSD. Scott's ridicule of drugs was ceaseless. So maybe it was just as well he was on his own. It gave him a sense of freedom that swept aside his fears and anxieties. He couldn't wait, now, to see what the night would bring.

Outside the van, he distinctly heard hooves galloping over cobblestones. It took him a few seconds to figure out that he had put his palms over his ears to blot out the voices around him. He lifted his hands and heard a gruff, urgent little voice: "How's it feel, man? You losing it yet?"

"Shut up, Mad-Dog," Edgar said. "What're you trying to do, push him over the edge? Ignore him, Mike, it doesn't come on that fast."

"I think I feel something. I'm not sure."

"Yeah? Maybe you're hypersensitive. That's good for the ESP, you know. That was fucking amazing tonight, you drawing that tire. Hey, guys, Mike and I had some telepathy going!"

"You told him about the risk of permanent damage, right?" Kurtis said.

"Lay off," Edgar said.

"I mean, me, I don't care. I don't want kids, but if you were planning on it, well . . . I hope you like flippers."

Mike realized, with a huge and superior amusement, that Kurtis was teasing him. He felt a stately warmth toward him— towards all of them. It seemed he could see them clearly in the dark, through a process of echolocation such as bats relied upon.

"Don't tell him shit like that," said Edgar, his guide and protector in this exotic new world.

"Fair warning, James, that's all. I mean, some people don't mind a little brain damage for the chance of seeing God."

GOD

. . . *god* . . .

The word echoed in the van. He could hear the creak of every spring, the rattle of every bolt in the metal shell that carried them; and all the parts picked up the word *god* and repeated it over and over again endlessly, each in its own peculiar, particular voice.

Suddenly Mad-Dog shouted, even louder than the inanimate choir, "Stop the van! Stop it!"

"He's gonna blow, Dusty!"

They lurched forward as the brakes screamed. The door flew open. Mike watched with remote amusement as Mad-Dog threw himself toward a storefront with a thorny hedge whose waxy pointed leaves glowed and crawled under the streetlights. Mad-Dog pushed his face into the thorns and proceeded to vomit with exquisite grace, as if he were a dancer, one arm thrust out behind him, the fingers curling like the fresh baby creepers of a newborn plant. Mad-Dog growled and barked and shook his head, flinging ropes of saliva. Everyone laughed. It all took forever. Mike gulped huge drafts of fresh air. In the new light, he saw into the corner where Kurtis sat with his arms around a dark-haired girl; he didn't know her name but her face was familiar from the Alt-School. Mad-Dog heaved again and curled up on the pavement like a pillbug.

Dusty said, "Someone go check he's not choking on his tongue or something."

"Yeah, Mad-Dog! Do a Jimi!"

Edgar stepped out onto the street. Mike felt suddenly afraid for him. Here it was solid, cagelike, secure; but beyond the safe black confines of the van, anything might happen. As Edgar approached Mad-Dog, Mike's vague nagging feeling of dread grew stronger, more definite. He felt certain that he would soon see it clearly.

The storefront pulsed with light. He saw with a delayed shock of understanding that the window above the hedge was not a window at all but an aquarium. Inside the tank, gray mannequins were swimming. They twitched toward Edgar in the cold glare of the streetlight, burlap fingers raking the dingy broth for sustenance. They would soon move directly into the light. Any moment now, he would see their faces.

"Edgar!" he screamed.

Edgar stooped over Mad-Dog, whispering. As he turned around, blindly nodding toward the sound of his name, Mike saw that Edgar's face had vanished. The eyeless, mouthless head had the texture of stretched canvas, but somehow it managed to grin. Mike struggled to free himself from the press of bodies.

"Open your eyes," said a girl.

He hadn't known they were shut. He blinked and light streamed in. He saw Edgar helping Mad-Dog to his feet on the sidewalk. The window was only a dress-shop window. The mannequins were simply and elegantly mannequins. They could never be anything else.

He looked over at the girl beside him. Deep brown eyes; a round white face with high cheekbones; pale hair pulled back from her high forehead, held in a bandanna tied off like a gypsy kerchief. His heart leaped with love, as if he had known her—desired her—forever.

"You're okay," she said.

Then the door slammed shut again, and the van took off.

It wasn't as dark in the van now. The air was full of lingering shapes—tumbling emeralds, complicated jewels, intricate pieces like interlocking light-flecks in a kaleidoscope. Leafy vines dripped down from a rainforest canopy. His body felt as if it were made of wind, fit with wings to carry him over the streets. But at the same time, he was one of a pack of wolves, all of them chattering and growling wolf-talk in a dark den. Wolf-monkeys. Was there any such thing? *There was now.* Somehow he had landed among them; he was a changeling among adopted siblings. Best of all, he had a beautiful sister he adored, one who loved him completely. Even now she was licking his throat, purring against him, clasping his paws with her own.

"Hey," Howard said, his voice slurred and blurry. "The dark, it's something you get used to when you're staring at the door like I'm a little kid and the light in the palace is coming from so far away. . . ."

"Man, Howie," Kurtis said. "That is really deep."

And Howard began to weep piteously. "You got no right, asshole! I was talking to Craig!"

"Sh, shush," said his wolf-girl sweetheart, and then she tore away from him, a painful separation that left him rocking in the rocking dark. As he heard her whispering to Howard, a vast and vicious rage began to grow inside him, or else revealed its immensity for the first time. It was as if he had merely peeled away a tiny shred of the protective leaden outer coating, allowing an evil radioactivity to seep out. Her voice, so gentle, seemed the essence of femininity, calm, comforting. Anger burned through him and destroyed itself, leaving ashes, desperation, loneliness. How could he rage against such beauty? Deserted, he would crumple here and die. He would make not a sound of protest or complaint. He would die gladly having kissed her only once—but he had never kissed her except in a dream, and his misery knew no limits. It filled the empty reaches his rage had eaten into him for eons.

It was a form of resurrection when her fine cool hands returned. "He's been having a hard time," she confided. "I guess his best friend died recently."

"Mine too," Mike whispered, not knowing himself exactly what he meant, but she squeezed him anyway and it was as though she had never left—as if she had been faithful forever. Her embrace promised a secret world of pleasure leading out of this world like a flower-stalk soaring up from the mundane worm-tunneled soil and blooming elsewhere, in a diamond realm. He didn't know or care if his eyes were closed or open now. He reached for her and felt her flow into him, as though they had been twinned together always, one body, one soul.

And yet, there was something new here. They might have been soulmates for eternity, but one crucial connection had never been made. It was a purely physical thing—unbearably so. He became suddenly and painfully aware of his dick, an adamant wand shoved into a pocket, gouging him insistently, bringing him down from the dizzy heights. His balls ached from the nearness of fulfillment, release.

Had she felt it, he suddenly wondered, nudging or prodding her? How could she not have? And who was she anyway? He didn't care, as long as *It* could finally happen. His rite of manhood; his initiation. Had it come to him finally, here and now? If so, he was willing to accept it even in the crowded van, where it was dark enough to forget everything else.

Then she drew away from him.

"Where are you going?"

"Goin' nowhere, man," someone answered—but not her.

"Where—?" He reached for her, but she was gone. He had repelled her for some reason, so she had left him. Just like that. And not for just *any* reason. His dick had done it. Beyond his control, like an outright enemy—traitor!—it had reared up and threatened or disgusted her.

"Don't be scared," she whispered in his ear. "I'm here, love."

But how could she be here when he couldn't feel her? She had been beside him, and now she was gone. Arms he thought he'd put around her were wrapped instead around himself.

He gulped at rational thought like a dolphin breaching for air, and then the descent began, the depth-sounding.

As the darkness grew impenetrable, he feared to move, feared his body might betray him in some mortal fashion. Spiders crept across him, furry tarantulas and chitinous shiny black widows taking delicate eight-legged steps, brushing his flesh daintily, extruding their hollow curved fangs to pierce him, poison him, and suck him dry. If he moved they would sense him in the web. He was trapped already, wrapped in sticky silk, doomed in the end like any other insect. If he could only stay still, prolong it—

But no. His body hummed like a piano wire, taut with repressed screaming. He hurled himself at the stretched-out moon that hung mockingly in the sky, a pale parallelogram. The air filled with shouting; birds and bats seized him in their wings, trying to drag him down, but he clawed his way through them, fighting to get at the light. Spiral galaxies, bright nebulae, exploding stars—all went streaming through the light, which from certain angles resembled a windshield. He had to get out, more than ever now that the spiders had started calling him by name.

Tenacious vermin, they dragged him back, threw him down on their carpeted web and sat upon him. Gulliver among invisible Lilliputians, prone on the floor of a rumbling cave.

A flash of light caught his attention, trapped his soul. Hanging in space like Macbeth's dagger, blood dripping from a serrated edge, he saw it take on form:

His key.

The lost, surrendered, stolen key.

Emotions and images streamed from the key. It was the radiant star that lit up every dread. He had kept his terror locked away for centuries—all his guilts and insecurities, his nightmares and doubts; and not only his alone, but those of all men. Every monster they had chased into the night and shut out beyond the fortress door was fighting for possession of that key. He had locked that door himself, as had Beowulf, and with this very key. But it was his no longer. The monsters needn't roar and pound at the gate. They owned the key, and no one but Mike knew it. They were free to come and go as they wished. When they wished.

Soon, they whispered. Very soon.

The key dangled before his eyes, but out of reach. The hand that held it poised unseen. He shut his eyes and saw it still, glimmering like a piece of the moon. It lay in his palm, beside a knife—a switchblade. He admired the way the moonlight caught its edges. Like the knife blade, it was silver. And like the knife, it was a weapon.

He was moving through a thicket, crouching low, with the key held out ahead of him like a lantern, or a magnet pulling him along. He smelled sagebrush, sharp and resinous; he heard footsteps all around him and saw the shadows of companions from the corners of his eyes. Abruptly the branches fell away and the key lit up with the full force of the moon. He stood on a hillside, craning up at a tall narrow house, sliding glass windows and wooden decks precariously stacked. He had never seen it from quite this angle, by moonlight, but he knew it was his house. Not a light was on anywhere inside it.

Terror and panic caught him in full flood, bearing him away through ears, eyes, and mouth. He was swept toward the key, and reached out as if to tear it from himself, to steal it from his other hand. But the tide of fear swirled him past and the key went rushing away, dwindling into darkness behind him. The currents swept him in the opposite direction. He gave up struggling, stopped swimming, let himself float facedown, sucking at the black waters, hoping he would drown.

Instead he washed up on a barren shore. Someone was dragging him into faint light.

Edgar spoke to him cautiously. "Mike . . . you okay?"

He opened his eyes, seeing red sparks pulling into distance. Taillights. Dusty's van was driving away down a dark street. He looked up at the moon, then down at the earth. He was sitting on Edgar's front steps.

"Yeah . . . you look pretty high."

Mike's mouth felt like a new instrument, not yet broken in. "Wha' happen?"

"Nothing. And everything." Edgar's grin was wide and knowing. "Know what I mean?"

He felt a sudden conviction that Edgar had been part of his visions, that Edgar had seen the key and understood the nature of the creatures that controlled it. Even as he thought this, Edgar nodded and put a hand on his shoulder.

"Riiiiight. No fear, okay? Let's get up. I want to try something while the acid's still fresh. We're past the main rush, but we'll be flying for a good long while yet. I should warn you, you might be feeling the effects for a few days, since this is your first time. We'll drink some beer later to bring us down; I've got B-12 in the house. For now, though, do you feel up to another ESP experiment?"

Mike rose and stretched, not answering yet. His body felt soft, elastic, as if strong water currents were rushing along his limbs. He took a deep breath and felt it spreading through his cells; he could feel carbon molecules snagging on the oxygen before he exhaled.

"This—I mean, everything you felt and knew and saw . . . that's what ESP really is," Edgar said, leading them back behind the house. "That's what I keep trying to say. It's weird . . . subtle . . . not like a regular voice talking, like I am now. It's people thinking the same things at the same time, so you can never say one of them thought it and the other picked up on it. It's more, both of them pick up on it simultaneously, right? Mutual arising, the Buddhists call it. Everybody creates reality at the same time, you know?"

Mike nodded. It made visceral, instinctive sense to him at the moment. He could almost see Edgar's words forming illustrations in the air.

He felt very close to Edgar, who had been with him at the darkest time in the van. Guide and guardian, he remembered suddenly.

"Who . . . who was that girl?" he asked as they went around to the back of the house.

"You mean Kurtis's girlfriend?"

"No, the other one."

"Up with Dusty, you mean? That's his old lady, Nancy."

"No, the other one."

"What other one?"

"The third one. She was . . . you know . . . with me."

Edgar looked at him strangely. "There wasn't any third one. It was just you."

Mike gaped at him. "But I—" How could he describe it? Words were unreliable. "I had my arms around her. I looked right in her eyes. She touched me and . . . and kissed my face . . ."

"No way," Edgar said with awe in his voice.

"She was there. She had blond hair in, you know, in a scarf. She was so beautiful. You had to have seen her."

His heart ached with the memory of her beauty, but Edgar only shook his head. "I'm telling you, Mike, there wasn't any third girl, and none of the other two went near you." He pulled in close, secretively whispering. "You know—you know who it must have been? Man, I can't believe it."

"Who?"

"You just met your anima. It was your *self,* Mike. Like, your female side. You know, in psychology?"

Mike shook his head, uncertain why he felt so frightened all of a sudden. Was it because she had been so real? Because he had known her so intimately, loved her so intensely? Or was it because he had been planning and hoping to see her again, and now had lost her more completely than if she had never been. Which, Edgar seemed to be saying, she never had.

"This is unreal," Edgar said. "My mom would flip if she heard this."

"She was a hallucination?"

"No, man, she was as real as you. She was, *is,* like your ally. Your twin. I can't explain it, but my mom could. It's in books."

"No . . . a hallucination . . . ?"

Edgar sighed and shook his head. "I am so jealous. You met your anima, and she was a fox."

This judgment was so crass that he could neither agree nor argue with Edgar. Instead he fell silent, wishing he could call her back again, summon her out of some deep place in himself. But she had come unexpectedly. What made him think she would return just because he wished it? How many times had he woken from dreams of a perfect lover to find himself alone in the narrow bed, the empty room, staring at the rolling minutes on his Glantz Appliances clock radio? A desperate pang always followed such awakenings, haunting him all day sometimes, until he went to sleep praying he would dream of *her* again. At least then he could console himself with the truth: that his ideal lover was only a dream. But this girl—he had seen her with his eyes. He'd been drugged, true, but wide awake. He couldn't bring himself to believe she didn't exist, and therefore he grasped even at the purely psychological existence Edgar offered. Maybe . . . maybe if he did more acid he would see her again. Yes—if he stayed close to Edgar, he would meet her eventually. Again. She had seemed as real as the tank full of mannequins—as real as the spiders, the wolves, the burning key . . . She's real, he thought, because I am real.

Edgar saw him straighten, must have seen the new look of strength and resolve in his eyes.

"Your power is definitely cracking tonight, Mike. I think you're ready for what I've got in mind."

Edgar's envy and exhilaration were infectious. Even with the sense of loss that filled him, Mike felt ready for anything.

"Come on. This is gonna blow your mind."

=18=

At the back of the house, Edgar unlocked the sliding glass door and went into his room. "Wait here," he said. A moment later, without having turned on a light, he returned smelling strongly of patchouli and carrying a crowbar.

"While the psychic link is strong, this is the perfect time."

"For what?" Mike asked, though he was starting to get an idea. Edgar's laugh confirmed it. There *was* some sort of unspoken communication going on.

"Craig and me . . ." He shrugged. "We were partners at this sometimes. Not Howard, he's too clumsy. But usually I work alone."

"Work," Mike repeated.

"You said you want to be a master thief. It's time you start learning the trade."

Mike had no reply.

"It's easy, really. All you have to do is stay quiet, calm, and alert. And use a crowbar."

The last few minutes had been a breathing space, a lull in the night's strangeness, but that interval of peace was coming to an end. After the compressed insanity of the van, his mind had found room to stretch and expand beneath the open sky. But

Edgar's words, his hinted schemes, quickly brought all Mike's fears reeling in again, cinching nightmares tight around him.

The acid effects had never gone away. Now, with the renewal of adrenaline, they began to ooze out again. He grew preternaturally aware of the slightest scrabbling sounds in the scrub around them; the wind in the sage sounded like a rough voice, whispering. Nature spirits lived out in the wilderness, their domains threatened by encroaching houses and streets. He thought he could see them lurking just beyond the reach of streetlights, warning him off. Edgar, also silent, listened with a similar intensity. He caught Mike's eye and nodded.

"Yeah," he whispered. "This is righteous. You're the best partner I've had yet. I mean, you're really tuned in."

But if Edgar was tuned in to Mike's dread, he didn't show it. He pulled on a pair of leather motorcycle gloves and rapped his padded knuckles on the sliding glass door.

"In every house around here, there's sliding glass doors, right? The ones that back up on the Greenbelt, like mine, have total privacy. Now these things are baby-simple to pop. We'll practice on my door, since we can make all the noise we want back here."

Edgar bent to point out the tracks in which the door slid. "This works almost like a window screen. You want to pry the whole thing up so it tilts in the frame." He demonstrated by slipping one end of the crowbar into the track, edging it under the door, and levering down on the other end. As the door tipped up, it slipped free of the simple latch and slid open at a touch. "You're in. If they've been burglarized before, they'll probably have stop-bolts built into the tracks. But I never hit the same house twice. Now it's your turn."

Mike declined without making a sound. The ESP was surely working.

"Well, then, come on."

Edgar led him along the crest of an eroded dirt embankment, a mound that had been piled behind the houses by bulldozers when the foundations were dug. Most of the houses dated from the first wave of development in Shangri-La. All were occupied, though tonight the lights were off in many. Looking between them as they walked, he caught a glimpse of his own house, one of a row running up the edge of the canyon. The lights were off there, too; Ryan must have turned them all off when he'd left for Dirk's. He suddenly remembered his vision of standing in the canyon behind his home, looking up at it. A wordless panic reached for him. Before he could say anything about it, Edgar beckoned him into the bushes, beyond the mound.

"From back here you can watch all the houses and no one will even know you exist."

From where they stood, well hid in the weeds, he could see straight into half a dozen houses, through the glass-paneled rears they had turned to the night—and to him. Like his own house, most had decks and sliding glass doors on every level. In many, drapes were drawn; but in a fair number the curtains were wide, showing dark interiors or vivid domestic displays. Kitchen scenes, people watching TV, talking on the phone, eating dinner, arguing. He watched in fascination, feeling his mind creep in among them, inserting itself into their lives. Ignorant, unsuspecting, all of them; as if simply because they saw nothing beyond their windows, nothing could possibly exist out there. Nothing could be stalking or spying on them. Not a one of them suspected his presence. It was as Edgar said: He might not even have existed.

The sagebrush whispered that this might be truer than he knew.

How often had Edgar sat here, spying? What a strange temptation—especially when the lives he glimpsed seemed, if anything, duller than his own uneventful life. Perhaps the strangeness of distance, the edge of paranoia, lent it all some slight curiosity. How would his own life appear to someone peering in at him? He couldn't imagine that it would look any more interesting than these.

"There's a girl down there—the window's dark now—I've seen her stripping. And there's a couple Craig and I saw fucking in their kitchen . . . right on the counter! Couple of geezers. We didn't watch *that* too long."

But nothing was happening now. It was all common and obvious. Only the incredible detail made it interesting. He might have been looking at an incredibly sharp film or photograph.

"Okay, so from here we figure out what everyone's up to. Now that house over there—they're out late tonight. Heard 'em telling my mom all about it."

Edgar pointed out one of the dark houses. Beyond the blackness of the rear glass doors, Mike saw dark rooms and dim shapes of furniture. Remembering the tank of mannequins, his uneasiness doubled. He was afraid of seeing Edgar's face go blank again, and this time no soulmate would remind him that his eyes were shut. The impersonal night offered no comfort. He felt as if the weeds were pushing him forward, expelling him into plain sight. The dark house drew him like a magnet, but the pull was terrifying. Why hadn't those people stayed home tonight? He had to find some way to get out of this.

"You're on lookout," Edgar said. "Try to keep our psychic connection. You know, think of that movie screen if it helps you. Imagine we're still together. Picture, like, a two-way radio between us. If you see anyone coming, I'll pick up your warnings and get out."

"What if that doesn't work?"

"Then hammer on the wall and run like hell. Don't wait for me, either. We'll have a better chance if we split up. If there's trouble?—I mean, if the cops come? You might not see me for a day or two. I've got a hideout back in the Greenbelt. That's my fallback, though I haven't had to use it yet. I'll hang around and test the water. You know, the cops might be onto me. It's always a possibility."

"Have you ever been caught?"

"Not at this. They've got fingerprints from some other things, though. Oh, yeah, take the crowbar. You'll have longer to get away and hide it. Okay?"

Mike shrugged. Cops, he thought. They seemed more unreal, more terrifying, than any of this.

"The main thing, like I said, is to stay cool. Just . . . feel it. Stay tuned to me, partner."

Edgar put out his hand, palm out, and Mike took it for a brief squeeze.

"No more talking. Let's go."

They crept over the embankment and darted to the back of the house. The house next door was all lit up, and patches of indirect light scattered on the dark house's patio. They kept to the shadows. An amber floodlight whose model number he almost remembered was mounted above the sliding glass door, but it wasn't on. Mike stared up at the bulb while Edgar worked the prybar into the track. He was remembering the day he first met Edgar—remembering Scott's shadow blocking out the hot light from the alley, Edgar coming in, the fall of lightbulbs, Mr. Glantz's anger and suspicion turning to slack, drooling blankness.

The door popped with a dull thump. Before Mike fully recalled where he was, Edgar handed him the bar and stepped into the dark house, heading down the hall toward a staircase.

He knew he ought to get back to the safety of the underbrush, but it was hard to leave Edgar alone inside. The more he strained to see into the black interior, the more he saw to frighten him. He had no desire to go in; the vast empty night, no matter how hostile, seemed preferable. He could not get in trouble with the law for simply hiding in the hills.

He moved off slowly. Dishes rattled in the house next door, making him jump. The sound had seemed to come from the dark house. A voice rose in anger. Was it aimed at him?

Looking down, he saw his foot was glowing. He had blundered into a patch of light. He jerked back, then sprinted around the side of the house where the shadows were deep and reassuring. Crouching against the stucco wall, he waited for his heart to slow.

Relax.

He crept to the front of the house and found a clump of bushes where he could sit and watch the street. It made more sense than going back into the hills, much as he might have liked to.

A pair of headlights swooped over the rise, heading east on Shoreview, coming his way. He tensed to escape. How long would it take Edgar to get down and out once he warned him? But the car pulled over before it had gone half a block, dousing its headlights. He took a deep breath.

Why was Edgar taking so long?

He looked the other way, since it was just as likely that the residents would drive home by the back road from South Bohemia. His eyes roamed across the canyon, coming to rest on the row of houses there. He counted them until he found his own.

A light flickered on in his mother's room. Jack had said not to expect them before two in the morning, but they must have come home early from L.A. He realized he didn't know what time it was. It might have been later than two. He thought he saw his mother moving past the bamboo shades; then the inner Levolors closed. He was guiltily grateful to see her taking precautions for privacy, knowing now—from firsthand experience—that anyone might be watching.

Who had Ryan seen that afternoon? Someone actually spying?

Then this was fair-play, skulking and spying. But what about stealing?

Well, Edgar was the one doing that . . .

Light bloomed on the street, another pair of headlights sliding forward. This time it was easier not to panic. A hundred cars must use this street each night; only one would come here. The odds were in his favor. The headlights went out, relaxing him further.

He tried to reach out with his mind and feel Edgar inside the house, to reassure him if that were possible. But whatever communion they had shared earlier, in the flood of acid images, it was gone. He felt nothing now but drained. His eyes wanted to close.

The crowbar dropping from his hand alerted him; he jerked himself awake with a gasp. No time at all had passed, for the car was still approaching, very slowly, its headlights still dark. There might be a party somewhere around here; the driver could be looking for addresses in the dark. He huddled tighter into himself.

Just then, he saw that it was a different car. Metallic brown. As it passed under a streetlamp, he saw the shine of a chrome spotlight mounted on the driver's door. It swiveled toward him like a silver eye, its lid of light about to open. It looked like an ordinary car except for that: unmarked.

He stumbled backward, tripping in the bushes; scrambled to his feet and rushed to the back of the house. He banged his fist against the glass, unable to draw a sound from his throat, hoping Edgar heard it.

Inside the house, Edgar made no sound. He wouldn't, if he was smart.

Split up, Edgar had said.

Get out of there, Edgar! Mike prayed fiercely, sending the message as urgently as he could. Get away from that house!

He didn't dare wait to see the result of his warnings. He was already running, lost in the bushes, trying to steer a course into the safety of the Greenbelt. He looked back only once, as light exploded around the house, surrounding it in a halo of glare. The powerful spotlight went roving down the path he'd followed a moment earlier. He thought the sliding glass door gaped wider than before, and hoped this meant that Edgar had come out already. But the glimpse of light redoubled his terror. He wanted only darkness now. So he ran.

He saw no trails. The ground kept folding into gulleys or ridges, deceiving him when he most needed trustworthy footing. Several times he fell and sprawled flat, taking advantage of the momentary stillness to listen. No sirens howled, no cop radios blared, but he might have run too far to hear anything. He thought not, though. His hearing was acutely sensitive tonight. It seemed as though he could hear crickets in the grass, waiting silently for him to move on. The infinite mindless patience of the insects inspired him.

He moved in a kind of overdrive for a time, a trance state that kept him from harm. In the moonlight, everything became very clear and obvious, even luminous. The individual plants had distinct personalities; they whispered to him of shelter, or cried out harsh warnings. He had not stepped into any cactus, though it grew everywhere here; it and the poison oak had voices unlike those of the other plants. He heard them long before he stumbled into them.

But that alien easiness passed eventually. He began to feel more himself again. Too much so, maybe. Every muscle ached.

It seemed that hours had passed before he came in sight of houses again, but it might have been only minutes. He had circled around Shangri-La to approach it from the southern corner. Squinting at streetlights, he blundered into barbed wire and backed off, gasping, with a gashed hand. Thoughts of tetanus coursed through him; his jaws were tight already, his teeth grinding so loudly that he feared they would draw his pursuers. He went crashing through brambles and came out in a clearing, sensing a faint trail in the dust at his feet. A spark of light glinted beyond a tumble of rocks. He moved toward it, following the trail to a high clump of bushes where it ended in a cavelike clearing among the brush. Interlaced branches closed over his head; the moon appeared broken between them, but there was enough light to show that the place had been hollowed out and trampled down. It was large enough to let him stand. His eyes were level with a small opening in the thicket, where branches had been bent and woven to make a frame, like a wicker porthole. The shelter was a hunter's blind, from which one could await the coming of deer, but it should have been facing the Greenbelt. Instead, when he looked through the hole, he saw only a lamppost and the thin strands of barbed wire cutting him off from the street.

Under that light was a house. Parked in the driveway of the house was a black van. Not the one he had driven in tonight, though. Sal's van.

He was still holding the crowbar, after all this time. He flung it deep into the bushes, as if it were poisonous. What if they caught him with it? Then he thought, what if this was a police blind, built for watching Sal's house? They must know what he was up to, dealing drugs and molesting boys. If they came here tomorrow to resume their vigil, and found the crowbar with his fingerprints on it—the same crowbar used in the burglary— what then?

Jesus, he had to get it back.

He crouched and looked after the crowbar, but everything was tangled and murky among the broken sticks. Something pale lay flattened on the ground below the branches. He touched it, and heard paper crinkle. It was a magazine. Seeking clues, he dragged it out where the mingled lights of street and moon could fall upon it.

The pages were stiff and brittle as a stale tortilla, glued together from nights of dew, grittily gummed by the elements. A musky, moldy smell rose from the pictures. It was hard to see clearly here, but he knew what he was looking at. Bodies. Besides being crinkled and so horrible to touch that he could barely bring himself to leaf through it, the pages were selectively mutilated. Photographs of penises, gleaming wet, going into cunts that were equally glistening; and women with their mouths open, taking in other cocks; or gripping them, more than one woman, more than one man. Little of this was entirely new to him—he had Scott to thank for that. But wherever men appeared, the pages had been scratched and torn. Their testicles were missing, ripped away, nothing but holes there. On the opposite sides of those pages, the same holes found awful correspondence in the models' faces; whole parts of their limbs and abdomens had been eaten away. By teeth or nails or acid.

Acid . . .

That's the trouble. I'm full of acid. It's dissolving me.

He could feel it burning through him, a fire in his brain and nerves. He was already crouched and in position—he had only to open his mouth and vomit a thin string of bile on the magazine. He couldn't avoid seeing that trove of desecrated flesh as his guts seized and spasmed. Now stomach acids burned through those rips and tears. The tears he squeezed out were acid, too, etching trails down his cheeks.

The cave of weeds was engulfing him. He thrashed free of it, finding his feet, reclaiming the open night again, running. The barbed wire didn't faze him. He slid between the strands without a scratch, only pausing to look down Shoreview Road toward the house they had burglarized earlier. When was that? How many people had he been since then, his mind running riot as he raced through the hills? Had everything happened on this one night? Wouldn't it ever end?

Two police cars sat before the trespassed house, rack-lights spinning. When he saw them, his heart nearly stopped.

Worse, the metallic brown car was parked in front of Edgar's house.

I sure hope you didn't go home, Edgar.

He took a circuitous detour back to his home, staying out of the cops' sight.

Only his mother's VW sat in the carport. It must have been earlier than he thought, or Jack's Volvo would have been there. He unlocked the door and let himself into the darkened house, wondering if a call to Edgar would tip off the police.

As he switched on the upstairs light, all thoughts of Edgar vanished.

It's another hallucination, he told himself. I'm having a nightmare. I may never wake up.

The solid glass dining room table had been smashed into ten thousand pieces; lethal shards covered the yellow carpet and chairs, making a gleaming ruin. As he took a numb step forward, he discovered that the mirrored wall also was shattered, though a few pieces clung there still, returning his horrified stare.

He turned around slowly, afraid to see more. Deep gouges scarred the dark blue walls, in sweeping arcs as wide as a man's reach. Dishes and crystal lay shattered on the floor; at the foot of the fridge was a clotted pool of sauces and jellies, swimming with the curved wet shards of broken jars. Raw hamburger, flank steaks and a whole chicken lay thawing on the linoleum. The oven door had nearly been wrenched from its hinges. He looked hesitantly into the living room and saw that the wood and glass shelves had been toppled. Albums were ripped from their sleeves and strewn about; the reel-to-reel was buried in festoons of tape. The white sofa and matching chairs were slashed open like members of a massacred family, plush foam and padding spilled everywhere.

He switched on the light for the lower landing before descending. Halfway down the stairs, he knew he shouldn't go any further. What if the intruder was still inside? He should run for the cops right now, while they were in the neighborhood. On the other hand, they might smell the acid burning through him and instantly throw him in jail.

But could that be any worse than this?

More gouged lines ran above the stair railing. The door to the master bedroom was open. He could smell spilled perfume and powders. Clothes had been torn from the closet and shredded. The mattress, hauled from the bed, was covered with dirt and strewn with petals. His mother's orchids were destroyed, pots overturned and broken. The thought of her grief at this scene made him burst into tears.

He shut off the light, unable to bear the vision, and went on weakly to his own room, expecting a scene of complete devastation as he opened the door. It would have been far more reassuring than what greeted him.

His room was almost untouched. Almost. A few books were off the shelves; then he remembered loaning them to Edgar. His desk seemed less cluttered, but at first glance he couldn't tell what was missing.

He looked at the walls, wondering if by some mysterious power, the gorgeous painted moon had saved him.

It hadn't. Not completely.

Beneath the moon, among the layered green hills, a foot above his pillow, the intruder had carved a hole. Three inches in diameter, roughly circular, it looked like a cave in one of the magic green hills—but a cave that could hold only horror.

He approached fearfully, because it had the look of a place in which something must be hiding.

Down in the dark hole, a rounded shape. It looked hard and metallic—not soft or wet or poisonous. Safe to touch. His first thought, ridiculous, was that it was an avocado. He put his hand in slowly, closed his fingers on the thing, and took it out.

He had only seen hand grenades in movies. This looked like one of those. Unreal.

Then he was walking down the stairs, scarcely seeing the slashed walls and shattered mirrors in Ryan's room. Ryan's back door opened onto the patio, where Jack had installed a redwood hot tub. Mike went down the stairs between the houses, out into the brush, and laid the grenade in the dirt beneath a sage bush, where he could find it again if he had to. Where it could explode without destroying the house.

Or what was left of it . . .

From here, he turned and looked up at his home. A strong wave of déjà vu washed through him.

It was the view he'd hallucinated earlier. In the bushes, looking up. He recalled a light coming on in his mother's room, a shape behind the bamboo curtain, blinds closing. That room was dark now.

From outside, knowledge of what the house held felt unbearable. Everything looked peaceful and normal; he could almost imagine that nothing had changed.

But the worst had happened. One night not so long ago, his

key had fallen into a monster's hand. The monster had finally used it. What else was there to fear?

What else but . . . the monster's return?

Thoughts of monsters were ridiculous, the dregs of a ludicrous hallucination. A man had done this, one with a face and a name. Who? Stoner had the grenades, but Sal's brother Lupe had vanished with the key. Were they working together?

His brain felt raw and bloody. Nothing made sense.

Shouldn't he confess now? Wasn't this finally the time to admit to Jack and his mother exactly *how* he'd lost the key? What was he confessing, after all, except that he had gone into the house after dark, when he'd been warned not to. That was such a small transgression, his original mistake. Sure, things were more complicated now, but why keep piling lie upon lie? The whole clumsy edifice had to collapse eventually under its own ungainly weight.

For the moment, he felt locked into the pattern he had helped create. He was more concerned about fitting into that structure, enhancing its apparent reality, than with tearing it apart just now. Maybe there would be another time for the truth, a better time, later.

But not tonight. Not with cops around and acid percolating through his bones and Edgar in hiding . . .

No way. There had been a good chance for honesty before tonight, an option of confessing and getting the locks changed. But that was in a simpler, more innocent time. The amount of blame that would fall on him now, after this incident, was inconceivable.

It was almost a relief to realize that the police would finally be involved. Let them take care of it. He would stick to his story.

The only trouble was, when the cops came around they would see no windows broken, no doors forced. Then his mother would remember the lost key and the blame would fall on him anyway.

He had to keep things straight. They must *seem* to make sense, so that no one would look any deeper. The real secret of the key must remain hidden. He knew what had to be done, and how to do it.

Looking up at the house, his eyes went dry.

No use crying, boy, he told himself. You're going to have to do it: cover up a monster's tracks because they overlap with your own.

He walked back up to the patio. Since Jack had only recently finished building the redwood tub, tools were still scattered about. It didn't take long to find the prybar Jack had used to wrestle the staves into position while he worked the metal straps around the tub.

Still want to cry? he asked himself.

Tears would get in the way with what he had to do, so he gave them a chance to finish up, get it over with.

Nothing came. He couldn't feel a thing.

Back at the bottom of the house, he saw the strobe of lights across the canyon. One of the cars was driving away.

"Stick around," he said softly, positioning the prybar in the track. "You can come over here in just a minute."

Breaking into his own house was, in Edgar's words, baby-simple.

═19═

Lupe ran through the sagebrush hills with a pack of shadows at his heels. The boys could have moved much faster, but they were patient with him, knowing that he carried a knapsack packed with cans and cartons, vegetables, eggs and bread, kidney beans and fruit cocktail—anything he had managed to stuff inside it. Delicacies, compared to the roots and nuts and cactus pears he'd been living on since finishing off the emergency cache he'd hidden away while living with Raymond.

It had been stupid of him to trash the house, a voice in his head said now. But that voice had been silent while he prowled, after passing through the door his key had opened.

You could have fed there again, he told himself. You could have taken a few things, only what you need for a few days, nothing they'd really notice, then struck again and again whenever supplies ran low.

Instead he'd gone wild. He couldn't help it. He'd snapped, seeing everything so neat and perfect that it mocked him. It was a life he would never know, the nuclear family in a TV house with dishwasher, garbage disposal, washer and dryer—all the fixtures sparkling, of course. He had wanted to destroy it—had been forced to settle with making it merely uninhabitable. Let them live in filth; let them see how their lives could have been.

As he smashed the mirrors that covered walls in several rooms, he was amazed to see what he looked like. His hair was matted, crazy, full of stickers and straw. He must remember to steal a comb. He took his time, on a stroll of destruction. On the second level, he entered a room full of plants. Flowers grew everywhere, on the outer deck and inside, giving a perfume to the air. He stared enrapt at softly speckled hoods of orange and violet, yellow and brown frills, swaying on dark green stalks. The flowers caught his attention, but it was the roots that fascinated him. At the base of several plants, thrusting up from the soil, were nutlike clusters, small and ovoid, of pale brown and green. He grinned at the sight and snapped a couple from the soil of one pot, breaking off the stems attached to them. They were firm, resilient, cool in his palm. He rattled them together for a moment, then—an urge irresistible as that of destruction— thrust them deep into one of his trouser pockets.

Now, as he hurried through the hills, he rubbed his palm against his pants, feeling the oval lumps near his crotch, jiggling them slightly in the pocket's pouch. He closed his hand around them and squeezed through the fabric. Tightened his grip, desperately dreaming of the agony and nausea he was supposed to feel.

But he felt nothing. He had trouble imagining—or remembering—what such pain might have been like. He reached into his pocket, pulled out the bulbs, and popped them into his mouth. He rolled them on his tongue. Saliva squirted, despite the bitter taste. The texture was all wrong, and they were too hard, poor surrogates. He gagged, fighting the reflex that almost made him swallow them. They might be poisonous. He spat them out. Not all vegetables were good.

But at least he had real food. And weapons. And shelter— grand shelter! He knew the hills and canyons thoroughly, from roaming them ceaselessly, day and night. He went to his cave only for the deepest and darkest of necessary sleeps. The rest of the time he moved stealthily, spying, storing information. Shuttling between Rim of the World and Shangri-La, avoiding the fire roads that linked them, taking more hidden paths. He had watched Raymond leave for Hawaii alone, keeping the house empty as a lure, a deliberate temptation. A trap, yes, devised by Sal. He had seen his brother in and around it, Sal and his boys, keeping watch in case Lupe returned. What Sal did not know was that he, too, was being watched. Sal's watchers, however, had lost heart after the disappearance of their clumsy giant.

Lupe still wasn't sure who had sent the big man. At first he'd thought the black van watching Sal's house held police interested in the drug deals going on. But Lupe had found a driver's license and Social Security card that both indicated he had killed a "William Stone."

He had chuckled when he read that. Killed a Stone with a stone.

Thinking of which, he wondered again if he should have taken Stone's strength, conducted an actual initiation. It had been an occasional regret ever since the killing. He was bigger and older than Lupe usually liked, but that might have been an advantage in the days ahead. He had looked very strong, despite the fact that his skull had cracked like an eggshell. All that power could have been Lupe's . . .

But it hadn't seemed right. Not only was he the wrong type, but the killing had been done without his special blade, in full sun. The glaring light, the heat and dust, had robbed the death of meaning.

More attractive to him was the growing appeal of the boy whose room he had entered tonight. He was already thinking of him—in the same way he thought of the Pump Jockey, the Junkie, and the Marine—as the *Artist*.

Imagine, an Artist for his collection.

Returning from the lower rooms of the house, he had noticed a door under the stairs, one he'd missed on the way down, in his frenzy.

He opened the door, found the light switch, and walked out into the hills . . .

It was cooler in there, with a breath of the night, as if he were stepping through a magic door into a dream. It was a room of green hills and soft, scented breezes. The full moon hung in a starless sky. Standing there with the rest of the house in shambles around him, he spread his arms and heard an owl hooting in the distance. Wilderness. Incredible hills. Squinting, he imagined roaming through the folds, down among the crevices the painter had left hidden. All it lacked, to make it perfect, was one decent cave.

The absence troubled him until he thought of how to remedy it.

With his knife in hand, cutting the hole, he had felt how right it was. Paradise. It was his cave he carved, he realized. The wall was a map of this very moment—or one a few nights from now, when the moon would be exactly as full and round as the one on the wall.

Backing away to put the cave into perspective, he saw a desk littered with pens and paper, crayons, brushes, paint. Tacked inside the closet walls above the desk were many sketches, some extremely violent, surprising in their starkness. A generous use of red for splattered blood. Dripping fangs, bloody swords and daggers, severed heads and arms. A man being drawn and quartered; scenes of torture. Lupe's breath caught in his throat, arrested by recognition. It was as if whoever inhabited this room had looked into his mind, reached down into his nightmares, wrenched them out and thrown them quivering on the page; as if the artist had stood beside Lupe in all the caves since the First Cave, watching his eyes, hearing his heart, drinking it in and putting it on paper. Here.

He crumpled a sketch in his hands, then realized he was destroying it. With wracking guilt, he tried to flatten it on the desk. Then he backed away, feeling he had damaged something irreplaceable—some part of himself.

At the same time, a feeling of jealousy began to warm within him.

He had drawn once, long ago. It seemed so far in the past that he could hardly remember. Why had he done it? How had he known what to do? What was the point of it all?

And why—why had he stopped?

Unthinking, he picked up a pencil, then a pen, and then handfuls of them. He thrust them into his pack, among the cans and loaves of bread. He grabbed a drawing tablet and stuffed that in, too. Suddenly he wanted these things more than the food, wanted to remember and reclaim whatever he'd once had. He could hardly understand his excitement, which felt as if, finally, he was about to find fulfillment—release.

He tried not to feed his hopes, for they had always betrayed and disappointed him. It was impossible that he would ever change. Still, it was impossible not to want to hold on to the promise.

It was then he conceived the idea of collecting not only the art, but the *Artist*.

Family photographs stood on the desk. One snapshot in a lucite picture-cube showed two boys with their arms across each other's shoulders. He studied their faces, thinking of what he'd seen in the house. The room downstairs belonged to one boy; there were soccer balls, baseball mitts, football helmets and posters everywhere. This other room, with its lovely scenic walls, might almost have belonged to a girl . . . might have, except for these sketches.

These were no girl's visions, of razors and murder and decapitation, of muscular men with absurdly buxom women wrapped around their legs.

He noticed a pencil sketch pinned up in the closet. It was the shorter of the two brothers, the one with eyeglasses. Labeled "Self-Portrait," it showed a boy with a dripping sword in one hand and his own severed, bespectacled head in the other. Both heads smiled grim identical smiles. He had used red pencil for blood, the only color in the picture—in most of these pictures.

That was him. The Artist.

It dawned on Lupe that this boy was the very one who had

left him the key. The one who had invited him in. The one who knew his mind and thoughts as surely as if they shared the same dreams.

The Artist understood him.

Lupe looked back at the wall, feeling that he should leave a gift, something special for this boy whose mind was so full of horror. Something, also, to make the map completely accurate.

Gentle as a lover sliding a flower into a buttonhole, he slipped one of his grenades into the wall.

Lupe stood still, gazed grinning at the hills, basking under the moon.

His boys gathered around. A breeze blew up from the canyons, from the cave that awaited him.

In the distance, he heard an owl call.

PART THREE

A WALK ON THE MOON WALL

=20=

The next day, on foot, Mike trudged up Old Creek Road. He had sworn off hitchhiking. It only led to trouble.

How can all this be happening to me? he thought. I'm not even old enough to drive.

After the morning's long house-cleaning, he had figured it was probably safe to call Edgar. Since he called every day anyway, it might be more suspicious if he suddenly stopped.

"Hi, is Edgar home?"

Ms. Goncourt recognized his voice immediately. "Uh . . . no, Mike. In fact, I haven't seen him since yesterday."

"Really? Wow. I wonder where he is."

"When was the last time you saw him?"

"Oh, uh . . ." He remembered that Ryan had seen them together yesterday. Better play it close. "Yesterday afternoon, till about five or six. We were going to go downtown but he changed his mind so I went alone."

"He didn't say anything about where he was going?"

"Nope . . . uh-uh."

"Well, gee. Okay. Would you do me a favor? Tell him to call me if you see him? There's . . . someone who needs to talk to him."

He sensed that she meant the police. She sounded worried,

which was unusual; she took pride in being unfazed by any of Edgar's schemes. She always seemed pleased not to have raised simply another zombie. It was she, Edgar confessed, who had enrolled him in the Alt-School, as if it might make him even more unorthodox.

"I'll tell him," he promised. "I hope everything's okay."

He hung up.

It was then he thought of finding Hawk, which would take care of two things at once: the key and Edgar's disappearance. Maybe Hawk knew Edgar's hideout. They could bring him food and water while he was lying low. Hawk might not do it if he knew about the burglary, so he would have to make up some story just to get Hawk moving. Let Edgar deal with the truth, later.

All he knew about Hawk was where he lived. There obviously wouldn't be any listing for a plain "Hawk" in the phonebook. For all Mike knew, his name was "Hawk Jones."

Half a mile up the canyon road, he realized he should have called one of the other guys in Hawk's gang. Kurtis or Howard or Mad-Dog. Any of them would have known the number. He wasn't thinking straight, though. He'd gotten so little sleep that it was hard just putting one foot in front of the other.

He had spent most of the night following cops around his house, eavesdropping on their conversations, answering their questions. Dirk's mother had brought Ryan home in the middle of the night, and after the initial shock, he joined Mike in tagging after cops. When the police asked Mike where he'd been, he blurted, "I went downtown. Alone." Only later did he realize that his story left Edgar without an alibi if he ended up a suspect in the other break-in. Since both houses had been entered in the same manner, on the same night, the two crimes would certainly be linked. Edgar might end up being accused of burglarizing Mike's house!

The cops said nothing about the other break-in; they were quiet, talking mainly to each other. The missing art supplies intrigued them. Jack, too, trailed after the cops and asked them pointed questions about the investigation, showing off a command of cop talk gained from "Columbo" and "Adam-12." Mike's mother sat on what remained of the upstairs sofa and wept, since the police would not allow her to straighten anything—not even to put her orchids back in their pots—until the crime lab had been through.

Around three in the morning, a short fat man in a rumpled business suit showed up to powder and brush the sliding glass door. He transferred the sharpest fingerprints to pieces of clear adhesive tape, which he then pressed onto white index cards for preservation. Ryan and Mike watched this procedure with an intense curiosity that overpowered sleepiness and even, in Mike's case, shame. Finally, along with Jack and their mother, the boys submitted to having their fingerprints taken.

That's it, Mike thought. I'm on file.

Since the government now knew who he was, he could forget about ever being a master thief or assassin or anything like that. Not that he'd want to, after this. His fantasies were spoiled.

Therefore he approached Hawk's residence with dread, since it meant a return to the domain of vaguely illicit activities. Hawk's One-Way Gang, the pack of juvenile delinquents whose company he had for some reason sought and cherished, all sickened him now. Or else he was getting the flu. He felt queasy and tired and feverish. The sun wouldn't leave him alone. Was it going to be summer forever?

Old Creek Road was packed with cars. Their exhaust made the heat seem worse; blue-gray tailpipe vapor darkened the sky without cooling it, like clouds that gave no shade. He passed the driftwood stockade of the art festival, where people crowded in by the score. Bohemia's festive displays couldn't cheer him; he felt more an outsider than any tourist. The town's population, bloated by the sun, didn't ease his sense of isolation. In fact, the crowds might simply offer more cover to the man with the key. Sal's brother. Lupe—or "Loopie." It sounded like a nickname, one that made his skin creep the way it hinted of both whimsy and psychosis. That wacky ol' cut-up "Loopie" might be following him even now, a guy in baggy Bermuda shorts, sunvisor, and a Hawaiian shirt. It was awful to realize that he didn't even know what Lupe looked like, though the guy must know him well by now—even intimately.

What kind of weirdo would take my art supplies?

The crowds faded out. He might as well have stood on a featureless plain, alone with his shadow and one other. The shadow of a man he couldn't see, a silhouette against the scorching sun. He felt as if he were being pursued by the shadow as much as the man. For now, Lupe was less substantial than the horror he inspired.

Farther up the canyon, things weren't set up for tourists. You didn't see sunbathers flocking into auto repair shops for souvenirs or snapshots—although compared to the sculpture exhibited in the festival, the corroding heaps of oily metal scrap outside the garages looked imaginatively composed. This was the real Bohemia Bay. People lived and worked here; not orthodontists or lawyers, not retired movie stars or brain surgeons; just people.

Beyond a junkyard, eucalyptus trees fringed a dry dirt lot. Hawk's trailer squatted in the sun like a lunatic's chapel.

He had always wondered about this place—never dreamed he might visit it. It looked like some kind of crazed miniature golf course, a blend of cemetery and scrapyard. The chassis of stripped cars and motorbikes looked like bones pulled from a tar pit. He trudged toward the trailer through the shadows of giant Candyland crucifixes.

The trailer door hung open, presumably for ventilation. Mike walked up the steps and stuck his head into an atmosphere of yeasty mildew. It was dark, but he could hear someone muttering.

"Hawk?" he called.

At the far end of the trailer, in the elevated niche that held the bed, a shrouded shape rose up. It was Hawk, in a tangle of sheets. "Who's there?"

Beyond Hawk, Mike glimpsed curves of flesh and realized he

was looking at a woman's buttocks. Hawk pulled the sheets over her as he dropped from the bed.

"Sorry," Mike said, retreating toward the door. At that moment, someone poked him in the kidneys and squeezed into the trailer. It was Dusty.

"Heeeey, how you doin', kid? Back on earth again?"

"Where'd you come from?" Hawk said. "Dusty, what's he doing here?"

Dusty shrugged. "Ask him."

Mike cleared his throat. "I, uh, thought you might know what to do with this."

He unshouldered his backpack and set it on the crowded little formica table. The pack was stuffed with a huge beach towel for padding. He dug his hand through wads of terry cloth and found the hard egg nestled safe at the cushioned center.

Hawk's eyes bulged when he saw it. He grabbed it from Mike, shrieking:

"What are you doing, you idiot kid? Where the fuck did you get this?"

He didn't wait for an answer. He rushed outside and for a moment Mike imagined him running into the road stark naked, causing an accident that would end in a movie-style fireball.

Laughing, Dusty pushed Mike out of the trailer. They watched Hawk run up the hillside behind the lot, where he set the grenade down gingerly in a pile of crispy bark and eucalyptus mulch. On his way back down, cursing, he grabbed a frayed towel off a drying line and wrapped it around his waist. Finally he stalked up to Mike and shook his index finger in the time-honored manner.

"Do you know what you were carrying around? Do you have any idea what it could do to you? You'd be lucky if they found your shoes! And then you have the balls to bring that thing into my house!"

"It's one of Stoner's, man," Dusty said. "Where'd you get it?"

"Yeah." Hawk hesitated. "Where *did* you get it?"

"I found it in my bedroom last night."

"Your *room?*"

Mike found himself abruptly on the edge of tears. Hawk's admonishment came close to the punishment he had been awaiting from his mother, but which had never come. He was tired, hot and dizzy; and sick of all this.

"It's that key," he choked. "Someone used it last night to break into my house. They wrecked the place. They cut a big hole in my wall and stuck that inside it."

Hawk looked at Dusty. "Stoner?"

Dusty shrugged. "How'd *he* get the key?"

Some kind of look went between them. Hawk shook his head. "Shit," he said, and went tiptoeing back to the trailer, avoiding all the bits of twisted wire and jagged metal that littered the lot. "Start your van," he yelled at Dusty.

"It was lugging last night, man, so I . . . I been working on it."

Hawk stopped, shook his head, sighed. "God help me."

"Jeep's okay," Dusty called out hopefully. "I haven't touched that."

"And you better not." Hawk went in and slammed the door.

When he came back out, he was dressed and ready for action. He squinted at Mike a moment before slipping on his sunglasses. "I tried calling Edgar, have him meet us up there. You know where he is?"

Mike shook his head. He hadn't cooked up a story yet.

"We might need him to find the spot again. I don't suppose you know the place he and Leo dug?"

"No." That must be his hideout, Mike thought with relief. Hawk knows it.

"Well, we'll give it a shot without him." Dusty was already in the Jeep. Mike started to climb in back until Hawk noticed and stopped him with a look.

"What do you think you're doing?"

"Going . . . with . . . ?"

"No way. You stay here till I get back."

Mike backed off, in no mood to insist. Besides, if he went with Hawk he'd have to do some explaining along the way, come up with a story, and he wasn't ready to be grilled. With mixed feelings—mostly relief—he went back and sat on the trailer steps. Hawk tore out into traffic, nearly causing a collision.

A story, he thought, a story. I have to come up with a story—something to protect Edgar and fool Hawk. Because once I start telling the truth, *if* I ever do, I won't be able to edit it just any old way I please.

"Hey. Kid."

He twisted around, looking up into the trailer. The woman from Hawk's bed stood above him, tugging a pair of bluejeans up over her hips. A flash of pubic hair between the zipper halves nearly stopped his heart. She pulled up her black sweatshirt and zipped herself. Her hair was tangled, her eyes dark and circled. A cigarette fumed between her lips. But he hardly noticed these details while the memory of dark curls blocked his mind's eye.

"Where'd he go?" She had a raspy smoker's voice.

"Uh . . . up the hill? Shangri-La?"

"Shangri-La, huh? What a fuck. Bailing some kid out of trouble?"

"Well . . ."

"Bailing *you* out, right?"

Mike blushed. "I'm sorry."

"Don't be. It's not *all* your fault."

She turned away, went deeper into the trailer. Mike heard her muttering as she banged drawers and cabinets. He thought she might be talking to him, so he leaned back inside. "Excuse me?"

"You know he's got, what do you call it, illusions of granger, right?"

"I don't really know him that well," Mike said.

"Oh, just well enough to ask for help when you're in trouble."

"I'm in trouble *because* of him," he said, which was a lie, but he needed some defense.

"That's Hawk. The more he helps, the more you need it."
She threw herself down at the built-in Formica table, clutching a pad of paper and a ballpoint pen. She lit another cigarette and started scribbling furiously, still muttering. "The fuck."

He watched the traffic for a while, acutely aware of her behind him. The glare made his eyes ache, so he was grateful when the woman, coughing, said, "Hey, come in here."

What if she seduces me?

He knew how absurd it was, but he couldn't help imagining her dark hair tangled around him as her tongue pushed into his mouth, tasting of cigarettes, sort of disgusting but *real*. He got to his feet without seeing where he was going, moving blindly toward her voice. Hawk's girlfriend, an older woman, experienced—she would show him how it was all done. Finally!

When his eyes adjusted to the dimness, he saw that she was holding out the pad. Big shaky words were scrawled across the top sheet. It looked like a third-grader's handwriting, with the letters all different sizes, some capitals, some in lower case. He couldn't believe an adult had written it.

"Immature," she said.

Did she mean him? "What?"

She thrust the pad up to his face. "Immature. Did I spell it right?"

He tried to find something like "immature" in the jumble of words, and found himself reading a letter he had no right to see—wouldn't have wanted to read in a million years. But she had it shoved right in his face and there was no avoiding it.

Hock—

Taday I had all I cud take. Yore obveussly not reddy for a dult rilashinship. I new you were immithur but I thot you were gone to be a man sumday. Now I see your jus trine to be a boy agen.

"Uh . . ." She doesn't even know how to spell his name! he thought.

"What? It's wrong, isn't it?"

"Well, not *all* of it."

"Shit. You do me a favor?"

Standing by the table, he found his eyes straying to the loose collar of her sweatshirt, glancing down at bare tan skin. A wisp of smoke stung his eyes, just as she looked up at him. He squinted, rubbing at the pain.

"Okay," he said.

"You look like an egghead. If I tell you what to write, will you do it?"

An egghead? he thought, seduction dreams evaporating. Jeez . . .

"Will you?"

"Write . . . your letter . . . for you? This letter?"

"You owe me." She put the pen in his hand. "Have a seat."

Numb, he sat down across from her.

"What have I got there?"

Mike ripped off the top sheet, put it to one side, and read it back to her as best he could. She started another cigarette and gazed at the ceiling, pondering.

"How's that sound to you?" she asked. "Sound okay?"

"Well—maybe I'll recopy it? Just to get it all spelled right?"

"Whatever you want."

He wrote a corrected version of her text; he couldn't bring himself to make suggestions. He was terrified that Hawk might return, find him here composing a "Dear John" letter, and see in his eyes that he lusted after his girlfriend. Then Hawk would drive him out into the hills, tie him to a tree, and write "Come and get it!" on his chest.

His fingers were shaking. He tried to control them because he didn't want to have to do this twice.

"Done?" she said, eyeing him sharply, squinting through her smoke.

"Uh-huh."

"Okay . . . let's see . . . trying to be a boy again, that's why he prefers their company to mine. Is that good?"

Mike shrugged. "If that's what you want to say."

"If that's what I *want*?" She slammed a fist on the table. "Of course I don't *want* it, but it's the fucking truth, okay? I know him a hell of a lot better than you. I knew him when he could still admit he was a fuck-up, a regular asshole like everybody else. At least back then, acting like a jerk kid, he had a good excuse. He *was* a kid."

Mike shrank back into the seat. "I just meant, how do you want to say it?"

"I don't care how the fuck I say it. Just write it down, all right? How his boys don't worship him like he thinks they do. They're just getting what they can out of him, and there's nothing left for me. So I'm going now, Hawk, you bastard. Going for good. And I sincerely hope you're very fucking happy with all your little pals."

Mike nodded, writing as fast as he could, repeating after her: "—hope you're very happy—very *fucking* happy—with all your little pals."

"Damn right," she said. "Does that sound mad? Because I'm mad, and I want him to know it."

"It sounds pretty mad to me," Mike said. "Pretty *fucking* mad." He suppressed a giddy laugh, but she glared at him anyway.

"Give me that," she said, and snatched the pen and pad out of his hands. "That's enough—more than he deserves."

She scrawled her name at the bottom of the page, tore it off, shoved it at him. Maggie, he read. At least he knew her name now. "You're sticking around, right?"

"He said to."

"Give him that when he gets back."

"Muh—me?"

Maggie swung around on the bench and started pulling on a pair of boots. That done, she reached for her cigarettes, saw the pack was empty, crumpled it with a curse. She got up, bootheels loud on the floor of the trailer, slung a big leather purse over her shoulder, and headed for the door. Mike sat watching her, folding the note nervously.

"Bye," he said as she stepped out.

She glanced back briefly. "Yeah, right."

He watched her through the dusty window. She stood at the edge of the lot with her thumb out, hitching east. Within minutes, a car pulled over and let her in. Some surfer-looking guy—definitely not an egghead. Within minutes, he supposed, they'd be pulling over and having sex in the back seat.

Oh fucking well.

Mike opened the note and reread it a few times. Maybe he should rewrite it, he thought. Soften the blow. Make it easier on Hawk. Make it easier on *himself,* when Hawk read it!

Then he remembered Maggie, her constant bubbling anger, and tried to imagine what she would do to him if she found out. Now, instead of thoughts of seduction (which had dampened considerably since he'd seen her handwriting) he pictured her long red fingernails gouging his eyes out, her smoke-stained teeth biting off his nose.

Leave the note, he thought, smoothing it on the table. Stay out of this. Go home and wait for Hawk to call. Give him time to get over her.

Then he thought about his room, once his sanctuary, and the condition it was in. He remembered the hole in his wall. After that, he couldn't bring himself to move.

=21=

Hawk stood at Edgar's door, the sound of chimes fading inside the house for the third time. He went back down the path to the Jeep, shaking his head.

"No help there, huh?" Dusty said.

"I'll find it."

He raced to the end of Shoreview Road, parking where he had the night they stashed the grenades. He gave the bug-flecked chrome crucifix a burnishing swipe with his cuff before jumping the gate. It was too hot to move fast, too dry to talk. Hawk looked for landmarks along the dirt fire road.

Stoner's goofy grin popped into his mind. "Told the fucker to leave those things alone," he said suddenly.

"He never said nothing about them to me, Hawk. And it still don't make sense. The key . . ."

"Nothing makes sense anymore."

"Well, yeah . . ."

"The only ones who knew about that stash were Stoner, Edgar and me."

"Edgar was with that kid last night," Dusty said. "I dropped the two of them at his house around midnight."

"Edgar's part of this, I know it. He can't keep out of trouble."

"What about that other kid?"

"I'm not sure about him."

"He's in the shit, though, that's for sure. I just can't see Stoner trashing his place."

They tramped through cactus and sage and thistles; everything looked brittle and prickly. It was a different land by day. Down in the Greenbelt canyon a creek ran through green meadows dotted with grazing cows, but up here everything was rust-colored, wheat-colored, brown or dead. Foxtails worked their way into his socks, stinging his ankles with every step. He knew he was on the right track when they passed through a thistle field and came out at the top of a slippery sandstone slope. After sliding to the bottom, Hawk slowed to check the base of every bush they passed.

Before long, he found a rope twist covered in dust.

"Here it is." He knelt and grabbed the rope. In a sigh of dirt, Edgar's hidden hatch tilted up.

He fell back gagging, caught in a cloud of stench. The hatch banged shut.

He had smelled death before, but never so concentrated. Fresh death, on the road, blood and bowels, hosed away before it dried, so the place would never stink of anything more than burned rubber and spilled fuel. He'd smelled mortuary death, a dusty perfumed pressed-flower odor, no more offensive than a prim old woman dressed for church. But never anything like this, never so hot and rank and carrion, so personal.

The closest thing in his memory was a cow's carcass, found in the hills in midsummer when he was a boy. He had smelled it from a distance, and never went farther than necessary to take a long, fascinated look at bones and flesh blackened like fly-crusted jerky.

But this . . . this was like falling head-first into the carcass. Like swimming in it.

Dusty knelt in front of him. "Jesus, Hawk . . . did you see?"

He had seen enough before the hatch fell. He didn't want to think about it.

Dusty left and came back with a long stick of bamboo. Hawk

sat cross-legged, letting him work. Dusty hooked the thick, splintered end of the stave into the rope loop, and hauled up on it. The bamboo bent, the hatch groaned open. The second wave of smell was not quite as bad as the first—that would have been impossible. But what he saw now, as the hatch fell open, was worse than he'd imagined from his glimpse.

Stoner's head—and it had to be Stoner—was black, as if syrup had been poured all over his skull and left to coagulate. Beetles and ants had come to feed. His eyes were . . . boiling. His body was crushed into a corner, as if the stench had shouldered him aside on its way out of the pit.

"Gaaah," Dusty said, pinching his nose. "Stoner, dude. You poor fucking loser."

Don't put it off, Hawk told himself. Do it while you're still numb. It'll only get worse.

He got down on his knees and began to crawl slowly toward the hole.

"What're you doing, man?"

It wasn't so bad if he looked straight down, avoiding direct sight of Stoner. But why should he humor his weakness? Couldn't he face death? Wasn't exactly this confrontation at the core of everything he believed, everything he preached? They would all come to this sooner or later, deserving or not, by means peaceful or violent.

Fuck that, he thought. I'm close enough as it is. I don't have to look him in the face. That's not Death there, not some Gothic-lettered symbol. That's my friend. That's Stoner. Or it was.

At the edge of the hole, he lowered himself to his belly. Eyes narrowed, he thrust his head over the edge. From inches away, the seethe of insects was deafening; he breathed through his mouth but it really didn't help. He didn't want to puke here; it would have been sacrilege, defiling Stoner's grave. But he might not have a choice.

He pushed himself forward until he nearly lost his balance and toppled in. At that moment, without having to be asked, Dusty clamped his hands around Hawk's ankles. He wriggled farther over the edge, dangling until he had a view down the dark tunnel into the little chamber.

There was just enough light to see that the little cave was empty. Gouges in the dirt showed where the trunk had been dragged—but that told him nothing.

He tried to climb back up but couldn't get a grip. "Okay!" he choked. Dusty hauled him out by the ankles.

He scrambled away, gasping for air, and was satisfied to vomit several yards away from the hole. Willpower . . . Stoner's expression hung in his eyes, so he forced them open, looking down to see his shirtfront covered with dust and stickers. He beat the dust from his chest, started to pull out the foxtails and burrs. It was something to do while the burning in his throat subsided.

"Well?" Dusty said.

"The whole crate's gone," Hawk said.

"You sure?"

"You want to look for yourself?"

"Shit," Dusty said, looking philosophical. He had seen more death, and at closer range, than Hawk had. "I never exactly trusted Stoner with all them grenades, but at least I knew the dude. You gotta wonder what we're dealing with now."

Hawk gazed into the pit for a minute. He would have met Stoner's eyes for a farewell, if the insects had left him any to meet. In a fury he took hold of the hatch board and flipped it back into place.

"What're you doing?"

"Burying him."

Dusty started to say something, then shrugged. "Guess we better, for now. Don't want to tip off we were here."

"I don't want to tip off the police either. I want that fucker for myself."

"You think it's the same one who killed Craig?"

Hawk just stared at him. He got to his feet and started kicking dirt over the board to cover it again. The smell pervaded everything, but that might have been because it had saturated every cell in his nose. He knew he would smell it forever. Olfactory nerves went straight to the brain; they would make sure he never forgot what had become of Stoner. What became of them all.

"I want to say a few words," he said.

"Be my guest."

Hawk clasped his hands and looked down on the hidden grave. He had practiced for years to prepare himself for moments like this, and the words came in a rush. Improvisation around a core of grief; a litany that felt polished, rehearsed, even as he invented it.

"Ashes to ashes, dust to dust, and all that other bullshit. Why Stoner deserved this kind of death, I'll never know. He was just a boy, Lord, a wild boy grown way too big for his body. He had a boy's heart, a boy's head, a boy's appetites. He was always searching for the fastest bike, the loudest explosion, the biggest tits. Stoner was no thinker. He believed everything he could ever need would come from somewhere outside himself, and for some reason, Lord, you never showed him otherwise. You never saw fit to raise him up and make him a man. When I talked to Stoner about the spirit or the soul, I know all he pictured was a spook in a bedsheet. He looked grown-up, Lord, but I was never fooled. I think that was a stingy trick to play.

"He never saw it coming, did he, dear sweet Jesus?"

Hawk turned on his heel and walked away. Bootsteps came crunching after him as Dusty caught up.

"Fuckin' Stoner," he said. "Amen."

As they approached the fire road, going wide through bushes to avoid the thistle field, Dusty said, "So what're you gonna do about that kid?"

Hawk felt mild amazement. "Why is he my problem all of a sudden?"

Dusty shrugged. "I thought . . ."

"I don't even— I don't know anything about him. He's Edgar's friend, and Edgar's responsibility."

"You tell Edgar that?"

Hawk stopped, threw back his head, and screamed at the sky: a wordless curse—something the usual obscenities wouldn't cover.

As the sound died, he heard cracking noises in the brush, startled animals. Dusty stood tense, looking nervously around. "Thought I saw someone," he said. "Musta been a deer." They listened for a minute, but heard only the expected sounds of the Greenbelt. Hawk sighed, spying the road ahead of them, starting forward again.

"Why is it, every time some kid gets in trouble—why do they come running to me?"

"Hey, I hate to be the one to break the news, but you set yourself up for it, preacher-man."

Hawk kicked a rock from his path.

"The boys look up to you, Hawk. I mean, you can't hold yourself up like some kind of hero, then just pull out when things get rough."

"I wasn't planning on pulling out. I want this guy. I'm gonna get him."

"Good for you. But meanwhile, that kid. He has no idea what's going on, you know? I don't think him and Edgar go back very far, you know what I'm saying?"

Hawk silenced him with a gesture. "All right, you're right, shut up already. So what do you think I should do?"

"Shit, I don't know. He's gonna need protection. Someone to cover his ass. You could see he's scared—but maybe not scared enough. He don't exactly look tough, you know. You gonna let him go it alone against whoever did Stoner?"

"Lupe." Hawk spoke the name with certainty.

"Yeah, him. Looks that way. Sal's bro."

"Why do you think the kid would have to go up against him?"

"Hell, seems to me the dude left him a calling card. Sort of like, 'Sorry I missed you, I'll drop in later.' "

"You don't . . . not a word about Stoner, not to him anyway. I don't want him more scared than he already is."

Dusty shrugged. "Cool. It shouldn't matter if he never knows. We'll all of us fuckin' take the guy out, that Lupe fuck, we'll all do it and the kid'll never have to know how close he came."

"All who?"

"All your boys. The gang. Say Lupe's gonna come back for that kid; say he can't help himself, right? So let's stake out his house. Like we did Sal's, but do it right this time, real thorough. Work in shifts, surround the place. Get some boys on the hills below the house, some to watch the streets, a couple more to check the fire roads in case the freak pays his respects to Stoner. It could happen."

Hawk considered this for a long time, while they walked on. He'd thought he heard twigs breaking while Dusty spoke, but they were gone now; nothing louder than lizards scuttled. Finally, reluctantly, he nodded. "Okay, let's do it. I just wish Edgar was in on this. He knows these hills better than anyone."

They finally reached the gate at the end of the road and climbed over. Hawk got in behind the wheel, lost in thought until something jarred him back into the world.

"Jesus." He stiffened. "How did that happen?"

His crucifix was missing from the hood of the jeep. Nothing remained but a jagged chrome stump.

"Fucking vandals!" Hawk jumped out of the seat and danced around the front, pounding on the hood. He bent to look under the car, but the asphalt was bare.

"Jesus fucking Christ! This is sacrilege!"

"Well, whoever took that mother better not go wearing it around his neck," Dusty said. "Every cop in Bohemia knows that chrome cross on sight."

It was late when Hawk returned to the trailer. He had covered Bohemia Bay from one end to the other, grabbing his boys when he saw them, visiting their hangouts, working up a plan with Dusty. After arranging for a meeting in the morning, he had dropped Dusty at a bar and headed home. He needed time to heal and ready himself for the days ahead. He was feeling worn thin, all his mental padding rubbed away. He looked forward to seeing Maggie. Sometimes a few words with her was all it took to get his head on straight. Her kisses had restorative powers.

Jesus, he thought, I can't even tell her about Stoner yet. And I know she loved him in a way . . .

He tried to fight the growing feeling of isolation.

He was amazed to see Mike waiting for him as he pulled into the lot. He had figured the boy would've gone home long ago, but there he was, silhouetted in the open door of the trailer where Hawk had left him half a day earlier.

Jesus, the kid looked pathetic. He hoped Maggie had given him something to eat.

He got out of the jeep and trudged toward the trailer, wondering about how much of the plan he should reveal. He could share his methods, but not his motives. He was proud of the scheme he'd worked out with Dusty: a net of watchers waiting to catch the killer. It should make Mike feel secure. He had spent most of the day working for this kid's benefit. In an altruistic mood now, he didn't expect anything for his labors but the satisfaction of a job well done. The real payoff would be getting his hands on Lupe Diaz. He doubted the boy could appreciate everything Hawk was about to do for him, but what the hell. Kids.

The twitching shadows of giant crosses swept the sides of the trailer, moved by the headlights of passing traffic. Mike wavered in and out of view.

"Hey," Hawk said. "Thought you'd be gone by now."

"You said to wait."

"Oh, well." Hawk chuckled. "I didn't mean forever. Maggie take care of you?"

"Uh," the kid said, blocking the doorway. "Maggie . . ."

"What?"

Mike handed him a piece of paper, folded so many times that it looked like a piece of crumpled Kleenex.

"What's this?"

"I'm sorry," said the boy. "She made me write it."

=22=

Sal's front door flapped like a jabbering mouth. Visitors went in and out, in and out, all day and all night. Neighbors in any other suburban neighborhood would have suspected what was going on, but it hadn't escaped Lupe's notice—little did—that when cars parked in neighboring driveways, they belonged to realtors showing houses. Sal didn't have many neighbors to bother.

Some of the customers swaggered up to the door and knocked loudly, not caring what sort of attention they drew. Others stood there twitching and sneaking nervous glances from side to side, jumping at every car that passed. Barefoot hippies in tie-dye bell bottoms and floppy knit caps; suntanned skateboarders in bathing suits and dark glasses; older men, neatly groomed, professional. Very few women came around; those who did were mostly hippies in sandals, long skirts, no bra. Lupe sank back deeper in his blind when they appeared, fearing they might feel his eyes from across the street. Women had intuition.

Twice a day, the cops cruised past. The prowl car never slowed, and the men inside hardly glanced sideways at the house, even though the curb was often crammed with everything from beat-up VW buses to shiny sports cars.

Sal had them fooled, he supposed. He put on a convincing

front as an art studio. Every afternoon, the garage door opened and a handful of Sal's boys went to work, laying sixteen or twenty canvases in rows on the concrete floor. They went down the lines, working them in sequence, like assembly-line artists. They sprayed the canvases with black paint, then globbed on thick ropes and blobs of color which they swirled and spread with spatulas. These hideous works left the house as soon as they were dry, tucked under the arms of Sal's customers.

At other times of day, Sal gathered his boys in the back yard, leading them slowly, in unison, through the poses of tai chi. At first Lupe shifted his vantage to watch the exercises, but they were always the same and he soon stopped bothering. He was more concerned about the few—very few—intervals when the flow of customer traffic let up, the boys cleared out, and Sal was left alone in the house.

Lupe kept laborious track of comings and goings, tallying a guest list and a schedule in his head. Eventually, he verified the fact that there was one time each morning when Sal was guaranteed to be alone.

Precisely at ten o'clock, the front door opened. Whoever had spent the night would spill out of the house and climb into the van, leaving Sal alone. For one hour, from ten to eleven, no customer ever dropped by. Sal must have warned them not to disturb him, because they wandered in at every other hour. Not long after eleven, the van returned with groceries and art supplies. The boys were like house slaves, out on errands while the master attended to his private rituals.

It was now five minutes to ten.

The morning was hotter than he liked. It exaggerated his sense that everything could see him. He dreaded leaving the shade of his shelter. He could already feel the sun burning his back and shoulders, even through the branches. He kept checking the breeze for the faint whiff of charring. When it didn't come, he relaxed a bit. Then he heard voices.

Two boys came out of Sal's house. Lupe had met them on the afternoon when he confronted Sal. Randy and Marilyn, that was them. They got into the van and drove away. There was no one in sight, no one watching. Lupe made his way to the barbed-wire fence.

Halfway across the street, he paused, thinking he smelled burning. He looked back but saw only clear sky above the brown grass, nothing else, no smoke from a brush fire, no reason for the smell.

Unless it was coming from him.

He hurried across the street and hammered on Sal's door. He could feel his skin beginning to smoulder.

It took Sal forever to answer the door. When he did, his pupils were huge. Sal had closed all the shades and turned off the lights. A candle flickered in the shadows. The sight made Lupe's spirits rise. Lupe had done a lot by candlelight.

"Guadalupe," Sal said. It sounded like a formal greeting.

Lupe pushed past his brother, trying not to show his relief at entering the dark house.

"What are you doing here?"

"You don't look very glad to see me. Is this a bad time?"

In the living room, a cushion rested in the center of the floor. A votive candle burned on a low table before it.

Sal said, "This is when I meditate."

He closed the door soundlessly. Lupe relaxed as it grew nice and dark again. Cavey. Sal followed him into the living room, looking remarkably at ease. Lupe had expected some surprise or tension.

"You have nerve coming around here, Lupe," Sal said.

"Why's that?"

Sal picked up a lit stick of incense that sat on the table, fuming. He waved it in the air between them as if dispelling a bad odor.

"I think you know."

"I came to say good-bye, that's all."

"I thought you were long gone. I mean, you show up, you disappear, you seem to show up again, but nobody's sure it's you. Now you're here to say good-bye? Why bother? I guess

I'm not part of your life, Lupe. Okay. I offered my love when you first arrived—and what did you do? I don't know what you did. I don't *want* to know. You're trouble, that's all. You could have gone off without bothering me again."

"That'd make you happy, wouldn't it?"

"I'd be happiest if you weren't the kind who needed to run. But since you are, I admit that I'll be happier knowing you're gone. I don't like knowing you're around my boys. Not after . . . not after that kid at the beach. If it's true, what I think."

"You always were trying to get rid of me," Lupe said. "Ditching me."

"Is that what you think?"

"I was looking for you when it happened, Sal. I was scared and I went out looking. You stirred everything up and left me in it."

"When *it* happened," Sal repeated softly. "You hold that against me? You think I—"

"I went looking for you, man. I looked everywhere, without the faintest idea how big everything was. You never told me how lost I could get."

"You think I don't wish I could have helped you—healed you somehow?"

"Don't you worry about that. I did my own healing."

Sal looked doubtful. "Yeah? I thought maybe you had, when I saw you at the Rock Lobster with our friend Raymond. I thought at first maybe you were like me, and had come to peace with yourself. But I don't think so anymore. You were only using him, weren't you? In a fucked-up, cynical way."

"Don't you dare judge me, not when it was your responsibility . . ."

"I'm sorry, Lupe, but you have to get past that. You're not a kid anymore."

"No?" Lupe said. "Then what am I?"

Sal shut his eyes in exasperation. He might be strong from his tai chi, but the muscles of his belly were soft where the knife went up inside him.

Lupe turned the blade as if twisting a key in a lock, and Sal's life rushed out and down his arm. His brother fell over gasping, clutching his navel. The cupped hands filled with blood but it kept coming, overflowing.

"Good-bye," Lupe said, alone now in the room.

How many times had he dreamed he was the last man on Earth? At odd moments, people would shift and turn to smoke around him; only he was real. All the things that hurt him seemed phony now. They were like devils that came from the back of his head, a game he played with himself, as if his mind were a magnifying glass held up to the sun, which made little things big and brought the hot smell of smoke out of his flesh to prove to him that he was alive.

Sal's blood drew Lupe's boys instantly. They didn't mind candlelight either. The nine of them gathered in the dark, hovering over Sal, looking to Lupe for guidance.

"Do what you want with him," he told them. "No initiation today. Take him far from here. I want him to hurt. Forever. Like I hurt. He doesn't deserve to be with us."

Sal still moved feebly, stubborn. Lupe crouched in front of him.

"Come on," he said, looking straight into Sal's face. "Get out of there."

Sal's eyes congealed.

A tenth shadow entered the room.

Lupe moved back from the body, giving Sal's ghost a place to stand. The faces of corpse and ghost looked equally confused.

Sal didn't speak. The dead can't talk. But he took one step toward Lupe and the gang closed in, blocking his path, forming a circle around him.

The Cherokee shoved Sal's ghost soundlessly into the arms of the Musician, who caught and thrust him away again, toward the Pump Jockey, who grinned spitefully and shoved him at the Marine, who whirled him around toward the gray-toothed Junkie. Sal went from one to the other, shoved with increasing violence. He soon stopped casting dizzy, pleading looks at Lupe. It took all his ebbing strength to hold himself together.

"Get rid of him," Lupe whispered.

The nine became a blurred cage of teeth and eyes and moving hands, with something like a frightened animal trapped inside. Sal didn't much resemble his brother anymore. He was hardly even a man: more like a fly buzzing between screen and windowpane.

They glided through the living room. Miguel leaped ahead to beckon and urge them on. Perspectives changed, the world warping around them. Blood spattered the Marine's fists and teeth; the Hopi threw back his head and howled silently. They kept on toward the walls, as if they might pass through them. Only then did Lupe see the window there, opening into a night city of ragged jet-black towers, a blue-black sky of weird blotches. Streaks and dabs of white on the buildings suggested broken windows; they cast a meager light on canyon streets between cliff-tall spires. It looked like a nightmare, the last place on earth anyone would voluntarily go, but the last bit of Sal dodged toward it, leaping up and away from Lupe's boys. A gust blew out of the painting, fanning the dying spark of Sal's ghost-light. Lupe smelled oil and asphalt, borne on the wind from the dark streets. A door opened in one of the buildings, framed by flickering light from a dim fluorescent bulb. Sal darted for it and slipped inside, slightly ahead of the boys. Then the door slammed shut, leaving them thrashing and snarling.

Abruptly the scene was only a painting again, a crude and lurid cityscape hanging flat on the wall of the drab room where Lupe stood alone with Sal's equally mundane husk.

He cursed at the canvas. After all this time, all his planning, Sal had gotten away.

His boys spun idly around him, waiting for further instructions. In frustration, Lupe pulled the knife out of Sal and slashed the painting till it hung in tatters from the frame. He hoped that Sal was still in it somewhere, cut to ribbons.

After that, he felt a little better. He had to be realistic and content himself with practical things. He had learned a hard lesson. He would be more careful next time; he would cut off all possible escape routes.

By the clock on the wall, it was not even ten-fifteen. He had plenty of time before the van returned. But there wasn't much left to do.

He grabbed the body by the hair and threw it facedown in the hallway, half on matted shag carpet, half on blood-slippery linoleum. He folded up his knife, stowed it in his pocket, and took out the other thing he'd brought along.

"Get his pants," said a distant voice, somewhere deep inside him.

=23=

Someone was watching the house. Ryan James was convinced of it. Mike and Edgar had laughed at him the night of the burglary, but he'd been right then—and he was absolutely, positively . . . well . . . *almost* sure of it now. He hadn't seen anyone moving down there today, but as it got darker, he became less sure of what he was or wasn't seeing.

For a couple of days—especially in the evenings—he'd seen movement in the gulley behind the house, creeps in the bushes. He couldn't tell if it was one person moving around a lot, or a few people hiding out in different places. Mike had looked upset and said he was crazy when he mentioned it.

It was probably kids. Ryan himself used to wander in the canyon, following trails through the brush. There were plenty of places you could hide where dense branches formed canopies and caves. But not now . . . nothing would lure him out now. The sliding glass door on his balcony stayed locked. Sure, his deck was on the second floor, but he'd scaled it himself and knew it wasn't hard.

Jack had installed security bolts everywhere. He was talking about putting in an alarm system, but that was a big project and might never happen. Ryan wouldn't mind if it did. What scared him most was the door near his bed, which opened out under the house, by the hot tub. It had a deadbolt and a spyhole in it, but Ryan couldn't help imagining someone standing right outside, out of the spyhole's view, listening to every sound he made. That was the first door in need of an alarm.

It was safe for the night, at least. Jack was out there, firing up the tub. Leonard and Davis, the homos next door, were throwing a party tonight, so Jack had offered use of the tub. There'd be a crowd in the way of anyone who tried to come through that door.

While Ryan was looking down into the gloomy canyon, he saw the door open behind him, reflected in the sliding glass. Jack walked in, drying his hands. The tub rumbled in the background.

"Whatcha doing, champ?"

"Watching. In case he comes back."

"Hey, it'll never happen." Jack tousled his hair. "Vandals like that are kids, probably no older than you or Mike, hormones going haywire. You know about hormones."

Ryan grinned and pushed Jack's hand away. "No . . ."

"It wasn't planned, Rye. It was an impulse thing, nothing personal, break in and wreck stuff up. It's not so unusual. I mean, I'm sure you've done a little vandalizing, right?"

"No way," Ryan said, indignant, thinking simultaneously of several instances of what an adult might call "vandalism," but which had seemed to him at the time like just plain "fun." He saw them differently now.

"Now, come on. I remember when I was about fifteen in Pennsylvania, in the winter we used to go out to the summer houses at this lake near us. We'd, you know, jimmy a window, climb in, throw parties, eat canned food . . . sometimes even mess the place up a bit. Nothing drastic, not like this, but . . . I can see how it might happen. Maybe this is my karma coming back at me. I wrecked somebody's place when I was a kid, now my house gets wrecked. Cosmic, huh?"

Ryan shrugged, still unconvinced.

"Rest easy," Jack said, than tramped away up the stairs.

Ryan scanned the room, even more depressed now that he had begun to consider his own behavior. Only a few of the mirrored tiles remained on the walls; the broken ones had been pulled down, leaving bare, unpainted patches lumpy with tile adhesive. Jack had patched the larger gouges here and there, but nothing was repainted yet. Sports posters covered the worst spots. Once it had been clean and white and bright in here, everything gleaming like the beach. That was how Ryan liked it. Now it all looked grubby and sad.

The head had even been snapped off his soccer trophy. Who would do that? Maybe somebody from the AYSO league, someone on an enemy team? What about that one goalie, the kid who'd gotten so mad when Ryan kicked the ball in his crotch? But how would he get here? Did vandals' mothers drive them to the places they wanted to wreck, wait in the street, then make a speedy getaway before the cops showed up?

He felt like killing whoever had done it. Hearing that it was probably a kid made him feel much better. A grown man might be too strong; Ryan would probably back down. But with a kid it was different. He'd choke him to death, or kick his face in with his soccer cleats!

It was getting too dark to see the canyon. Suddenly he realized that standing at the glass with the lights on, he was totally visible to whoever might be watching. He jumped back and lowered the silver metal Levolors.

So what was he going to do? Dirk was out of town with his parents. He'd been bragging they would leave him home all weekend and he would throw a kegger for his friends, but that was a typical Dirk lie. He could read: He was halfway through *Super Cops,* which wasn't like the boring books they assigned in school. But he didn't think he could concentrate on that. He had to be in the mood. *Night of the Living Dead* was on TV later; that was a possibility.

Maybe . . . he blushed excitedly at a thought. Maybe Mike would go out tonight, and he could check out his stash of porno magazines. Mike didn't know Ryan knew about them. The other night, when he was following the police around the house, one of the cops had rummaged through Mike's desk drawers and uncovered them. The cop had pretended not to see them, though his smirk said he had.

"Ryan?" his mother called. He went to the foot of the stairs and looked up at her, hoping she couldn't read his face. She was brushing her hair, not even looking at him directly.

"We're going next door to the party for a while. Do you need anything before we go?"

"No."

"There's ice cream in the freezer."

He'd already eaten half of it, but didn't say so.

"Did you have plans for tonight?"

He shrugged. "Dirk's out of town. I guess I'll watch TV."

"I asked Mike to keep an eye on things, but we're only next door if you need us."

"Okay," he said. She blew him a kiss and walked back into her room.

Shit, he thought. Mike *would* have to stay home on the one night he might have had the house to himself.

A steady thudding started up, pounding through the walls from next door. Disco music, like a heartbeat, boom-boom-boom. Chattering voices grew louder in the space between the houses. He checked the peephole in his back door and saw nothing but the bubbling tub.

Quietly he undid the deadbolt and opened the door a crack, peering around the edge of the frame to see who was out there. Candles in colored glass globes were set on the steps that ran down the hillside between the two houses. In the wavering light, he could see a few couples sitting on the steps or standing in the little sculpted patio garden under the neighboring house. They were all men, of course.

The neighbors, Leonard and Davis, were nice enough guys, Ryan had to admit. As the only homos he knew personally, he found it hard to hate them the way he was supposed to. They'd hired him to carry rolls of sod down the stairs to their lower garden last weekend, and they never flirted with him or anything. They were pretty regular, really. He might not have known they were fags at all if his mother hadn't told him. They'd both been married and Davis even had kids.

Most of their friends, though, were more obvious. Listening to the fruity voices rising and falling, the high-pitched laughter, the musical way some of them talked, he thought they sounded like they were making fun of themselves, mocking all the jokes he and his friends cracked about fags. He watched until he saw two men press together in the shadows. Kissing! At that, he pulled back into the room, locking the door as if the danger level had just shot up into the red.

Stifling laughter, he ran upstairs. Jack and Mom were already gone. He knocked on Mike's door and went in.

His brother was lying on the bed, a sketch pad propped on his knees. He dropped the pad and Ryan saw it was blank.

"What do *you* want?"

"Did you see next door?"

"What about it?"

"Thay there, thweety . . . the boyth are having a pah-tee."

"Why are you so interested?" Mike said.

"I'm not—not at all. But they're all over out there! It's hard to ignore."

Mike picked up his sketch pad again. "I've managed so far."

"What are you drawing?" Ryan took a step closer, only one, since he hadn't actually been invited into the room. Mike didn't seem to mind.

"I'm not. I'm doing an experiment."

"More of that ESP stuff you and Edgar were doing?"

Mike nodded. "I was trying . . . to reach him."

"Reach him? How?"

"It's stupid. I'm trying to imagine I can see what he sees. I thought that would show me where he is."

"And . . . ?"

Mike pushed the blank pad toward him. "See for yourself. It's not working."

"You think he ran away?" Ryan said.

"Why would he?"

"I heard the police were looking for him."

Mike's face twisted up.

"You don't think Edgar . . . ?"

Mike jumped off the bed. "Don't be an idiot. I was with him that night, while it was happening."

"That's not what you told the cops."

"Because, I told you, Edgar was doing drugs. I couldn't tell them that, could I?"

"No . . . Did you do any?"

"No!" Mike looked both angry and scared. "He asked me to watch him, in case he had a bad trip or something."

"Wow . . . what was it? Heroin?"

"It was marijuana."

"Oh. Dirk did that once, he told me. He said he could get some more and we could try it. He can get all kinds of stuff."

Mike stared at him steadily. "I wouldn't."

"Why?"

"Because of what happened to Edgar."

"What happened to him?"

"I don't know. He never got home, that's what. He ran off and that's the last I saw of him."

Ryan swallowed—a painful gulp. "Man . . ."

"Right."

"I wish I knew who broke in. Wouldn't you like to kill them?"

"Yeah."

Ryan walked over to the wall and stared at the nasty, crumbling hole. On an impulse, he stuck his hand into it.

"Don't do that!" Mike grabbed his wrist violently and yanked it out.

"Ow!" Ryan pulled his hand free and swung it at Mike, who flinched and ducked, barely avoiding the blow.

"Watch who you're messing with!" Ryan said.

"You watch out, I'm older than you."

"Older and weaker!"

Mike shoved him backward, trying to force him out of the room. Ryan fought to keep his place. They grunted and groaned, straining to overpower each other. Ryan usually won fairly quickly in contests of strength, but Mike must have been desperate because somehow he managed to push Ryan all the way to the door and out into the hall, which almost never happened. Usually he just fell down kicking and gave up. Ryan grabbed the door frame and clung with all his might until Mike shoved hard one more time, catching him off guard. He flew so far that he hit the top step and would have gone backward down the stairs if he hadn't caught hold of the stair rail.

Ryan, gasping for breath, saw Mike's face hanging over him, white with fear. "Are you okay?"

It took him a moment to answer, to pull himself up. "Yeah."

"Jesus. I'm sorry."

Ryan got to his feet. "I'm okay."

"You could have broken your neck. You almost went down the stairs!"

Ryan looked down. He had never quite seen the stairs in such a light before. It was hard to imagine falling and injuring himself in such a way, but now that Mike had planted the idea in his head, he couldn't get rid of it. He kept seeing himself slamming hard against the wall at the bottom, lying there limp with his eyes rolled up in his head and blood trickling from his mouth.

Dead, he thought. I could be dead right now.

Then he thought, *No way!*

Backing away from Mike, he pretended to trip on the stairs. While holding tight to the rail, he windmilled one of his arms and let out a yell. Mike's panicked expression made him laugh. He bounded down the stairs, half expecting his brother to pursue him.

When he hit the floor, he heard a man's voice speaking outside the door: "It was murder!"

Upstairs, Mike's door slammed shut. He had gone back into his lair.

Ryan put his eyes to the spyhole and saw two men in the tub, arms spread out along the rim, heads lolling back. A bottle of champagne and three glasses rested on a shelf near the edge. A third man, naked and covered all over with curly hair, gasped as he lowered himself gingerly into the steaming water, moaning as the bubbles came up to his neck. He went all the way under for a moment, then burst to the surface, shaking water from his hair, wiping his eyes.

"So you heard about Sal?" he said. His voice, a growl as deep and loud as a radio announcer's, carried over the rumble of the tub.

"I still can't believe it," said one of the other two. "He was doing so much good for our community."

The third man worked his finger in an ear, as if to drain it. "The thing that gets me is, you know the papers won't mention any of the details."

"Denny's covering it for *The Advocate,*" said the second man. "You can bet the truth'll come out there."

"Preaching to the converted. John Q. Public won't know it was pure homophobia."

"He wouldn't care anyway. He'd applaud!"

"But the details are so grisly. I should think the newspapers would eat them up. Besides, there's the whole drug-dealing angle."

"Right, the drugs," said the deep-voiced man. "As if that was the only thing he did. Forget about his community service, the help he gave to those confused kids, the runaway shelters he funded. The drugs are a tragedy because they cloud the truth. They're convenient propaganda already in place for the papers to paint him as a villain."

"And once the *cops* figure out that Sal was a dealer, not to mention gay, they won't even bother with an investigation."

"Yeah, they'll conveniently forget he had a steel crucifix shoved up his ass. As if it were an insignificant detail."

"The only thing that could have made it plainer would be if the cross had been burning."

The name Sal finally called up a picture. Wasn't Sal the Kung Fu Faggot, the guy who drove the black van that all Ryan's friends knew to avoid? It had to be. Could there be another queer Sal in Bohemia Bay?

"Well, we can't expect miracles from the Bohemia police. This'll never turn into a civil rights test case. They caught the bastard who did it, and that really is the main thing right now."

"I hear Randy found him."

"Randy? Oh my god, that poor kid!"

"Yes. He told Kent he sent the cops straight to the killer. He knew who did it, that biker-preacher from the canyon. He'd been making threats . . ."

"I always knew there was something dangerous about him."

"Tell me about it. Some of his boys came after me once on the beach below the Lobster. They almost killed me."

"I remember. And what did the cops do about it?"

"Absolutely nothing."

"That's what I'm afraid of now."

"Well, the evidence is undeniable, from what Randy said. Strong enough to keep him in jail for a while, anyway."

"I hope he rots there."

"Poor Sal. Do you know—has anyone heard if he . . . you know?"

"If he still had his balls?"

"Oh, Lord, please don't!"

"Isn't that what everyone's wondering? It has to be the same guy, doesn't it? That other kid, the one they found in the Central Beach tunnel, wasn't he one of those gang boys?"

"So?"

"Don't you see the connection? This preacher character must be seriously repressed, surrounding himself with boys. Sound a little familiar? Maybe there was something between him and that boy, something he couldn't handle. Maybe Sal confronted him on it."

"Well I haven't heard a thing about the state of Sal Diaz's

testicles, and I hope I never do. It's the whereabouts of the champagne I'm concerned about . . ."

Ryan raced for the stairs, taking them three at a time, and launched himself at Mike's door. He threw it open without knocking this time, and surprised Mike at his desk, the drawer pulled half open, a flash of pink briefly glimpsed before his brother slammed the drawer shut.

Mike rose up, enraged. "What do you want? I told you to knock!"

"Whoa, wait till you hear!" Ryan was so excited he didn't even care about the magazines. "They caught the guy who killed Craig Frost!"

"What?" Mike's face flooded with color. His eyes seemed to fill the lenses of his glasses.

"I just heard them talking about it at the party."

"What did they say?"

"He killed somebody else. You know Sal, the fag up the hill, with the black van?"

"Yeah?" Mike said slowly.

"The karate guy?"

"I know who you mean!"

"Well, he's dead, and the same guy did it, but this time the police caught him. He stuck a cross up—a cross up Sal's butt!"

Mike stared at Ryan as if he were insane.

"Swear to God! The guy's in jail. Can you believe it? A murder two blocks away!"

Mike sat down hard on his bed. His whole body trembled and he let out a huge sigh. "Man," he said, shaking his head. "I can't believe it. . . ."

"Isn't it cool?"

"Yeah . . . yeah, really cool." Mike began to laugh. "They really caught him? You're sure?"

"Everybody says so."

"They know who it was?"

Ryan shrugged. "It'll be in the papers. Wait'll I tell Dirk!"

Suddenly the clock radio caught his eye. "Hey, *Night of the Living Dead* is starting. You gonna come watch?"

Mike shook his head and lay back on the bed. "I'm going to draw, I think. Suddenly I feel inspired."

Ryan suppressed a comment about the magazines. If he let on he'd seen them, Mike might make them harder to find. He closed the door behind him, then went upstairs to the kitchen. With a half-gallon drum of ice cream in one hand and a spoon in the other, he descended to the TV room and threw himself into a beanbag chair before the set. Seymour, the mysterious gravel-voiced old joker in a cape and black gaucho hat, introduced the movie with a bunch of wisecracks. Ryan methodically stirred his ice cream into sludge, the way he liked it.

By the second commercial break, he had finished the tub. He walked back up the three flights to the kitchen and tossed the empty carton in the trash. The party next door was still going strong; he could hear his mother's laughter above the thumping of the music.

The massive infusion of milk and sugar had made him logy. Yawning, he headed for the stairs again, still seeing how easy it would be to trip and fall two flights from up here—fall to his death. Broken neck, bloody mouth . . . the movie was making him nervous.

As he grasped the stair rail, extra cautious, he heard a sound at the front door, and stopped.

There was a grating noise. The knob rattled.

It must be Jack, drunk and fumbling with his keys.

Ryan reached out and opened the door.

There stood a boy, probably older than Ryan though he couldn't be sure. Maybe Mike's age.

Seeing Ryan, he stiffened and jerked his fist back.

"Hi," he said, in a small voice that made Ryan wonder if maybe he was younger than he looked. "I was just about to ring the bell. Is Mike home?"

Ryan nodded anxiously. The movie would be starting any second now and he'd already been too long. He wasn't about to let one of his brother's dorky friends make him miss any.

"Come in," he said. "Just hurry!"

=24=

SEASCAPE, WITH DEAD STEPFATHER

Being:
A Comedy,
Although nightmarish to its participants
(And particularly its Narrator,
One Rupert Giles of Balmy Beach, California;
Age 15)

152 (one hundred and fifty-two) stairs lead down a sheer cliff to the Naked Beach. How many times hath my stepfather Wally tumbled the whole flight, to land smashed and bleeding at the sandy bottom, only to summon his last ergs for a crawl to the top, so that I may push him down yet again? "A myriad," I am happy to report.

Ancient steps they are, all of crumbling gravel embedded in a matrix of sandstone and coarse cement like that which encoffins Wally's feet in my merriest dreams, when he sinks beneath the kelp beds, gulping with diminishing cause at the poison-finned sculpin and circling lurid garibaldi. "¡O bony day-Glo orange beautiful yet inedible STATE FISH OF CALIFORNIA!" the killing of which is a fear-ridden pleasure akin to that derived from ripping tags off mattresses one has no intention of purchasing; though within each garibaldi ("Not to mention Wally," he said, mentioning him) are gobbets of green, brown and liver-colored goo, so much nastier than mattress stuffing. God forbid we should commit such icthycide beneath the Balmy Beach cliffs where game wardens and rangers daily sit their unpredictable vigils, binoculars trained on us, always engaged in violation of some state code or other--mussel murder mayhem, for instance. As rewarding as garibaldi (or Wally) assassination, though lacking the thrill of outright illegality, our former mad hunts for mussel pearls entailed the wholesale slaughter of live mussels by the score. You should have seen them, helpless mollusks, torn in weedy clumps from searocks bared by outrushing waves, then smashed to pieces in small tidal pools until the miniature cisterns were creamy with soft orange intestinal matter, a filter-feeder's lunch, now sustenance for lucky crabs and anemones; for which savageries we were rewarded with a (very) occasional tarnished nacreous gray pebble the size of several sand grains glued together, and about as valuable. I once pried open a mussel and ate it, liberally smothered in cafeteria taco sauce squirted from a plastic packet, crunching a pearl between my teeth so hard it chipped a filling. "Just revenge for earlier massacres!" piped a voice from the mussel beds. So I crushed them all, gathering up their shattered shells for that ultimate day of glory when I shall embed them individually in Wally's skin and force him to roll in a tub of kosher salt liberally mixed with rusty jacks and broken microscope slides, symbolic ruins of my innocent childhood, from which Wally has wrenched me forever. (I feel I should also mention, not as an aside but for completeness' sake, that hermit crabs were often pulled from their shells and fed to the friendly (else why always waving?) anemones, which fattened on our attentions, benefiting so greatly from human association that they still show affection and kiss my toes stickily when I visit tidal pools. So don't pity the mussel alone. Personally, I feel crabs were somehow the most pathetic of our victims, for they had popping eyes and useless claws that gnashed futilely and little guts that dripped all over everything when we'd been too rough in extracting them from their shells, as, sadly, we usually were. Perhaps it is because of crabs that we left

●ff pestering crustaceans and turned ●ur attenti●n t● fulltime harassment ●f the nude, s●metimes badly sunburnt bathers, wh● were mature humans and theref●re able t● defend themselves, m●re ●r less.)

But I must speak n●w, with gr●wing excitement (can y●u n●t hear the quaver in my v●ice), ●f Wally, _Wally,_ wh● lies festering in the sun ●n a black terrycl●th shr●ud, magg●ts w●rming in his gut and cringing with a sizzling s●und each time he gulps fr●m a tankard ●f lemon-scented Pepsi. P●●r magg●ts! Hearing my typewriter, Wally l●●ks up fr●m his Har●ld R●bbins n●vel, emitting a fart which scarcely relieves the purulent swelling ●f his abd●men, gase●us result ●f his well-deserved decay. S●●n I will take this l●ng, p●inted instrument especially designed f●r cleaning black c●tt●n lint fr●m the inky small "●" ●f my typewriter (currently dedicated t● a m●re imp●rtant task), ●r the sharp edge ●f ●ne ●f my mussel shards (d●es that have the same res●nance?), and prick him. Or perhaps the feeding insects, with their sharpened m●uth-saws, will d● the w●rk, letting him burst expl●sively, spattering the ●ther sunbathers with the bypr●ducts of Wallyesque r●t, all●wing me finally, and in g●●d c●nscience, t● clean these keys . . .

Mike had already roughly sketched Wally's corpse half buried in sand at the base of the crumbling flight of stairs. You could actually count all 152 steps. He began to work at the splintered bones poking out of Wally's skin. Maggots were next. He tried not to make "Wally" look too much like Walter—in case Walter happened to see the illustration when he sent it to Scott.

Ryan's news had flooded him with freed energy. He had been ruled by fear for longer than he'd realized. And fear had locked his thoughts up tight, put clamps on his imagination, so that he was afraid to dream, afraid to turn his mind loose for fear of where it might wander. When he narrowed his eyes, he could still almost see the whorls of his acid trip, shadows tipped with fangs, but such moments were fading. A wave of unreality had covered his life, and as it slipped away, it had threatened to leave him in a world far worse than the one he'd inhabited before the trip. For days there had been room for only one terrible thought in his head:

He was bait.

Since Hawk had seen the hand grenade, everything had changed. Suddenly Mike was the center of the One-Way Gang's attention. At first he wasn't sure what had made him so important, but gradually he'd realized that he was only a means to an end. Hawk's real goal was Lupe; and Mike was just a convenient way of luring him in.

Whenever Mike thought about it, the plan infuriated him. Why should he be the bait? Why couldn't someone else sit and wait for the psycho to pay them a visit?

He'd even wondered if the whole plan weren't Hawk's revenge on him for helping Maggie write that letter . . .

But now all that was over. He didn't have to question anyone's motives. Lupe was in jail. His life was his own again. He could say goodbye to Hawk and Dusty and Stoner, to Kurtis Tyre and Mad-Dog Murphy and Howard Lean. He could even say so long to Edgar, whenever he showed his face again, though Mike had a feeling Edgar was on the road, maybe hitching in Mexico by now. Somewhere the Bohemia cops wouldn't follow.

All the subconscious power he'd wasted on worry, diverted to thoughts of Lupe and his own survival, now came rushing back free and clear. It was as if a lever had been thrown, switching his mind to full power. He could think of no better use for the fresh energy than drawing. He didn't need to fish for ideas, either. Dozens of them had been wriggling morbidly away in the back of his head, sprung from the text of Scott's novel. So he had pulled out the dogeared manuscript, refreshed himself with the first few pages, then set to work.

The sound of footsteps on the landing above didn't distract him for more than a second, nor did the murmur of voices. It was one of Ryan's friends, or someone from the party next door.

The next thing he knew, the footsteps were right over his head, as he worked at the desk in the closet. He found himself hesitating, listening as they paused on the landing outside his door.

Someone knocked, and Ryan peered in. "Hey, a friend of yours is here."

It must not be Edgar or he would have said so. Puzzled, Mike put the pencil down and went to the door.

The hall was dark. He didn't recognize the kid at Ryan's shoulder, even when he stepped toward the light.

"I don't—"

A silver gleam stopped the words in his throat. The boy held one hand up, offering the key. "I thought you might want this."

Mike abruptly grasped that everything he believed was based not on truth, but on desire; his world was a fake. One moment, believing one thing about this world, he'd been frigid with terror; the next moment, believing something far more insubstantial, he'd felt relaxed and vigorous. How was he supposed to feel now?

Ryan was already halfway down the stairs, leaving them alone. He called back, "Show's just getting good, I gotta hurry!"

Mike stood facing the stranger. The boy? Lupe.

He took a step back before the other stepped forward. Lupe came into the room, holding the key ahead of him. He brushed the door, closing it quietly behind him.

"You can have it back," he said.

In the brighter light, among the painted hills, Mike could only stare. Not a boy after all, it seemed. Not quite a man either. It was hard to be sure about anything. The sharp, unpleasant smell of sage flowers filled the room—it was stronger than the animal smell of sweat. Lupe's face was round and smooth, full-cheeked, dark Spanish eyes set in nut-brown skin, swept by dark oily hair that looked freshly combed. He had the body of a pioneer—one who had hiked ten thousand miles, cut down sequoias in the North woods, broken boulders with his hands. But it just didn't go with that babyish face. The voice was especially wrong.

"Go on," he said, soft and fluting. "Take it."

Mike reached out automatically, desperate to regain the stupid key that had started all this. As his fingers closed on the tiny bit of metal, he felt much more than that pressed into his hand. Lupe grabbed his wrist, seized it tightly, and forced his fingers closed around something he couldn't see, but which he knew by feel.

It hadn't been that long, after all, since he'd held the other hand grenade.

He managed to choke back words, knowing they would only get him into trouble and solve nothing now.

Lupe worked quickly. He had a length of string, thick scratchy jute, which he wound around and around Mike's hand and the grenade, binding them together. Mike waited like a spectator to see what would happen next.

"Okay," Lupe said, apparently finished. Without releasing Mike's wrist, he turned the hand palm-upward, as if showing off his workmanship. He had left the trigger free. Now he curled Mike's fingers around it, forcing them down tight.

"Don't let go," he said, as he pulled out the pin. "You see how I tied it? You can't throw it away now. And you can't untie it without letting go, not one-handed anyway, not till I put the pin back in."

"Please . . ."

"You'll be fine." He held up the pin, grinning. "I'll give this back, too, when we're in a better place."

"What—what did I ever—" Mike's voice rose to a high-pitched shriek until Lupe clamped a hand over his mouth and put the pin to his lips.

"*Shhh.* You don't want to go making a lot of noise."

Mike backed toward the window. Lupe didn't stop him. The key lay on the floor between them. The disco music thudded steadily, but he could hardly hear it over his heartbeat. For an instant his mother's laughter pierced the spell. He looked down at his hand. It was white as marble, and shaking. If he relaxed his grip, the room would vanish; a huge hole would appear as if by magic. This house, and probably those on either side, would be destroyed. His mother, Jack, Ryan downstairs—how many would die in addition to himself? All for the sake of killing Lupe.

Lupe grinned at him, tossing his head toward the moon wall. "I like this a lot. You did it?"

Mike tried to shake his head. It came out as more of a spasm.

Lupe looked disappointed. "No? But you're an artist, right?"

Mike choked. "S-sometimes."

"Only sometimes? You mean you can turn it on and off?" He shook his head. "I wish I could do that."

Why isn't he in jail? Mike thought, oblivious to Lupe's words, remembering suddenly the news Ryan had brought, which he had relied on. Craig Frost's killer . . . and now Sal's, too. The cops were supposed to have him, but here he was.

Who was in jail, then? Who had really killed Craig and Sal?

Lupe spun the pin on his fingertip to catch Mike's eyes.

"I'd like to stay longer, but I don't want you thinking you can, you know . . . get away in there."

He was looking at the painted hills. *Get away how?* Mike wondered.

Lupe started toward the door, then turned back abruptly, as if remembering Mike. He beckoned with the pin.

"Come on. You don't want this getting away from you."

Mike shook his head.

"Put on a jacket, something with pockets. It's chilly. Fall's on the way."

Mike grabbed a sweatshirt. It was hard pulling it on one-handed; his swollen fist barely squeezed through the cuff. Lupe offered no help. His eyes were on the painted moon the whole time.

Lupe went behind him up the stairs and out onto the front porch. Men from the party were climbing into a car next door.

"Put your hand in your pocket," Lupe said.

He could hardly move his arm; the elbow had locked up. His entire hand was numb. He couldn't feel his fingers. What if they started opening?

They waited until the car pulled away, splashing them with light, then Lupe nudged him across the carport and into the street.

"Which way?" he asked.

"Up."

Lupe walked beside him, up the hill and across the vacant lot where he had hid his first night in Shangri-La. Dry grass crackled around their legs, his shoes and cuffs caught in stickers. On either side, lights glowed in shaded windows, but no one looked out to see them pass. It had been the same on the night this all began: people safe in their homes, none knowing what went on outside.

In the middle of the lot, he wondered if Hawk's boys were out here. Maybe Hawk himself was hiding in the shadows. But why would they, when everyone thought Lupe was in jail? It didn't make sense. Who had they locked up for the murder of Sal Diaz, if not Lupe? Who else could have been mistaken for him?

It came to him then.

A cross, Ryan had said. A cross up the butt.

The cross was Hawk's thing. If the cops found a cross on Sal's body, Hawk would be their first suspect. Stories would come out about the night with the key and the shotgun, the avocado smear, and who knew what else?

Hawk was in jail.

He felt certain of it suddenly.

Lupe jabbed in him the ribs. He had stopped dead, there in the middle of the field. "Keep walking."

So none of the One-Way Gang was here tonight, watching over him. With Hawk in jail, they were probably in hiding themselves. Without a leader, they'd be helpless. The field was empty. No one would help him. His life wasn't bait, or even a sacrifice. It was just going to be wasted.

He could hardly walk. He was without hope. At Lupe's urging, they threaded their way between houses, emerging on the farthest street of Shangri-La. It was darker here, as always.

The thought occurred to him that he would never live to see this neighborhood fill up.

Mike looked over at Sal's house. It was completely dark tonight. He remembered Sal standing silhouetted in that doorway, shapes pouring out around him, one of them Lupe. He felt sick at the thought of Sal's death. Because of him . . . yes? A stupid prank that backfired, bringing Hawk to the rescue, and now Sal's death in order to distract the cops from Lupe.

My fault, all of it . . .

"Keep going."

They crossed the street and clambered up the dirt bank. Lupe had to help him up the slippery slope. Glancing back from the top, he saw the neighborhood spread out behind him, the ramparts of houses facing the wilderness like little forts grouped together for safety on a hostile plain. From now on he was beyond their pale. He desperately hoped to see Hawk's boys streaming across the street after him; hoped he was wrong about Hawk being in jail. But he knew he was right, and he saw nothing.

Lupe spread the barbed wire for him and he ducked through.

On the other side of the fence, they went on walking. His eyes adjusted slowly to the dark. Moonlight made the distances deceptive. Sometimes he thought he was on firm ground, but then he would step into a hole. Once he tripped and barely caught himself one-handed. He walked into bluffs and brambles. Lupe seemed to know the way intimately; he walked at Mike's side and never stumbled. They moved in silence over the uneven ground, and the full moon shone steadily down.

I'm alone, he thought. Hawk isn't going to save me. Not now, not ever. No one is.

He's going to—to kill me. He killed Craig Frost, didn't he? Now he's killed Sal. What chance do I have? I'm not nearly as tough as either of them.

In self-defense, Mike's mind clenched like his fist. He would not think of the future, for that was only death. He would think of nothing but the urgency of each and every moment. He would survive this moment, and this one, and the next. That was all he could ask of himself. He wouldn't try to look beyond the instant, wouldn't wonder where Lupe was taking him, since there was no resisting anyway. The grenade was only one way Lupe controlled him; there were many more, subtler. The night—the entire universe—might have conspired to bring them here together.

Full moon. Blue-black sky. Hills rising and falling in the distance. It all looked artificial, and somehow familiar.

With growing certainty and little sense of shock, he realized that he was walking on the wall of his room.

Yes . . . it was so right.

He hadn't left the house at all. The acid trip had never really ended. The strangeness wound on and on, carrying him to new levels. He had walked right into his bedroom wall. Lupe had stepped out of that hole gouged in the hills, right out of his nightmares, and dragged him up into a two-dimensional world. No wonder he couldn't run or shout or even think. This wasn't real! It was less than a dream; it was all taking place on a small, flat space. On the moon wall.

How fascinating to explore it finally. He had so often wondered how it would be to roam these hills, exploring unpainted canyons that only the painted moon could see. He and Lupe were the first through this place, apart from the artist. Now that he could see it for himself, it was a revelation.

He looked back from a ridge, before they started their descent into the canyon, and saw lights. They might have been street-lights, or windows in the farthest row of houses; but it seemed more likely they were seeping through the blinds in his room, falling on the wall from the party next door. As they started down, the painted hills rose up to hide his lights. The painted moon hung full overhead. He could hear the clock-radio on the nightstand by his bed; its rolling numbers crackled as they turned to midnight, making a sound like wind in weeds. If he could only penetrate the illusion for an instant, wake up enough to make out the dimensions of his room, then he would happily lapse back into unquestioning dreaming. But he couldn't quite manage the trick. And sometimes, in a nightmare, even waking was a dream, proving nothing.

The trail followed a dry streambed that brambles gradually choked. Cactus fingers poked from dusty soil, moonlight glittering on the spines. The trail led steeply downward, seeking and then finding a deeper ravine to trace. At one hand was a sheer drop; at the other, gray cliffs rose up. Far ahead of them, the canyons opened into a broad darkness of fields and meadows where a thin silver stream lay peacefully gleaming in the moonlight. He hoped that might be their destination. It was beautiful.

Lupe stopped him with a word: "Here."

Here, Mike thought. Here we are. Time to die now. Time to step off the wall and back into reality.

Then he looked up, and found he was on the wall after all. It was another false awakening.

Above the trail, partially hidden by bushes, was the mouth of a cave. The very cave Lupe had carved on his wall. Mike looked over at Lupe in surprise and saw a knife in his hand. Lupe pointed at the cave, making a stabbing gesture. Mike thought he was trying to enlarge the opening, gouging the moon wall still further.

He scrambled up a few yards of rugged sandstone, one hand flailing for balance, the other, throbbing, thrust deep in his sweatshirt pocket. He began to cough at the clouds of dust that rose. Lupe climbed up next to him, waited for the dust to settle.

"Give me your hand."

Lupe fit the pin into the trigger, then slowly untied Mike's hand. Needles pricked him as the blood worked slowly through the skin and through his joints. Even with the twine undone, he could not straighten his fingers. Lupe pried the grenade from his hand; the knuckles snapped as he forced them. Finished, Lupe dropped the grenade into his own pocket. He nudged Mike toward the darkness, relying on the knife now.

Ahead, there was no light for his eyes to grow used to. He found himself on a steep uphill slope; he kept stumbling and falling to his knees, several times thinking that he was about to slide or roll all the way to the bottom again. Each time, Lupe grabbed his arm and pulled him to his feet.

Once, when he fell, his half-clenched hand closed on a strange brittle shape, smaller and lighter than the grenade, and far more mysterious. He tried to understand it as he climbed. It felt capsule-shaped, about two inches long, an inch in diameter; the texture was that of brittle, compressed twigs. He realized that he was treading on more of the things, crunching them underfoot. He clung to it as he climbed, as if it were a talisman; besides, his hand was locked in the perfect shape to hold it, since his fingers still refused to uncurl.

Suddenly the slope leveled out. Misjudging a step, he fell face forward. They must have come nearly to the crown of the hills, high inside the cliff.

He got slowly to his knees, robbed of breath, dust in his mouth, clutching the capsule of twigs. Looking back, he saw a pale glimmer of moonlight far below; the cave's entrance looked like a dead eye.

A match hissed. Light filled the chamber, flickering over smooth sandstone walls, hardly penetrating several black niches. In the choking dust, his eyes began to water and his nose to sting; he sneezed several times, then gasped for breath. He could smell wax and ashes and sweat, urine and rot and faint perfume. Lupe touched the match to a candle stub, which he set on a small rock shelf. As the light settled down, the shadows took up assigned places.

Glancing down at his hand, Mike saw a tiny fanged skull staring at him—if stare is the word for eyeless sockets—out of a dense mass of little crushed bones and clumps of matted fur. He dropped the pellet in the dust; many like it littered the powdery ledge. He brushed his hand clean, working to uncramp his fingers as he looked around.

Lupe had managed to find what was probably the only true cave in Bohemia Bay. It was deeper than any he'd ever dreamed could exist in these hills. All the "caves" he'd seen were merely shelves of rock, pocks in sandstone faces. Up here, the main chamber had a high, almost domed ceiling. Overhead, fifteen feet up the farthest wall, was a dark pocket full of shadow.

"Big old owl lives up there," Lupe said, noting his interest. "Only he's not here tonight."

The chamber had numerous alcoves, recesses so dark they looked like doorways into other caves. Lupe must have been using some of them as toilets, judging from the rank, putrid smell. Only the coolness kept it bearable.

Pushed back against the middle of the far wall was a large green trunk with black letters stenciled over it: PENDLETON.

Stoner's hand grenades, he realized. That whole trunk must be full of them.

The trunk was in use as a makeshift table, holding neat rows of pens and colored pencils, lined up next to a drawing tablet. Mike recognized his own materials.

"These were for you," Lupe said. Mike found the "were" ominous. "I—I was going to have you draw my boys, all of us together. But then I remembered how I used to be pretty good at it myself. And I thought, well, why not? It's been so long . . . I was rusty. If you don't do it, you lose it, I guess. But I don't know, they're better than I thought I could do. Maybe I should have stayed with it. I mean, you're an artist. What do you think?"

Lupe set the grenade on top of the trunk like a paperweight, took a stack of pages from underneath the tablet, and shyly handed them to Mike. He seemed timid in the face of a critic. Still, there was that knife.

Mike started to thumb quickly through the pages, nodding and making approving noises to calm Lupe. But when he realized what he was seeing, the urge to lie went out of him. There was no need.

The sketches, gritty with dirt from the cave, smeared by grimy hands, were very fine. Lupe had worked deftly in pencil, pen and ink, with only slight shadings of tint. He couldn't help thinking of the sketches in Da Vinci's notebooks, quick strokes that captured an essence of nature. The grubby, aged condition of the paper added to his sense that he was gazing at the works of an ancient master, idle scribblings in a genius's notebook.

On every page Lupe had drawn a different boy. Mike wanted simultaneously to linger on each image, and to rush through seeing them all.

One was so thin as to be crippled; sunken-faced, skeletal, with teeth that looked broken and jagged; lank greasy hair. In one glance, Mike felt that he knew everything about the boy—could see his entire miserable (and probably brutally short) existence clinging to him like a coat of grime. Abuse, addiction, unending despair and waste. He had one hand out, palm up, begging for something. Anything. Begging for the world.

Another, a black kid, wore a guitar on a strap over his shoulder, staring out from the page with a resentful, brooding look. Here was a musician who had never played a note, never sung a tune. The guitar was unstrung. The set of the boy's mouth told him he was mute. The anguish of the boy's unsung, unwritten songs was overwhelming. He felt as if the boy were standing there before him.

A small brown-skinned boy—his bitter expression mixed with spiteful humor—glowered at Mike, or at the artist. Though young, he was no innocent. To judge from his eyes, he had already seen far more than most adults, and dreadful sights had warped him into something most adults could only fear. Uncivilized, a wild boy held in chains, caged by the lines of Lupe's sketch, his ferocious power strained to break free.

And then a boy masquerading as a man, with closely-shaved hair, dressed in military fatigues. Fear haunted his face, and he had a whipped look. But there was brutality there, too, as if he were more than ready to take out his fear and frustration on anyone who crossed his path, eager to pass down the line his share of the suffering life had handed him.

Next an Indian youth with long black hair, black eyes, endless loss and hopelessness carved in the bones of his face. In one sketch Mike read the story of an entire culture destroyed, its remnants torn and scattered. The anonymous agony of extinction was invested in this lone boy, who had no one to speak for him but Lupe, in strokes of violent skill.

And then came someone familiar. It took Mike a moment to recognize the boy, because he had never seen Craig Frost so simply and directly. Never really *seen* him, while he was alive. As a boy, nasty and stupid, vicious and vindictive: yes—a *boy*. In one glance, Mike knew him better than he had after years of studied avoidance. But with recognition, the pages began to tremble unbearably in his hands.

He glanced up sharply.

The candle lit only Lupe's eyes, specks of glare that hypnotized him. Here they were again, on the wall of his room. He could hear the thud of disco music from next door, tomtoms booming in his ears.

"Well?"

Lupe's hesitance was horribly at odds with the power he commanded.

"They're really good," Mike whispered.

"They are? You think so?"

"I've never seen anything like them."

Lupe stepped closer in swirls of dust. As he did, the hazy echoing cave seemed to fill with people. The dust was on the verge of solidifying into columns of misty flesh. He tasted acid in the back of his throat, and felt an LSD twinge. For a moment, cast upon the dust, taking form within it, he clearly saw the faces of boys—*these* boys.

One stepped toward him, stirred up by the suction of Lupe's movements. A dim, familiar face.

Edgar. His friend's eyes flashed and were gone.

"No," he said.

"What's that?"

He stammered, looking down at the next page, to which he had turned with hardly a glance.

And there was Edgar.

Edgar, sketched in perfect detail, convincing Mike that all the others had been taken from life and were equally true to their models. His wide thin mouth, his unmistakable nose. And in the eyes, his sad hollow eyes, Lupe had in a few simple strokes captured Edgar's desperate need to find something beyond the mundane, to penetrate and partake of all mysteries, to merge with the shadows, transgress all boundaries, and take hold of the truth—even steal it, if that was the only way.

Mike, however, could hold on no longer. The sketches floated from his hands. He looked for another glimpse of his friend, but the dust motes were swirling and Edgar was gone. Only his image remained, fluttering facedown on the floor.

"Hey, are you crazy?" Lupe said. "What's the matter with you? Didn't I respect your art? Didn't I?"

He came angrily forward, slashing the air with his knife. Mike backed toward the niches at the rear of the cave. Avoiding a silver flash, he tripped at the threshold of one alcove and tumbled backward, striking his head on the stone wall. He landed on something soft.

Someone. There was *someone* under him. Cold skin. Hands and arms and a face. All sticky and wet with a cloying scent he finally recognized, the smell that made his eyes and nose itch and water. Patchouli. Whimpering, he thrashed around trying to regain his balance and free himself, even if it meant rushing back into Lupe's arms. Lupe had him by the ankle anyway, and was dragging him back into the candlelight. But he become tangled with the other, and they both tumbled out together. Not exactly face to face, but close enough.

At his third vision of Edgar, Mike wept.

Lupe pulled him back, but not before he saw the red gash gaping in Edgar's throat, the many other wounds caked with blackish-red mud, slathered like paint upon the pale skin. Worst of all, his eyes went irresistibly to the slashed rags of Edgar's sex. He should not stare; he should not possess the cold, clinical part of his mind that observed how the scrotum had been opened and emptied of its contents, like a cut purse.

The stench of patchouli was everywhere. An empty vial lay

in the dust at the mouth of the niche. Lupe must have poured it over Edgar's corpse to mask the smell of decay. Instead it had created a new, charnel fragrance—one he felt he would remember even in death.

In death . . .

Lupe rolled Mike onto his back and straddled him, knife drawn. His full-moon face shone down. The candle danced above his head, sending sparks through his wild black hair. Lupe put his free hand on the waist of Mike's bluejeans and fumbled at the silver buttons.

"Get his pants," Lupe said, as if he were talking to someone else. "Come on, boys. Come help."

Mike gasped as Lupe's knees dug into his thighs. He gazed up at the high roof of the cave, wishing he could believe it was only the ceiling of his room, but knowing that no one would hear him if he screamed.

Frustrated with the tight fly buttons, Lupe started hacking at them, nicking Mike's flesh through the denim. Mike pissed his pants at the cold pain, as if that were some defense.

Now, Mike thought. I'm actually going to die!

Lupe hesitated, looking down toward the cave's mouth. Mike heard faint noises advancing in the sudden silence. He twisted his head sideways, daring to look.

In the moonlight at the opening stood a crowd of shadows.

When he saw them, Lupe smiled. "Come on," he said, nodding frantically. "Come on up. I got another for you. An artist!"

Mike watched in growing horror as they stepped into the cave, moving soundlessly in the dust, gliding up the slope and merging with the blackness of the tunnel.

"Oh, they're bright tonight," Lupe said gleefully, sharing his excitement with Mike—as if only another artist could appreciate or understand it. "I think drawing them, really concentrating, made them stronger." He looked back at them. "Come and help!"

"Lupe . . ."

Hearing his name whispered caused Lupe's smile to die. He jumped to his feet, leaving Mike as he rushed to the top of the slope.

"You can't talk," he said.

"No? Why not?"

The boy who spoke stepped into sight. Mike knew him only slightly from around town. What he was doing here, Mike couldn't imagine.

Randy was his name. Randy something.

Behind him was another kid with bleached blond hair, his mouth a smudge of lipstick, his eyes a smeared mess from weeping. Behind them, still more boys were on the slope. Sal's boys, he realized. The same who had chased him that first night.

Lupe didn't seem to know what to do. His fingers tightened on the switchblade's handle.

Mike crawled slowly toward the back of the cave, out of the way, as quietly as possible.

"You killed Sal," Randy said.

"Get away!" Lupe said.

"You killed your own brother. And my lover."

Lupe raised his knife, then lowered it, remembering all the power behind him. He rounded on his heel and saw Mike, only inches from the trunk and the grenade that lay atop it.

Mike screamed and grabbed the grenade first, but Lupe's hands closed around his own. They were strong hands, strong enough to make him feel as if his fingers would be ironed permanently into the metal. But no sooner had Lupe grabbed him, than they were both engulfed in a rush of bodies.

Mike sucked in a lungful of dust and started choking. Lupe's switchblade swept down at his hand, but someone deflected it. The blade clashed against sandstone, throwing sparks, and snapped clean off.

Lupe howled and buried his teeth in Mike's fist.

The pain was unbearable, but the crushing weight of bodies was easing. Since the boys could not manage to pull Lupe off

Mike, they were pulling Mike away from Lupe. A united surge of strength left him feeling torn in two. They all flew backward. Some of Sal's gang went tumbling down the slope.

Lupe sprawled against the wall, panting. Crouched at the edge of the high chamber, Mike looked down at his hand, covered with blood and purple tooth-marks, throbbing. He turned it over slowly, reassuring himself and the others that he still had the grenade. There was a communal sigh.

Lupe chuckled and raised his own hand. The trigger pin glinted in the weak yellow light.

Then he turned slowly, still grinning, and began to unsnap the latches on the trunk.

While Lupe looked down, Mike's eyes flew up to the owl's roost near the ceiling of the cave. He felt no fear. He didn't quite believe in the legendary power of grenades. He had carried them twice now, and nothing had happened. Even so, without a second thought, he gave this one an underhand toss.

It sailed straight into the bird's hole, as if he had practiced the shot every day.

Lupe glanced up at the clattering sound. "There's my bird."

And that was all Mike saw, because Randy grabbed him from behind, hauling them both backward down the slope. He never had time to find his footing; it was faster to fall. The other boys had already hurled themselves outside.

Seconds later, the moon blinked at him; but it came from the wrong place, shining between his feet. He went tumbling through bushes, down the hillside, into the canyon and a dry stream bed.

He was still falling when the hillside exploded.

The moon went out. The sky turned black. Dust and rock blasted from the cave, as if from a cannon. A cannon around whose barrel he had wrapped himself.

The explosion echoed over the hills, demolishing the Greenbelt's peace, rocketing out through the night and back again. Dogs began to bark by the dozens, a whole pack baying in pursuit of the thunder.

He lay a long time listening to the thudding of disco before he realized that it wasn't music at all, and it wasn't coming from next door.

It was his heartbeat.

The dust finally settled and the moon reappeared. He found that he had landed beneath a ledge in the dry creek. Crawling out slowly, he looked up to find that the cliff had crumbled, collapsed, fallen in on itself. All the other boys were coming out to look as well, but he supposed he was the only one of them who saw the moon wall lying in ruins.

=25=

Food in the Bohemia Bay jail was the same stuff eaten by waterlogged, sunburned and dehydrated tourists who straggled up off Central Beach to the Plankwalk Cafe. Instead of the true nourishment they so desperately needed, the beachgoers received a variety of burned, fried, stale and soggy meats and starches. Hawk was relieved to discover that at least the café did not noticeably worsen the food it prepared for prisoners, probably because Gus, the ex-con "chef," felt compassion for those inmates who would eventually open the lukewarm cardboard boxes featuring the Plankwalk's tantalizing emblem: skull and crossbones on a flapping black buccaneer's flag.

Last night he had been too tense to eat the hamburger and fries provided. But this morning, waking after a remarkably deep sleep, he felt a fresh optimism that enabled him to wolf down the congealed home fries, cold scrambled eggs and almost half of a warm, mealy apple. He could bring no enthusiasm to the slightly brown coffee, which looked and tasted like hot water from a rusty pipe. But he said his prayers all the same. He suspected he had plenty to be thankful for.

Late in the night, as he lay tossing on a wire cot that left honeycomb patterns on his skin, he had heard a *boom* echoing through the hills and canyons of the Greenbelt. This was followed by a frenzy of cops in corridors, shouting and yelling, doors slamming, sirens going full blast as what sounded like every available patrol car raced out of the lot.

After the sirens faded, his nervousness increased in proportion to the silence. He had a fair idea of what must have caused the sound, and he couldn't help imagining all the possible outcomes. Worst of them, somehow, was the picture of the James house in ruins, bodies strewn everywhere—his boys among them.

Later, the cops began wandering back, loudly disappointed, sourly informing their station-bound peers as to the outcome of the call. In the cement-walled jail, their echoing conversations were easy to follow.

According to their speculations, the explosion had been caused by a stash of old, unstable explosives in a cave. The site was deep in the Greenbelt, away from all possible harm to Bohemians. It had shattered a hillside, woken some residents, but nothing else. There were no witnesses.

Hawk relaxed then. His words must have gotten through to Randy. Otherwise a body or two would surely have been found.

Yesterday afternoon the police had descended on Hawk's trailer, interrupting him in the middle of trying to convince Maggie to give him one more chance. He hung up the phone and went peacefully.

During the interrogation, they let slip the whereabouts of his missing chrome crucifix, and Hawk realized that Lupe had set him up. He must have followed Hawk and Dusty on the fire road; skulking, he had listened to their plans, then run ahead to prepare a distraction that would give him the best shot at Mike James. Hawk knew better than Lupe that as soon as his boys heard about the arrest, there would be not even the pretense of a vigil. Lupe would get his chance, all right, and Hawk's vow to help Mike would come to nothing. That troubled him more than his own arrest and the charge of murder—which was far from being proven, after all. Even the cops could not believe he would have left such an obvious marker, and sensed that it had to be a frame-up.

"I could understand why you'd do it and all," one of them had said. "Fuckin' faggots—I can't stand seein' it either."

"I *didn't* do it."

"So you said. Then who hates you and Sal both so much he'd try to take the two of you down in one move?"

He was not about to mention Lupe. He still clung to the notion that he might somehow catch the killer himself, though how he was going to manage that in his present position was a problem he couldn't quite figure out.

When it was time for his phone call, instead of seeking a lawyer, he called Sal's house.

Randy answered. Hawk knew he didn't have much time before Randy would simply hang up, so he tried to talk as fast as he could, describing his thwarted plan while Randy hung on in what might have been shock or disbelief.

"You've got to believe me, Randy," Hawk said at last. "I had nothing against Sal. Nothing. I want the same thing you do—to get the guy who killed him. You've got nothing to lose by watching this James kid's house. I mean, look, if I'm the murderer, they'll nail me for it. I'm already in jail. But if I'm not the one, then Lupe's still out there. And only you can stop him now."

"I have to go," Randy said. His voice was thick from crying. Hawk wondered how much—if any of it—had gotten through.

"Will you do it?"

"I'm going now."

Maybe he'd done it, Hawk thought. Maybe it was going to be okay.

The cops had also informed him (playing along hypothetically with his insistence that he didn't know the details) that Sal had been murdered sometime between ten and eleven o'clock that morning. Hawk had been alone then, asleep, with no particular alibi since neither Maggie nor Stoner was around anymore to vouch for him. Even if Randy succeeded, it would be tricky to defend himself, especially once Stoner turned up. He had stayed vague about his activities, waiting to see what they already knew for certain, but eventually he was going to have to account for his time. It would be best if Lupe turned up with a confession. But Hawk had the feeling that Lupe was buried under a load of rock.

If not, then things were about to get much worse all around.

He couldn't convince himself to worry. He swilled down the last of the coffee and settled back to wait.

He was torn, in the moment of relative inner peace, between working on a sermon about the dark night of the soul, or rallying his defense. He decided that a sermon would be premature; things could still bottom out. As for his defense, he had some things in his favor. Not many, but some: Dusty had been working on his jeep, despite all Hawk's threats and pleadings, and the vehicle was completely kaput. Unfortunately, there was a working motorcycle on the lot, Stoner's old Harley. Everyone who knew Hawk knew he didn't ride anymore—but that wouldn't necessarily persuade a jury faced with an ex-con biker accused of murder. He knew *how* to ride, and there was a working bike at his disposal. So . . . the transportation defense left something to be desired. If he'd only broken down and taken the fucking bike to go see Maggie—as he had been sorely tempted to do that morning—he'd be safe now. He'd have an alibi.

Give up on it, he told himself at last. You won't find salvation in logic or arguments or even evidence. And if you have to take the fall for this one—well, hell. What's a martyr for?

It was then he heard footsteps, and with them, startling him, Maggie's voice.

The cop who had sympathized with "his" murder of Sal brought her to the cell, winked and walked away.

Hawk went quickly to the bars. He wanted to kiss her, but she wasn't close enough. She watched him with a wry, amused expression. He decided not to appear overeager.

"How'd you get here?" he asked.

"Dusty and me came over. He had to call a cab, if you can believe that."

"The final indignity." Hawk grinned, though it felt out of place. Nothing was certain yet. He shouldn't be so happy.

"Someone named Randy called him. Dusty said to tell you it was all taken care of."

"Some of it, maybe."

"We're getting your bail together."

Hawk nodded. His hands were on the bars. She stepped forward and wrapped her fingers around his knuckles.

"Hawk," she said, "I'm so proud of you."

He looked around in amazement. Where they in the same room together? "Proud?"

"You kept out of it for once. I know how hard that must have been for you, and I appreciate it."

"Hard?" he said. "It wasn't hard or easy. I was locked up!"

"If that's what it takes." She grinned. "This could be a turning point for you. For us, I mean."

He smiled, shrugged. "Well . . . maybe you're right."

"I want you to know," and here she lowered her voice, "I've got your alibi all ready."

"What?"

"That little, you know, fight we had yesterday, on the phone?"

"Yeah?"

"You just tell me when we had that conversation, how long it went on. Jog my memory."

He started to chastise her for lying, but he realized it was the only way she knew how to help. It was a genuine offer. She wanted to save him, so she would take his blame. She'd share the risk. How could he turn her down?

He said, "We fought all morning, didn't we?"

"Yeah. It was bad, wasn't it?"

"Between, say, nine and noon, on and off all day till the cops broke us up."

"Ever since you got out of bed, and you could hardly sleep all night for thinking of me, you poor thing."

"No, I couldn't."

"It was bad, honey, wasn't it?"

"That it was," he agreed. "But we were right on the verge of patching it up when the cops broke us off."

"That's right, and it's all fixed up now," she said. "We're way past that verge, aren't we? Everything's straight between us?"

"If you say so," he said.

"As long as you don't keep thinking you're some kind of Peter Pan, you and your boys."

Peter Pan? he thought. It was not a suitably serious or Biblical image. It shocked him into wondering how he really appeared to others.

"No," he said.

" 'Cause I'll tell you something, honey. I ain't no Wendy. I'm not that fond of boys. And this sure as hell ain't Never-Never Land."

"No," Hawk agreed. "That it ain't. Isn't. I mean, *ain't*."

=26=

Autumn rode the wind in from the sea. The sky was thick
with gray this evening, allowing no rainbow sherbet sunset, no
ultraviolet bars of cloud, no color at all, anywhere. The summer
was dying without a struggle. The ice cream parlors and souvenir shops, the seascape galleries, toy stores and seashell boutiques
looked depressed and withdrawn, reacting badly to the seasonal
death of crowds. Many had closed early tonight, and looked as
though they were shut down for the year.

Mike walked in the early chill, cocooned in coldness. He felt
as if he might never emerge from his thoughts; he had to keep
reminding himself of where he was, that everything was fine.
The scars on his hands had healed—barbed-wire gouges on the
left hand, teethmarks on the right. The blisters raised by the
poison oak he'd fallen in after the explosion had long since
scabbed over, sloughed away, leaving his skin unblemished. But
shallow wounds were always the first to heal.

School started tomorrow, and he almost looked forward to it
as a kind of coma into which he could dive and take shelter,
barely functioning while the world went on without him.
Whatever was going to change inside him, whatever healing lay
in wait, it could run its course while he hibernated.

At the end of the boardwalk he came to a small playground,

deserted at this hour, on this day. He sat in one of the swings, buried his heels in sand, and stared at the sea. His thoughts joined the last gulls shrieking overhead, circling over the floodlights like vicious moths. He took his sketchpad from his pack and flipped it open.

It was not a new pad, but every page was blank. He forced himself to look at it until he could no longer bear the sight of so much nothing. How long had it been since he'd drawn even a doodle? A month or more? It was torture to keep trying to force himself to draw—but not as torturous as his inability to come up with anything. Yet he had to keep on. He was an artist. It was how he'd defined himself for years. Without that, what did he have?

The problem was, he kept seeing those daunting, perfect, grubby sketches. Created so hastily, then lost forever in the blast. He was the only one alive who'd seen them; they haunted no one else. No one would ever liken them to *his* pictures—no one but Mike, that is. And his would always suffer in comparison. How could he ever do anything to rival them? How could he forget them and go on with his own work?

He couldn't even remember what his own work was. Dragons and swordfighters? Did he expect those to sustain him for a lifetime? Yet that was all he'd ever drawn—unreal scenes, fantasies, wet dreams. It was all he was any good at, but it was ruined for him now.

Soft steps padded over the sand of the playground. Someone took the swing beside him, rattling its chains.

"Hi," she said. "What're you drawing?"

His heart jolted. That voice . . .

Looking over, he saw blond hair pushed up in a bandanna; dark eyes, high cheekbones. She was wrapped in a light, many-colored sweater.

It was her. The girl from the van.

His anima.

So this is a flashback, he thought, experiencing a delirious flood of fright. He tasted a brassy tang in the back of his mouth, an onrush of panic bringing LSD memories and making them inseparable from reality. Dreams had broken out beyond their borderland. Now there was nothing to keep Edgar from reaching up out of the sand to drag him down. If his anima could come to him so easily, then nothing would stop Lupe from walking out of the surf, dripping kelp, with deathless eyes and drawn knife . . .

That particular wave of fear crested and broke, leaving Mike gasping as it subsided and slid silently away.

She remained.

Mike swallowed and closed his tablet. "Nothing," he finally answered.

"Don't I know you?" she asked.

"I think so," he said, not daring to believe it.

"Are you a friend of Kurtis Tyre's?"

He ducked his head. "Not exactly. A friend of a friend."

"Oh, now I remember. In the van. Yeah!" She laughed. "I got talked into tagging along that night; my girlfriend knows Kurtis. It was pretty wild."

"Yeah, it was," he agreed, his tongue feeling thick for another reason now. Stupid, stupid! What should he say? That he had fallen in love and lost her in the same night? And that Edgar had convinced him she couldn't possibly exist? Edgar, who was always looking beyond the obvious answers, and Mike, gullible enough to believe him.

"I guess you made out all right," she said. "You were pretty unhinged there for a while."

He nodded, avoiding further thought of what had followed that night. Instead he tried to remember her sitting close to him in the van, touching him. She was close enough now that if he leaned over slightly, he could kiss her.

"My name's Mike," he said.

"I'm Anaïs."

"You mean like Anaïs Nin?"

"You know about her?"

He nodded. "My mom's always reading her diaries."

"I never met anyone, you know, our age who's heard of her. I was named after her. My dad's a professor out at Irvine; he teaches literature. We just moved here this summer from Torrance."

"You live in Bohemia?" he said, hardly daring to believe it. She nodded. "I guess we'll be in school together, then."

Something about the way she said "together" electrified him. "You want to walk?" he asked.

Without answering, she got up from the swing and put out her hand. It was warm. He held it delicately, as if she might break, burst, fade back into his mind. But Edgar had been wrong about her. She was real enough to squeeze his fingers in return.

They walked along the boardwalk toward the Dumas Père restaurant. Remembering the last time he had eaten there, he glanced down.

They were crossing the tunnel where Craig Frost was murdered. Horror surged up in him for perhaps the millionth time. Fear was an aftershock; he was never so afraid in Lupe's cave as he had been afterward, imagining over and over again how things might have come out. But for the first time, he refused to clutch at the fear. Released, it ebbed away, leaving only a dark stain on his soul like a high-water mark. It would always be there, faintly blood-tinted no matter how faded, until some greater tide surpassed it. But he could not imagine—and prayed he never saw—anything to rival it, no matter how long he lived.

He veered from the boardwalk and tugged Anaïs laughing over the grass, toward the lights of the street and the shut-down stores. He wanted to see her clearly in case she vanished again. He wanted to study the face he had thought was only in his mind, a figment of his desire, but which had turned out to be real after all.

He knew now, suddenly, what he wanted to do. Sketching wasn't enough anymore; it didn't encompass half of what he felt.

He would take up painting. He would teach himself to capture all her colors, the bright cloth and pale hair, her flushed cheeks and pink lips, against the gray subdued sky of the last twilight of summer.